Girl In the Mirror

Girl In the Mirror

Jools Abrams

Matador
Unit E2 Airfield Business Park,
Harrison Road, Market Harborough,
Leicestershire. LE16 7UL
Tel: 0116 2792299
Email: books@troubador.co.uk
Web: www.troubador.co.uk/matador
Twitter: @matadorbooks

ISBN 978 1803130 873

British Library Cataloguing in Publication Data.
A catalogue record for this book is available from the British Library.

Printed and bound in Great Britain by 4edge Limited
Typeset in 11pt Sabon MT by Troubador Publishing Ltd, Leicester, UK

Matador is an imprint of Troubador Publishing Ltd

For Stuart, Isabella and Joseph

April 1928

Edith Muriel, two first names and no need to choose between the one or the other, held her head high and tripped her Saturday shoes down Moss Lane. Rain was falling, a fine drizzle that she worried would turn her newly bobbed hair frizzy. It drove her to seek shelter under the shop canopy of Handforth's Hardware. The windows were still dark, goods shadowed as she waited, buckets, mops, washboards and ladders static in the grey light. There was nothing useful there. Nothing she wanted. Her prize was on a back shelf behind the counter. Something that would make her dance shoes sing, the only way to spark up and elbow her way out of a crowded house and into the spotlight of a brighter life.

It was early still; she'd sneaked out of the house while her mother was distracted. Her father wouldn't be happy if he knew she was spending her chore money on frivolities. Clarence agreed with the need for self-improvement. He would rather his daughters had their head in a book than were dancing. He didn't want them to become mill girls like the ones next door with their raucous Saturday afternoon parties. Edith Muriel had heard her parents argue about it, their words mumbling up through the floorboards as she listened.

'Must have money to burn,' Clarence grumbled.

Edith knew her father was a prudent man. He didn't much like his daughter's newly bobbed hair either, she'd heard him complaining about that to their mother.

'Look like bloody flappers, they do, Edna. They'll be swearing and smoking next and hanging out at cafés in town on Sunday evenings, laughing and joking with the boys.'

He didn't know that Edith was always hanging out with the boys, all the spare friends her brothers kept around. Four brothers and two sisters. She preferred the boys' games to playing with the one doll she and her sisters shared. She preferred to be out in the street, kicking a ball, catching a ball and running races. Clarence's strict rules couldn't contain her spirit and she'd already tried to argue against him, building up words like a storm and earning herself a thick ear.

Edith shivered in the spring morning and glanced down at her sister's old shoes. They were hardly Freeman, Hardy and Willis, but they were new to her and there was still plenty of life in them. Flo had thrown them across the bedroom at her the day before with her customary casting-off.

'You can have these, I've no use for them now Mother's getting me new ones for Whit Week.' Edith Muriel bit down on her envy. She'd show Flo that her old shoes would have a new life on her dancing feet. She had picked them up and inspected the worn black leather; the heels and soles were still intact. Their father mended all their shoes, resoled and reheeled them on the last he kept at home, until there was barely any leather left of the originals.

'I suppose they'll do for now, with some segs fixed on them. I'll get new shoes too after the dancing competition,' she said.

Flo laughed. She would never put tappers on her shoes, she preferred quiet steps. She didn't want anyone knowing she was coming down the street, rat-a-tat-tatting a beat that everyone recognised as Edith Muriel Cook.

'I don't think so, Edith, there's only enough money for one new pair of shoes, and they're for me,' she said.

Edith resolved to prove her wrong. Her hands clutched around the pennies in her pocket outside Handforth's. She had exactly enough for a packet of Blakey's segs.

Edith sprinted home from the shop with her segs in her pocket, imagining she was one of the women athletes who would be running for the first time in the summer Olympics that year. Their participation meant the girls could do athletics at school. Mrs Black had said they could even lay out a track in Alexandra Park. Edith could run as fast as any boy and dribble a ball like the best Man City player. She rounded the corner and barrelled into Mrs Padgett as she was coming out of her front gate and the old lady spun in her wide skirts.

'Slow down, giddy kipper,' she scolded. Edith did indeed slow down. Mrs Padgett was her hero, a kind widow who ran her own plumbing business from her house on Moss Lane. Her own business, no husband to take her money. She had a nice house too.

Edith hitched her dress through her belt a little more. 'I'm sorry, Mrs Padgett, I'm trying to get back home and get Father to fit my new tappers before he goes out to work.' A passing tram tore up the tracks and screeched like a dying crow. 'My dad is a better driver than that,' she said, shaking the packet in her pocket so it tinkled like a bag full of stars. 'I'll be sure to come back later and show you how they sound on that nice stone in your front garden.'

*

The shoes' first performance was in Edith's own home. She danced by the wash house, tapping out beats on the stone floor and making a sound that rang true and clear around the back yard. It was enough to bring her mother to the back door, a baby balanced on her hip. Edna granted her daughter a round of applause.

'Well I think you'll make that dance group, no trouble. Now give the clattering a break and come and help me with the washing before it starts belting down again.'

Edith glanced at the clear blue sky. Wash day was always Monday. Her mother was hanging out the sheets on a Saturday. It wasn't done. The neighbours would talk. Maybe Edna had too much work for the coming week and needs must. Her mother wiped a damp hand across her face and leant against the back door.

Edith rarely saw her mother sit down. Leaning against the door jamb was the closest she got to sitting. She even stood up knitting, waiting for the pie to brown. Edith shook her new bob, pierced with a sudden longing for another life, a better life. She saw herself bathed in the golden light of a spot lamp on stage, and rang out a few last defiant taps. When she was a grown-up, someone else would do her washing. She tightened a calf and sprang on tiptoe, arms outspread, and threw her head back below the high red-brick walls. She spun like a top until she felt she could almost take off and fly over the thick, squat houses.

'I'll be in in a minute, Mum. Hey, look, Harry, watch me spin!'

Her baby brother clapped his chubby hands. Edith's shoe caught on a flagstone and she tripped and staggered. She tumbled against the privy wall, cracking her head. The pain made her shout out, but she didn't cry. She could see her mother watching, blurry, nearby. Edith knew her mother would not pick her up. She'd say it was her own daft fault, that her whirlwind daughter should learn some quiet.

*

After the family had gone to bed that night Edith twitched, restless, between her two sisters. Flo, being fourteen, had the only pillow, Rose, at six, had the edge of the bed, and Edith, at ten, was the filling in the sandwich. It was a better situation than that of her older brothers, who shared a truckle bed pushed up against the opposite wall. Their room smelled of carbolic soap, damp linen and a touch of the Manchester smog that settled across the open sash. Moonlight shone between the thin curtains at Meadow Street as Edith wriggled. She wished she was still small enough to be with her mother and father in the back room. It would be nicer than having Rose's feet pushed up her nose and cowering from the dark shadows that flickered on their ceiling. The dark shadows wouldn't dare venture into her parents' room.

A cat called outside. The wash house waited in the cold night. Edith's skin itched and prickled under her nightdress. She sat up. She yearned to go out and practise. She was desperate to be a part of the dance group at school. No, not just a part, she wanted to take a bow and bouquets after a stunning performance like Joan Crawford. She thought of her shoes snuggled in the small hallway, shod with their shiny new tappers, and swung her legs over Flo, bringing a sharp mutter from the pillow end of the bed.

'Where the bloody hell d'you think you're going?'

'Privy,' she whispered.

'Use the bloody po.' Florence had discovered swearing early and was using it liberally whenever her father was out of earshot. She knew he'd box her ears if he heard her.

'It's full,' Edith answered. 'I need summat else anyway, unless you want me to fill the po right over and stick it under your head? Would curl your hair better than those rags.'

Flo turned away. 'You're disgusting, Edith.'

Edith crept down the stairs, took her shoes from the hall and raised the latch on the kitchen door. Outside, the rows of terraced houses sat tight back to back. Their walls of dense red brick looked black in the thick dark. She crossed the yard to the wash house, her bare feet stinging on the cobbles, four steps – maybe five until she dared to slip on her shoes and flick out one leg, rolling heel to toe, making the tappers spark a new song into the night. Four streets away a dray horse pricked its ears and echoed the sound with a stamp of its hoof and a curl of steam. Edith tapped again.

'One-two-three, one-two-three, two-two-three.' She panted with effort as her body lifted, nightdress flapping, white sails filling the small space. High on exhilaration, warm on dance, she spun and spun, feet flashing, world blurring. Like Joan in *Our Dancing Daughters*, or a funny Charleston flapper, moving like the little mouse she'd seen in *Steamboat Willie* on the Plaza screen.

A window shifted above, rattled in its frame and the other houses stirred, waking.

'It's 4 a.m., girl, you're waking the dead, your dad's got work at six and your sister's got her gala tomorrow and now you've got the neighbours yammering too,' her mother yelled, sleep-raddled.

Other windows stirred and voices echoed up and down the ginnel. A dog barked its contribution like an echo in a tin can as a chorus of complaints built along the Moss Side terrace. Edith thought she could carry on, but how could her audience see her in the dark, and she wanted to be seen. She tripped across the yard and returned her cold body to the warm bed amid grumbles from Flo.

'You waking me up again, you daft 'a'p'orth? I've got my swim tomorrow.'

Edith stared at the ceiling and wondered what her dance shoes would sound like on the poolside.

*

It was a tram ride to Victoria Road Baths. Edith pulled her mother's coat over her cold shoulders. It smelled like a pack of damp Woodbines and was stiff with age, cracked at the joints like Edna's early arthritic fingers, but it kept the draughts at bay. They rattled to a stop and pushed through the crowd to join the Swimming Club queuing outside.

'Look at the gargoyles up there, Flo, they look like you!' Edith teased.

She whipped her hidden tap shoes from Flo's bag as her sister gazed skywards, distracted, just before their teacher strode towards her charges, her long face flushed. Edith hid her shoes behind her back.

'Pleased to see you are all so punctual. I will take the competitors with me now. Family members may enter through the pay office and make their way up the stairs to the gala gallery on the first floor. You are not to enter any other part of the building before, during, or after the event. Entrance and exit only through the pay office. If the lavatory is needed, please use the attendants' entrance.' She cast a shrewd eye at Edith, who slid behind her mother's coat.

Edna sighed. 'I best go now then. Good luck, Florence. Save me a seat, Edith.'

Edith itched with Mrs Black's rules. There were so many of them; she would never remember them all. She changed her shoes and followed the line into the building, tapping her impatient feet across the tiled floor.

Her teacher froze. 'Who's making that noise?'

Edith held her breath and balanced on tiptoe the rest of the way past the mosaic fish that swam up the staircase, green and shiny like they were underwater. She shuffled along the gallery and folded down two seats.

When her mother returned from the toilet, she drew her attention to Flo. 'There she is, Mum, second in line.'

They waved and Flo pushed her shoulders back, proud. She wore a long-legged bathing suit embroidered with the three letters VSC, Victoria Road Swimming Club, 'the Water Babies'. Edna had taken it in, but her clever stitches could not disguise the fact it was still too big. Edith had helped sew the letters on herself. The C was just coming away; she'd left the end of her thread empty and dropped a double stitch. It wouldn't be enough to come loose, but it would be enough to let her older sister know Edith intended sabotage. She had seen Flo swim before, she could go and watch on club nights, but she had never seen her swim in the first-class males' pool. That was used for galas only.

Edith swung her feet, itching to try out her shoes in this grand place, and tugged at her mother's sleeve. 'Mum, I need the toilet. Now!'

'Go on then, it's downstairs, but be quick about it or you'll miss the race.'

Edith tiptoed down the far stairs past the shampooing room, the tepidarium and caldarium, her feet sliding on the steamy floor. She sneaked under the balcony with bathtubs where they had played a few weeks before, the water warmer than the pool. Packed in like sardines, Edith, Flo and Rose with their legs spreadeagled over the side of the baths.

'Feet as black as the hobs of hell,' Edith had said dramatically. She stopped and slipped behind the curtain of a poolside cubicle, flung back the curtain to make her grand entrance and ran along the tiled side, revelling in the smart, sweet beats of sound that echoed round the pool. A roar of applause came from next door. Edith took a bow, imagined it was for her, and tapped out her light feet, cross-stepping faster and faster behind the wall, bursting through the partition to the main pool with clattering shoes as the final whistle blew and her sister touched the side, first.

Mrs Black leapt off the poolside bench, her clapping hands like fluttering wings. 'Splendid win, Florence, splendid.'

Florence bobbed, grinning, wondering how her sister had got down to the pool.

Her mother thought the same, gave her a thick ear later. 'Where did you go? You missed the race. And what the bloody hell have you got those shoes on for?'

Edith rubbed her head, her stomach cramped as she gazed up at her mother. If only she could make her as proud as Flo had.

*

The opportunity came soon enough. Mrs Black formed a tap class of willing ten-year-olds. Edith couldn't wait to stay after school, tapping in the rays of light from the triptych windows. She knew she was the best dancer in the group and longed to show what she could do with her clever feet. When they made it to regional finals in the town hall, she didn't sleep for nights before.

Her mother cleaned at the town hall and was proud her daughter was performing in such a grand place. 'It's a palace in that main hall, right enough. They've got lovely paintings on the wall, they're called murals, like Muriel, eh!' She choked on her tea, and wiped the splatters off her wide black skirts. 'Oh our Muriel's on the wall!'

Edith considered the joke. Her full name was Edith Muriel, but she only heard it used when she was in trouble. Chanted like a warning, it gave her time to run before she got a thick ear again.

Her mother continued, 'They were painted last century by a famous artist called Ford Madox Brown.'

Edith considered this piece of information. She repeated the name, let the words roll on her tongue, two names, like she had. A whole house of a name that sounded more like a place than a person.

Edna had settled into her story, pleased to be teaching her daughter something. 'They say it took him six months to paint them all, lying on a platform. He supposedly fell off one night, caretaker had already locked up and gone home, so the poor man lay on the floor till morning.'

Edith thought if her mum had been around then, she would have found Ford Madox and taken him home for leftover hot pot and a warm by the fire.

When the day of the performance came, Edith waited outside the town hall, bouncing with excitement, clutching the clammy hand of her partner and best friend, Joyce, in one palm and her hat in the other. It was a breezy day and she didn't want to be chasing it across Albert Square. Not on the most important day of her life. The town hall towered above them, its walls crenelated and woven with brick embroidery.

'Don't you think it's dead grand, Joyce? It's a palace.' A bell rang once from the tower as a clutch of policemen marched past the girls.

Joyce sniffed. 'It's a police station, not a palace, Edith. My mum said they keep a load of bad 'uns locked up inside.'

Edith shook her curls. She didn't think anything bad could be contained in such a beautiful building. 'Grand hall is still open to the public, though, that's what my mum said, and she works here.' She didn't tell Joyce her mother was just a cleaner. She thought Joyce might know anyway.

She trotted up the steps, pinched with a little disappointment that her parents were not there to see her dance. Her father found dancing fanciful and could not get time off from driving the trams anyhow. If her mother sympathised with her middle daughter's passion, she rarely showed it. 'Can you see me and your little brother in there? He'd be wailing the place down within minutes. No, you go and do your dance, you show 'em what a graceful little thing you can be, but none of your mucking about now, do your best.' She'd made sure Edith's dress was clean and pressed for the occasion.

Inside, Edith was awestruck. She had never seen the like. It was a place the likes of her never usually went, they wouldn't be let in, as her sister Flo had jealously reminded her. 'Are you getting ideas above your station again, Edith? Your dancing's just fit for back-yard prancing. I'm surprised they're letting you in the town hall.'

Edith had shaken off Flo's barbs. She was here now, wasn't she? The chandeliers sparkled overhead, as bright as her mother's best birthday brooch. The tall church windows sent colour pop reflections onto the yellow stone. The girls' tapper-shod feet rattled on the fine mosaic floor as they snaked behind their teacher into the grand hall. Edith gasped in the doorway, hesitating at the entrance. The hall was lined with the most beautiful pictures she had ever seen, more lovely than the stained illustrations of the full colour plates in the fat family Bible, tucked on the top shelf. Joyce shoved her forwards to join the line and she gazed up at the murals of Ford Madox Brown wrapped around the walls that enveloped her in their riotous colour. Her pulse quickened. She loved them immediately, although their beauty felt too much for her heart to hold. They bewitched and terrified her in equal measure, they were so full of life, of movement. She felt a rush of blood to the heart and wobbled.

'You all right, girl? You've gone white,' Mrs Black said.

Edith took a deep breath. 'It's just, oh, Mrs Black, they're beautiful.'

Her teacher smiled. 'Indeed they are. You can have a look around over there while we wait for our section to be called if you like.' She gestured to a row of benches beneath the first of the murals.

Edith perched and eagerly read the inscription. '"The Romans building a fort at Mancenion". Do you think that means Manchester, Joyce?'

Her friend picked her nose and shuffled her shoes. 'I see the Manchester Grammar girls are here. Look at all the ribbons in their hair.'

Edith glanced at the opposite row. The yellow ribbons of the girls were outshone by the splendour of their surroundings. She looked back to the mural of the Romans where a proud man with sturdy footballer's calves gave directions from under a flowing red cape. There must have been a stiff breeze that day too. The artist knew the Manchester weather then, she thought. Each painted face pouted back at her, proud and purposeful. There were splashes of blood-red paint everywhere, it hastened her blood. She imagined Ford Madox grinning below his bushy beard as he brandished a brush and pointed across the wooden pallets laid flat for a stage, between the waiting gaggles of schoolchildren to a painting where a half-naked man crouched in a font, as if he were about to dive off the top board in the gala pool.

'Look over there, Joyce. Is that Jesus?'

Joyce's eyes widened, and she scanned the hall, expecting the messiah to be waiting his turn on another bench. 'Where?'

'Over there, in that painting.'

Mrs Black leant down to whisper to her charges. 'Young lady, that is not Jesus, it is a depiction of the baptism of Edwin.'

Edith focused again on the white, waxy skin of the figure and let her eyes roam to the next mural where a child in rags clutched a loosely wrapped baby. Edith shook her head. 'That baby's going to catch its death like that! There's a dog in that one too. Its head is as big as mine.'

'Big head,' Joyce giggled. 'Better watch out the dog doesn't bite your bum.'

Edith could not respond as she would normally do. She was bewitched by the art. They were not quiet little watercolours, like the prints in her mother's parlour, they were full of action and violence. Each mural seemed to have a struggle at its heart, a tussle for life. She wanted to stand on her bench and climb into their other worlds.

A bell chimed and the hall fell under a hush. Edith stepped forward when her group was called, standing tall at the back with her sailor dress and shiny black hair. She flung her arms wide and mastered her flashing feet. Inspired by the paintings she was made into something other than herself, and danced a dervish. She gathered in the admiring glances from scuff-kneed boys and prim mothers and, in the last beat, with her hair damp and muscles twitching, saw something for one moment that spun and spangled just beyond her reach. A desire and ambition that dissolved like a spin of smoke on a bobbin behind the layers of varnish on the town hall murals.

May 1931

May shifted hope and a lighter mood settled over the smoke-clouded city. May Day at school and Edith Muriel was crowned the May Queen. She ran home to tell her mother the news.

'I'll be leading the dancing in Alexandra Park. I'll need a white dress, white gloves and shoes, and a bonnet.'

Her mother was proud, beaming, but Edith sensed the smile was fixed. 'We'll see what we can do,' she promised.

Edith knew her dress would be Flo's, her gloves and shoes the result of a visit to the pawnshop, and her bonnet borrowed from an aunt, but that was no different to anyone else. She longed to dance, to find a way to flash out all the bright sparks inside her. Poets had their words, Ford Madox his paintings. Edith Muriel had her feet. Edna provided a new dress (not white), gloves and resoled shoes to showcase her daughter's dance skills at the fair.

Edith performed her molly dancing in the bandstand on a clear May morning. The group of girls a whirlwind of white, the girl with the fastest flashing feet at its centre, clutching her prop, a trusty broom to brush the bad luck away. But the bad luck was stubborn. It had infected her family before, and it was back again. It followed Edith as she stepped from the bandstand stage and held her broom aloft like a cat's tail.

'Leave your brooms by the steps, girls, follow the May Queen!' she laughed. The other dancers grumbled and deposited their brooms behind the stage of the bandstand, following Edith across to a clearing behind the fair where three unsteady poles, garlanded with flowers, wobbled. Edith took her duties seriously. She bossed the group, showing no favouritism, not even for her best friend Joyce, whose dress was far too long. Joyce's mother had not managed to pin and tuck as well as Edith's. She pulled her friend's dress up through the yellow ribbon tied fast around her waist and tutted. 'Just follow my lead.' She was enjoying the leadership that being the May Queen bestowed, even if it lasted only a day. Her subjects must do as she said. She shepherded the girls into their places, like white daisies in a fairy circle, and checked to see that her parents had a good view.

They were there, front row in a belt of people. Her mother raised her hand and gave a small wave and an uncertain smile as Edith waited for the music and began to dance. She perched on the balls of her feet and bounced like a tennis ball, in and out of the pairs of children, weaving the ribbon closer and tighter around the pole, her black hair flying. Her arms strained across her chest to the partner beside her, a small girl who kept her eyes locked on Edith's flashing feet as she was dragged in a circle. It was hard to keep up with someone who had learned all the moves by heart, and also invented some of her own.

The girls bounded like puppies in ever decreasing circles and the crowd clapped in time. As she whirled, Edith checked her parents were still watching. She could see her father's cap-bobbing head and shoulders above the crowd, and just before the final ribbon unfurled in rainbow flutters she released her partner and spun solo, carried away from the others by her own enthusiasm. She could hear the applause as she whirled like a dervish and she stopped, panting, took a bow (not a curtsey as she had been instructed) and lapped it up.

When she turned to smile at her proud parents, they had gone. Edith was panicked. She scanned the crowd and spotted them some way ahead by the steam carousel, her father clutching her mother's elbow tightly. Clouds covered the sun as she scurried behind, feeling the shame of a performance interrupted, and the attention she had been given for all the wrong reasons. She lost sight of them as rain began to fall, staining her dress and making all her mother's effort for nothing. She lifted its hem and sprinted the rest of the way, rattling her shoes between a network of terraces until she skidded to a halt. Somewhere she had taken a wrong turn. They had only just moved, again, and in her anxious state she had run by mistake to their old house on Meadow Street. No matter, she gathered herself. She was a mere three streets away from their new house on Florence Street, which was a little better and bigger with fewer bodies to a room.

Florence Street had been a hopeful move after a series of ups and downs. One rented house after another, until her father had received a small inheritance and moved them all out to Old Trafford, to a bigger house with a bigger back yard, big enough for a milk-dealing business.

She had helped haul the churns through the ginnel after they were delivered from Cowburn's Dairy. She and her siblings washed them out and refilled them. The business had almost worked until new regulations had come in on hygiene, and the cost of making their Old Trafford house up to new standards too much. They'd returned to Moss Side. She was pleased to be back among friends, and her brothers delighted to be closer to Maine Road, but it was a disappointment for Clarence. Edith turned and ran back until she came to the right house.

She found her father boiling water in the kitchen, his face one whole crease of worry. She could hear someone crying, faint sobs that leaked down the back stairs behind a man who was descending, his sleeves rolled up above the elbow. He was already starting to unroll his shirtsleeves, work done. He had clean hands, not a shadow of dirt under any of the nails. A doctor, she thought. Her stomach dropped.

'I'm sorry, Mr Cook, nothing could be done,' the doctor said, packing up his bag.

He shook her father's hand, money was exchanged and her father shrugged slightly: nothing could be done about nothing. The doctor left through the back yard and her father latched the door behind him, stumbling round the kitchen making a pot of tea.

'Where's Mum?' Edith asked, watchful as her father mashed the pot and poured tea into their best cup. He didn't answer. He wasn't used to carrying a teacup and saucer and the brown liquid splattered.

She blocked him on his way upstairs. 'Let me make it, Dad. I'll put it in a mug, it'll be easier to carry.'

He leaned against the sink as she poured the rich brown cure-all tea then took the mug off her, his hands shaking a little. He pecked her on the cheek, a rare blessing. 'Now you be quiet down here, Muriel. Don't put on any of your loud radio music today. Look after your brother and Rose, would you?'

She watched him climb the stairs. 'They're all still at the fair,' she called, hopeful she could go back there too. She could fetch Joyce and buy some candyfloss. Try and win something on the hook a duck.

She perched on the bottom stair, smoothing her dress. Her father's use of her other name confused her: something was wrong. Why had he called her Muriel, not Edith? She was always Edith Muriel, her full name a roll call when she was in trouble. Her first name her everyday name, they hardly used her second. Perhaps two names were too many for one person now she was older. Maybe her father wanted her to be Muriel now, maybe that was her grown-up name? She watched his receding broad back. He was dropping tea on the bare boards. Edith Muriel stood and clattered up the stairs behind him.

Her mother came down from the top stair, leaning heavily on the banister, and the three of them stopped, stacked like milk bottles on the step. Her mother looked wrung out. There was the faint smell of an end of day butcher's shop, masked with rose cologne. Edith Muriel connected the smell, her mother's pale face and the doctor's visit. She'd seen the doctor come and go up and down most streets they lived in. Knew the pawnshop visits that would follow to pay his bill. Knew that if his visit came shortly after a new baby was expected, it meant the baby had been lost. Her friends' mothers had lost children, some of them right near the end, like Joyce's mum. It had scared her so much she wouldn't have another. She made Joyce sleep with her and they pushed the wardrobe across the door together on Saturday nights when Joyce's dad came home late and drunk.

Edna wobbled on the stair. 'Are you all right, Mum?' Edith Muriel asked.

Her father reached out his free hand. 'Get back to bed, love,' he said softly.

'The tea won't make itself,' Edna snapped.

Clarence stepped back and bumped into Edith Muriel. He spilt more tea on the stairs. 'Edna,' he hissed. 'You've lost a baby, never mind the tea. Edith Muriel can make it, or I'll send her to the fish shop.'

Edith Muriel stepped backwards in her dance shoes and her segs sparked, made it sound like a routine on the narrow stairs, tap, tap, tap. It was an honour to be asked to go to the fish shop on her own. She'd ask for scraps for all – that might make her mother feel better.

*

Her mother's miscarriage shifted the mood of the house back to frustration. Edna was impatient with her daughters. She would not tolerate the girls bouncing on the bed or tickling Harry on the rag rug. Her frown had become permanent, knife deep between her eyebrows. She kept to long skirts, even when the summer heat rose. Her mother was shrouded in shadows and it made Edith Muriel uneasy.

She complained to Joyce, 'Rose wets the bed most nights, stinks like cold fish. Flo and I strip the sheets before

Mum gets up, save her the job, fling them over the pulley, the fire gets them dry most days.' It did, but they smelled of bacon fat and smoke.

Late May and Edith Muriel sat on her bed, her feet dripping into a new day. A single dog barked, calling a reminder that there was a bigger wash house in the new back yard and new stones to tap her feet-beat on, but Edith Muriel had stopped answering that call. She was a sensible girl.

'Can't go flighty in my nightie.' She giggled. 'Too tired anyway.' Thirteen meant helping her mother with the housework, more so now Mother had taken to her bed for most of each day. Between cleaning, washing, shepherding and supervising the younger ones, cooking when allowed, school and Sunday school, she was grateful to climb into bed each night and sleep. She twisted her new white gloves against her white Whit Week dress until they showed the light stains of perspiration and thought about the day on the stairs when her father called her Muriel. It was her name, her second name, part of her first. Would she rather be an Edith or a Muriel? Edith was too staid for a new girl emerging from her chrysalis. Muriel sounded like mural, that's what her mother had said. Mother, who had taken Muriel's old, outgrown dress and bleached, scrubbed and mended it for Rose. It was all her mother seemed to do these days, bend silently over laundry in the back kitchen.

Flo burst into the bedroom and pinched her sister's ear. It bloomed like the sting of a bee. 'I've been waiting downstairs for you, while you're up here doing nothing. You ready yet?' Muriel rubbed her ear and glowered at her sister. Why Flo should have a long, sophisticated white dress while she was still in short skirts, she couldn't fathom.

'Stop your mithering, our mum's not ready yet anyhow.'

Something passed across Flo's sharp features. Edith Muriel thought her sister was losing the bloom of youth already. She had shadows under her eyes and the first flush of beauty had left at least a year ago when some lad from the biscuit factory took off with her best friend instead of her. She pouted. There was no way she would let anyone do that to her.

'Mum's not watching today,' Flo said. 'She's lent her best shoes to her sister for the walk. Besides, she's got to get all our things ready for the holiday, hasn't she?'

Edith Muriel didn't believe Flo for one moment, she suspected it was something else. Their mother had grown quieter by the day since the miscarriage. The holiday was planned to give her a break. She peered around Flo to admire herself in the dressing-table mirror. Despite the length, she looked like a lady in her white dress and gloves. She resolved her hands would never be soaked in endless suds like their mother, her skin would remain smooth, she'd get someone else to do the work for her.

Flo pinched her other ear. 'Stop that right now, Edith, I know that look, you're daydreaming again, getting ideas above your station, are you?' She stomped out of the room leaving Edith Muriel wanting to peel off any name that Flo used, like one of her gloves.

She lifted herself off the bed and pulled the window open to the street. A new decade of noise had begun. There was an art to the noise, she thought, like one of those beautiful town hall murals had come alive with modern sounds, new sounds that bellowed in the close streets. Sounds of the cinema, radio, cars, buses, trams and newspaper sellers.

She called out her name amongst the clatter. 'Edith Muriel, Muriel Edith, Muriel, Muriel, Muriel.'

The milkman looked up as he clinked bottles. His horse huffed into the May morning. It was going to be a long day – the crazy girl at number twenty-two was already yelling into the street.

She waved one gloved hand from the window and laughed. 'Good morning there, I'm Muriel.'

The milkman waved back.

Joyce had reached the house and called up to her friend. 'You ready then, Edith?'

Muriel rested her hands on the sill, marking her white gloves. Was she ready for the two-mile walk into the city centre? Part of the sea of white, twenty thousand people and more that year.

She shouted back, 'You can call me Muriel from now on.'

She had been pegging out the washing across the yard, waltzing between the billowing sheets as she went, when she heard her father berating her mother through the back door. Her mother sat hunched over a bowl of potatoes, their peelings stuck to her red-raw hands.

'I'm not having some other bugger taking my job for the sake of a few days away but you need a rest, Edna – what about Booths Hall? I know you're not so friendly with your mother but surely she'd be pleased to see you and the children, given the circumstances?'

Edna shuffled her chair closer to the range. 'She won't want a bunch of Moss Side tykes mucking up her grand bedrooms. Can you see our Muriel clattering down the main stairs in her tap shoes?'

Muriel crossed her fingers and wished. The family didn't talk about Granny Cowburn much, but when they did it was in hushed, reverent tones. She had made good for herself by marrying into money. Muriel wrapped herself in a sheet and imagined it was a silk ballgown. She wouldn't clatter, she would glide down those stairs. She longed to see the house. She burst into the kitchen, still draped in the bedclothes.

'Muriel!' her mother scolded. 'You're dragging dirt all over my clean sheets.'

Her father unwound his daughter with rough hands and cuffed her ear. 'Why are you making more work for your mother, you selfish girl.'

She pursed her lips and railed against him. 'Why should Mum do all the housework? You and the boys could help out now and again.'

Her father's face clouded with cumulus clouds for the coming storm. Muriel stepped behind her mother's chair, her father reached to undo his belt buckle, but her mother stayed him.

'Now, Clarrie, don't go taking offence at the flighty girl. She didn't mean it, did you, love?'

Muriel gripped the back of her mother's chair. She did mean it, every word. She was sick of taking on all the chores just because she was a girl. It wouldn't do.

Her father sneered at her. 'Think you're too good to get your hands dirty, don't you, girl? Think you're better than the rest of us? Well, just you go and see how the other half live then, see if they think you're one of them.'

Muriel glanced around the small kitchen with its blackened range and stone floor, filled by three bodies, stuffed by nine when all the family was home. They'd moved to a new house so many times, each time somewhere a little bigger, but never big enough. Maybe Granny Cowburn would have room for one more in the space at Booths Hall?

*

Muriel travelled with her mother, two sisters and her youngest brothers by train from Piccadilly to Knutsford. They boarded the bus to Ollerton and walked the rest of the way. Her feet hurt. She had insisted on wearing her dance shoes, despite her mother's weary objections. It was just in case someone should see her and ask them straight into the house where she could demonstrate her dancing skills to Granny. Her feet rang like horses' hooves along the back lane, pausing by the gate where the gardener was to meet them. Harry was swinging from her hand. He kicked his shoes into the bluebells nodding against the high brick wall. A wall to keep the likes of us out, Muriel thought.

'Will they have horses, Muriel? Will they have boats on the lake? Can we swim in the lake? Can we swim in there today?'

She released her brother's hand. She was excited too, but there was no use showing it here – this was a refined place. 'Remember your manners, Harry. I hope you haven't left them at home.' She flapped her cotton dress. It was hot. Harry was right, a swim in the lake would be nice, so would the cool tiled floors of the house on her sore feet. 'When can we go in the house, Mum?' she asked.

'We've been invited for high tea on Wednesday, if you behave,' her mother answered.

The gardener opened the door and a new world glittered before the family. Flower beds that nodded with hollyhocks and beds of carefully tended vegetables, gravel paths through the kitchen garden which they crunched along as they followed round a fountain that gushed between the nodding lavender and across the soft lawns that wrapped around the huge house with its glittering walls of windows. Muriel thought she saw a figure move behind a window. Perhaps it was Granny Cowburn watching the pity-worthy branch of the family tread across her manicured gardens. She had only seen a picture of her mother's mother once. A sepia crumpled photograph that showed a stern-looking woman in swathes of black silk. She looked as though butter wouldn't melt, but Muriel thought she saw a spark in her dark eyes and noticed her small feet peeping from under her skirt. Dance shoes, she thought. There must be so many dances at Booths Hall.

Muriel had already made the decision that she would be moving in. She could live in the big house for ever and ever and never go back to Moss Side. She lagged as they snaked past a horse chestnut in the lower meadow and leapt onto the bench that encircled it.

'Hey!' she shouted. 'Do you think Granny Cowburn might leave the house to me when she dies?'

Florence turned round. 'Don't be daft, why would she do that?'

'I am the best grandchild after all, I'll be her favourite.' Muriel emphasised this with one of her theatrical bows.

Florence marched back and grabbed her by the hand.

'Don't be ridiculous, why would she single you out above all of us? Get down and stop mucking about now.'

Muriel thought it was obvious why she should be the favoured one. She was the dancer, the entertainer, the one with the looks. Her father said she was blooming into a lovely young lady.

Flo yanked her towards the cottage. 'There's no chance we'll get anything after Granny dies. The house is her husband's, it'll go to his side of the family. Anyway, girls don't inherit places like this.'

Muriel thought this unfair, but she kept quiet until they reached the cottage.

There she fought with her siblings over the best room, beds made up with clean white linen and whitewashed walls. A fire had been set in the parlour. Her mother started to unpack while the children ran down to the lake. Muriel picked a bunch of daisies outside the front door and offered them to Edna in a jam jar. The cottage already felt more like home than home did.

She found a quiet nook beneath a drooping willow and peeled off her dress, shivering slightly in her undergarments. She wanted a swim, but dark shadows flickered beneath the surface.

'It's just fish,' said Harry.

'Do you think they bite?' asked Rose.

Leslie slid behind his little brother and pushed him sharply. 'They can swim, unlike you, Harry,' he shouted.

As Harry's feet tripped he flung his arms out to catch on to one of his sisters, but he only snatched a willow tendril, and he hung there for a split second, a surprised look on his little face as the branch snapped and he toppled backwards into the water. Rose screamed. Muriel leapt in as he went under, the thick water clouding green over her own head. The shadows caressed her white ankles as she felt herself floating down into the darkness. She fought against it. It was Flo who grabbed both her and Harry by the neck and dragged them to the bank. Flo the champion swimmer. Muriel had to take Harry back to the cottage and explain to her mother why all of his clothes were wet. She got a thick ear for her trouble.

'That's a great start,' her mother said.

*

When Wednesday arrived, the children were dressed and polished in their Sunday best and made a procession across the sun-warmed meadow up to the grand portico, allowed through the main entrance, just the once. The front porch was as big as their front room. Muriel tapped her feet tentatively on the tiled floor and got a slap from her mother for her efforts as a long-faced servant girl opened the door and ushered them forward. The hall yawned around them, mosaic tiles beneath their feet circled with vines and leaves while white marble columns held up the ceiling, topped with curls and swirls like an iced wedding cake.

The servant girl addressed them all. 'Would you and your children please wait here, Mrs Cook. Tea will be served at four in the drawing room. We will call you then.' She left them waiting and disappeared round a corner.

Edna took a seat on a velvet chaise and reached out and felt the waxy leaves of an aspidistra. She could wait, if her children could not. Muriel's impatient feet tapped the floor and the sound echoed up to the crystal chandelier and shook the dewdrop glass.

'Quiet!' her mother shushed, but she knew it was no use. She closed her eyes, just for a moment's peace, and was soon dozing.

The children would not wait. It was Muriel who spotted the open door first and beckoned them to follow her into an empty room with a parquet floor and the chairs pushed around the edge.

'It's the ballroom,' she gasped, snatching Rose and waltzing her across the polished floor, giggling under the heavy oil portraits. They reminded her of the town hall murals a little, but they weren't as bright. 'Who do you think the people in the paintings are?' she asked.

Flo answered from across the room. She had leaned on the marble mantelpiece to light a cigarette and was already blowing smoke up the chimney. She let Muriel have a drag as she waltzed up, but drew the line at Rose.

'They'll be his family, I expect, from years ago. I can't see one of Granny Cowburn though,' Flo said.

'They all look really bored,' Muriel said. She ran her finger over the fine carvings on the marble frieze. 'Could these be angels?' she asked.

Flo peered at the creatures with bodies intertwined. 'They're naked bloody angels if they are.'

'Like Hell's Angels?' Muriel asked.

She'd seen the Howard Hughes film amongst many more. Films fed her fantasies and she had started going to the West End cinema twice a week. It was a barn of a place where the doors opened straight out onto the street so the fog would come seeping in. With the cigarette smoke and usherettes spraying disinfectant in the air, her view of the screen was obscured, but it was cheap, just a few pence for a seat and a block of chocolate. When Muriel sank into her seat and watched the silver screen she watched the modern women in the newsreels and dreamed of following them on their adventures abroad. She could slap the bonnet of a shiny car with her leather driving gloves and laugh into the camera. She could be a carefree explorer like the women who swam the channel, went motor racing and flew to Australia.

It was Florence who shot her dreams down. 'Girls like us don't cross the world, Muriel,' Flo told her. 'We work in mills and factories, offices if we're lucky, and marry decent men.'

Weary men with the steadiest jobs they could find, thought Muriel, men who didn't gamble or drink their wages away in the company of others, men who didn't raise their fist to you. Men like Nelson Eddy singing to Jeanette MacDonald. What would it be like to be loved by someone who sang across mountains for you? She'd not marry a weary man.

'I'm not working in a bloody mill and I'm not marrying a boring chap either. I'll marry someone who'll take me places, an adventurer, a hero!' That gave Flo a good laugh, but it made Muriel think. Where would she find someone like that in Moss Side?

They left the ballroom and explored the house up the grand oak staircase past a vast painting of a naked woman wilting in a dark grove.

'Maybe that's a painting of Granny Cowburn,' Muriel said.

'Why don't you tell her that when you meet her,' Flo sneered. 'I'm sure she'd be dead chuffed to be compared to a goddess.'

'What do you mean?'

'I've seen it in the art gallery in town. Bert took me.'

Muriel prickled. Her sister got to go courting into town, and to the art gallery as well. She hadn't been there yet. She'd go on her own as soon as she was old enough. Muriel pushed open yet another door into a room with high glass windows, where a forest of washing hung from ranks of pulley maids. A girl not much older than her sat darning a sheet across her knee as a bell rang and she put her mending down.

'You lot shouldn't be up here. That's the tea bell, you'd better come with me.'

The children trooped down a set of back stairs, narrow and plain for the servants, and emerged into the kitchen where a large wooden box on the wall flickered persistently with one yellow light.

Muriel pointed up at it. 'What's that?'

'The bell box,' the girl said. 'It's Mrs Cowburn calling from the drawing room. She'll be wondering where you lot are.'

There was a voice from the doorway. 'I was wondering, but I decided to come and find them myself, thank you, Nancy.'

A tall woman leant against the door frame. She wore a dress of dark blue silk, her neck strung with ropes and ropes of pearls. Her face had fewer lines, but the same slant as their mother's, without the shadows under the eyes. She smiled, a proper smile that lit up her face and lifted her pencilled eyebrows. Muriel thought she was the most beautiful woman she had seen, apart from Greta Garbo of course, but she was on the screen, not a real person.

Mrs Cowburn drew deeply on her cigarette holder and exhaled smoke-smooth words. 'Hello, children, I could hear the racket from the other side of the house and the ballroom smells of Woodbines. Would that have anything to do with you?' Florence blushed. Mrs Cowburn wafted a pink Sobranie in a cigarette holder towards her. 'You should try these, my dear, they're better for your health. I could hear someone's dancing footsteps too. Who is the dancer?'

Muriel stepped forward. 'That would be me,' she said bravely and stretching her arms gracefully took several steps of a foxtrot around the table in her white Whit dress, willing her granny to approve as she spun past the copper pans. She would be the girl who could dance and entertain visitors at evening soirées – she didn't know what soirée meant, but it sounded good – let the others go back to Moss Side. Booths Hall could keep her.

Her granny applauded the performance with light claps. 'Well, maybe we could have you up for the dance on Friday. Arthur has invited most of the village and we could do with some more entertainment. Can any of you play the piano?'

Both Flo and Rose nodded.

'I can sing too,' said Rose, emboldened by Muriel's display.

Her older sister shoved her out of the way. 'And I'm a champion swimmer,' Flo said.

Muriel glared at her. What use would a swimming display be?

Granny Cowburn drew on her Sobranie. 'We do have a swimming pool here, filled with fresh water from our own well.'

'I swam in the lake!' Harry piped up.

'Did you now, young man?'

'He fell in,' mumbled Leslie.

'I was pushed,' said Harry, kicking his brother's shin.

Muriel inched towards her granny, putting herself centre stage in front of her siblings. 'We would love to come to a dance,' she said.

They climbed the stairs back to the drawing room, the best stairs this time, and their grandmother wafted her cigarette to the painting Muriel had mistaken for her. 'That monstrosity of a painting is called The Death of Dido. I detest it, but my Arthur likes to have something impressive on the wall.'

'Muriel thought it was you,' Florence sniped.

Muriel shoved her sister and tugged gently at her granny's sleeve. The silk melted in her hand. She wished she could wear silk. 'Have you seen the paintings in Manchester town hall, Granny Cowburn?'

Her grandmother gently removed the girl's hand as she opened the drawing-room door. 'If you mean the Ford Madox Brown murals, yes, I've seen them, many, many times.'

Muriel beamed. 'I was named after them, Muriel, that's my name.'

Flo sniggered. 'No you weren't! "Mad Muriel", that's more like your name.' She tripped her sister and Muriel stumbled against her granny, falling at her mother's feet.

Edna hauled her upright and brushed her down, her

face like thunder. 'Please behave yourself, Muriel,' her mother begged.

Granny Cowburn perched on the edge of her chintz sofa and placed one hand on Muriel's soft curls like a blessing. 'I'm quite impressed with this one. She's interested in art and dances like a dream. Perhaps she can come again.'

Muriel squeezed her eyes shut in silent prayer. 'I can stay if you like, Granny. I could help you around the house.'

Edna shot her daughter a warning stare, but Flo couldn't help herself. 'What makes you think Granny would want a scruffy tyke like you round the house?' she yelled. 'You've been behaving like a stuck-up cow all week, Mural Muriel.'

The sparks ignited and Muriel flew at her sister, erasing her words with flying fists. She got a good handful of hair before the maid parted them, pinching an ear in each hand. Granny Cowburn waved them away, less than charmed.

She pointed at Muriel. 'Take that one down to the cellar, keep her out of trouble. Show her the wine, Nancy, and let her choose a bottle for Edna to take home with her.'

Muriel's heart sank. She had slipped from the chosen one to 'that one' in an instant. Her opportunity dissolved into the shadows.

March 1935

Muriel's mind had settled flat as the tram tracks that ran past another new home. It was a bigger house on Princess Road opposite the Grammar School with three bedrooms and a loo downstairs. Corporation-built in the 1920s from shiny, oiled canvas polished brick. Modern by all standards with solid square rooms and an indoor bath, a plane tree in the front garden, a piano in the front room and a carriage clock on the Victorian credenza sideboard next to the Philips cabinet radio. That was Muriel's favourite item in the whole house. She spent many a time twisting the dial to Radio Luxembourg, while her father twisted it back with a 'tut' to the BBC.

It was inevitable Muriel would follow her sister Flo, her schoolmates and Joyce to the biscuit factory, drawn like treacle on a spoon. She remembered there had been Crumpsall biscuit tins at Booths Hall, stacked on wooden shelves in the pantry. Any opportunities to visit the grand house again had withered since Granny Cowburn passed away. The other side of the family turned the cold shoulder on their Moss Side relations. Muriel's hopes of taking up residence were blocked. There were no invites to dances or high tea, although they went to the funeral. They kept seven steps behind the family car, six crow-black figures, their heads bowed in deference. Muriel had held her head high and dared the stares of the villagers who lined the route to the church in Ollerton.

Muriel handed her biscuit factory wages straight to her mother; all the girls did. Good job too, there wasn't much coming in from the men in the family and the house was full. Her older brothers, Clarence and Alfie, were out looking for work every day, walking so far their father couldn't keep up replacing the shoe leather on their soles. Money was scarce for extras, so she had to cut down on cinema visits and dances, but there were other ways to find it. She'd heard of girls charging for a dance at some of the dance halls. She wasn't quite that desperate, not yet, although it was easy enough to find gullible partners.

Crumpsall's was a decent place with a club for its workers and a recreation ground for strolling, if there was any energy left after a ten-hour day standing. Yet it wasn't the outdoor pursuits that tempted Muriel, but the events and the dances at the social club. It was not as grand as The Ritz in town, but as good a place as any to hone her skills. Partnering with Joyce, she would work out the foxtrot, waltz and tango, copying the more experienced dancers and memorising the steps she had seen on the silver screen. There were a few men there and with her trim figure and light feet she was always asked for a dance. They thought she was a dance teacher. Muriel could have taken advantage, but it seemed unfair to charge them when she knew they had as little money as she did.

Her brothers found ways to bring in luxuries, usually through the son of a neighbour, Mickey Evans. Mickey had latched on to their household from a young age and now he spent more time there than he did at home, flirting with Flo and kicking a ball round Alexandra Park with Harry. He had watched Muriel always with a sly smile, like she was a horse ready to bolt. He had been a family friend since they were children; now he was the man to go to if you needed knock-off cigarettes or stockings. He'd even procured stewing steak one week. Her mother was delighted. Muriel less so: the blood had leaked through its packaging and stained the jacket of his ill-fitting suit. She'd been given the job of soaking his jacket and he stood far too close to her as she scrubbed Omo flakes in the sink. She could smell Mickey, attractive and repulsive in equal measure, with his watered-down cologne and dried blood.

'How about a kiss for me, Muriel, and I'll get you some chicken next week,' he said.

She pushed him away with soapy hands that left two wet imprints on his vest. 'Get away with you, Mickey, I'm not one of your Saturday girls.'

He looked her up and down. She knew he was getting the measure of her, watching as he always did like a fox on the prowl. 'Stockings then,' he suggested. 'Got to be worth a kiss for stockings?'

She shook her head and turned back to the sink. 'Not even stockings.'

Muriel had mixed feelings about Mickey. It wasn't that she was behind the door. She'd witnessed her sister's fumblings in the back alley with boys who were keen and she and Joyce giggled over her older brother's magazines.

And there was something in her too, a flickering passion that she could charge up and unleash if she wanted. It was hard holding it at bay. Mickey had been around so long it would be easy for them to couple up. He was standing so close it would be easy for her to give in to thrill and turn and kiss him. She knew if she let it happen once it would happen again, and she couldn't be sure she would be the only one. She'd not seen him with the same girl twice walking down Princess Road on Saturday strolls. She'd seen him with new male friends too, and there was one that made her blood quicken more than Mickey Evans ever did. She only kept Mickey close because he could introduce them.

At work she had tried to set herself apart from the other girls. She had been noticed and asked to participate in some publicity shots for Crumpsall's. Muriel agreed readily – there could be some extra money in it. She tucked a stray black hair under her mob cap that was set skew-whiff on her curls, and rearranged her face into a serious frame, imagining she was posing for Ford Madox. Since the town hall murals, he'd become something of an obsession. She had discovered more of his work in The Whitworth and spent free days cloaked from the rain in the plush corridors, steaming dry by the lush paintings. She fancied herself one of his subjects, maybe that dark-haired Irish girl clutching a tiny sprig of heather, only here she was, clutching a wafer biscuit in front of a photographer who had plucked her from the ranks. She had hoped for more.

'Hold still, love. Could you stand at the table and open the tin a little more so we can see the biscuits?' he said.

Muriel's heart shifted down a gear. Biscuits? Who

needs biscuits when they could have a portrait of me? she thought.

Joyce called across the factory floor. 'Hey, Muriel! Watch the birdie!' she yelled above the rattle of the boxing machine.

Muriel waved back. She loved the din of her workplace, the factory bursts, mechanical rattles and clunks like a thousand tap dancers belting out a routine.

The photographer sighed and put his camera down. 'Listen, love, I need you to look at the biscuits, not your mates. Make your face demure. You know what that means, don't you?'

She frowned. 'Of course I do.' Flo had often teased her for her use of words at home. She said she sounded like she had swallowed a dictionary.

'Well, do it then,' he said.

Muriel leant over the table, allowing the stifled air to leak under the top of her overalls. Despite the constant sweeping and wiping down, bone-white icing sugar settled over everything in a fine veil. She pinched a pale pink wafer between her thumb and finger and folded the paper flat, revealing the neatly stacked biscuits. Crumpsall's biscuits were shipped all over the world, loaded on pallets for America by the boys who worked in packing. Boys that whistled after Muriel and her friends. She flirted back, nothing serious, mind. They might be promising dance partners, but she had her sights set higher than a packer in a biscuit factory. Anyone who promised a ticket out of there. It was hard to be uncontaminated by the sheen of grease in a biscuit works, enveloped in the aroma of melting sugar and fat. The smell drew dopamine rushes from all who passed by. Muriel too, enchanted by the aroma.

'Aaaah biscuits,' she breathed as she cycled to work in the morning, her skirt tucked in her knickers. She glanced back at the photographer.

He'd introduced himself as James Prince.

'But you can call me Jack,' he said, winding an extended handshake into a snakelike embrace around her waist. She allowed him, momentarily caught off guard by the flutter his name brought. She'd just met another James, who said she could call him Jim. He had made a dent in her heart and quickened her pulse and she wanted to see him again. She knew he was a good friend of Mickey Evans. He was tall and fair, not like this photographer James, who was dark with a square jaw like Clark Gable, hair parted sharply in the middle. Just a little too plastered with oil to be attractive. Photographer James was a disappointment, just a man with empty promises whose patience was wearing thin.

He had tried to sweet talk her at work behind the packing shed. 'You're an attractive girl ... if you were prepared to do a few private pictures for me, we could make a bundle selling them to my more discerning clients.'

She'd brushed him off like sugar dust. 'I'm having none of that, thank you. You'd have better luck with the sixpence dancers at The Raby.'

Muriel broke her pose as Jack packed up his gear. She shuffled back to work, moving some boxes onto a sack barrow, her forearms flexed with well-developed muscle. Speed was the thing at Crumpsall's.

She sidled up to her friend. 'What you doing tonight, Joyce?'

'Friday, isn't it? Stoppin' in and doing my hair, shampoo and set, the usual.' Friday night was Amani night, a hair wash once a week with a setting lotion for perfect curls. The girls got the bathroom to themselves while the men in the family went out. 'You in tonight too?'

Muriel pushed her hands into the small of her aching back and straightened. 'Where else would I be? Between working all hours here and doing the chores when I get home, there's bugger all time left for going out. I've got a new frock to finish anyway.'

'Would that be to catch the eye of anyone special?' She had confided in Joyce about the James she had noticed on Princess Road.

'Ah, get away with you. Jim wouldn't go to The Ritz – he doesn't dance.'

'You could teach him though.'

Muriel dropped a box and kicked it with her foot. That would be all the biscuits broken.

*

Muriel went dancing often. The dance halls were the dream palaces for all, grand halls offering thrills and sophistication that provided a frequent diversion from a substandard life. There were two dance halls within a twenty-minute walk from Princess Road, local places that satisfied her three-times-a-week habit. A habit her father objected to.

'You should do something more improving with your spare time, lass. Take an evening class or some piano lessons, like Flo,' Clarence said.

Her mother nodded assent as she was sweeping up the smuts in the grate. Muriel bristled and turned up the volume on the radio. She couldn't imagine anything else would come close to letting her express her restless spirit.

'It's no use agreeing with him, Mum. I'm not ending up stuck in a kitchen with a dustpan while I could be out dancing.'

Her father clipped her ear. 'Don't be cheeky, madam, you'll do as you're told while you live under my roof.'

She bit her lip and pressed her small teeth into her lipstick – she wouldn't give him the satisfaction of tears. If she had her way she'd be out from under his roof as soon as she could.

Muriel defied Clarence's rules and sneaked out to as many dances as she could. To the Victoria Road Baths, where she had tested out her first tap shoes. The gala pool was boarded over in winter with floral baskets hanging from the balcony and potted palms placed across the changing-room doors. As the orchestra struck up 'In the Mood' the dance leader quipped, 'Has everybody brought their costume?' The band wore fluorescent clothing that glowed when the lights dimmed. In her white dress Muriel complemented the dancing host of angels gliding across the boards. Dancing on water, she thought.

Saturday, she and Joyce went to The Raby. Joyce hung behind her friend in the new crêpe polka dot frock Muriel had made for her, a little too much like a day dress, but shy enough to suit Joyce. Muriel wore something more flamboyant in blue cotton with a gored skirt and flutter sleeves. She'd longed for silk but had only pennies enough for offcuts.

'I heard it was a blood bath here last week,' Joyce gasped as the girls entered the hall.

Muriel cast a glance around the flip-down seats and withered paper lanterns. The floor beneath her feet was sticky, splattered with beer and cigarette butts. She imagined it splattered with blood. The band was good though and playing the music she liked. Smatters of jazz that echoed the flibbertigibbet flickers in her mind, Radio Luxembourg favourites and the sudden rise and fall of a running, hopping trumpet.

'It's a right dive,' she agreed. 'Father would kill me if he knew we were here. Music's good though.' She pulled Joyce into a quickstep across the open floor before they changed their minds.

The band paused as the band leader announced, 'Ladies and gents, time for the tango!' A collective groan emitted from the few scattered men in the hall and a group bolted for the door.

Muriel spotted her fifteen-year-old brother Leslie amongst them. 'They'll be sat in the nearest pub with a pint until they think the danger's passed, Joyce,' she said.

She cheered when they returned, hoping that Jim might be with them – he frequented The Eagle a few doors down from The Raby, she knew that, along with his inseparable drinking buddy Mickey. There was no Jim, just her stumbling younger brother with his mates.

'Can't take the pace, can you, Leslie?' she yelled, wondering how her father would react if he knew Leslie was there. It would be a different reaction if he knew she was at The Raby. She danced out her disappointment in her own tango. Muriel had to lead – her friend couldn't quite get the hang of the cross step. She would have preferred the woman's part, curving her body into the sculpture of the *ocho*. She flashed her quick feet into a leg hook anyway, dipping a confused Joyce as the lilting violin finished with a flourish.

*

She had met Jim on Princess Road while she was strolling, her arms linked to her sisters', on a walkabout past the railings of Alexandra Park. She was too old to dance in the bandstand, but she still liked to go there and listen to the bands on Sundays. The girls were eyeing up the boys on the opposite side of Princess Road and the boys were eyeing them up in turn. The monkey walk, they called it. Hand in hand, arm in arm, marching heads high, eyes fixed in front, a symphony of orchestrated laughter with their heads thrown back. Muriel couldn't hold in her laugh that day, playing the giddy kipper. It belted out and shook the budding plane trees. Jim heard it. He knew who it came from.

Saturday, Muriel took her savings into town and splashed out on a salon perm in the city. She spent the whole morning cooking under a helmet hairdryer and emerged into a fine drizzle that threatened to turn her carefully sculptured curls to frizz. Pulling her scarf tight, she'd lowered her head and trotted to the tram stop in Albert Square, until she recognised a figure coming down the town hall steps. Muriel pressed her lips together to even-spread her lipstick red and waltzed through the crowd until she was level with his broad back.

'Hello, James Burns, have you been in trouble then?'

Jim turned to the compact figure, her big dark eyes set in a wide face that shouted 'Look at me if you dare'.

Her eyes sparked with mischief. He could look at them for
hours. Jim was smitten. He leaned towards Muriel outside
the town hall. She smelled of Pears Soap and damp wool.
'I've not been in trouble, you cheeky rascal. I've been in
there for an interview,' he said.

Muriel thought he looked dignified in his suit, but not
stuck-up. She'd heard him laugh with the rest of the lads at
some crude joke, but he had tempered his behaviour when
she was around – she liked him more for it. She'd overheard
him talking about her near Alexandra Park. He was leaning
against the railings with Mickey. She had yanked Flo's arm
and made her walk past slowly, deliberately behind so they
couldn't see her, but she could hear them.

'She's got movie star looks, that Muriel Cook,' Jim had
said.

Muriel beamed. Didn't she know it?

'Makes my heart lift when she smiles,' he continued.

Mickey had shrugged. 'I know Muriel, she grins a little
too often, that one. One buttie short of a picnic, if you ask
me.'

Muriel had revealed herself with a swift kick to Mickey's
shin and marched past, head high, dragging Flo behind.

She hadn't seen Jim since. He was handsome with
fair hair and light blue eyes, four years older than her so
had been out in the world a little longer. The same age as
Mickey. The same age as her sister Flo, but she was pleased
he'd taken a shine to her over her sister. She liked him more
for that too.

She touched his sleeve on the town hall steps. 'Interview
with the police? Did you get in?' she asked.

He shook his head. 'I was half an inch too flaming short.'

Muriel had made it her business to find out all about Jim. She knew he cycled everywhere looking for work. He'd been a butcher's delivery boy for a time, cycling to Timperley out along the canal. So, he was fit and had a sense of adventure, she thought, maybe a bit more ambition to get out of Moss Side and see the world, though Cheshire was hardly another continent.

She pointed at his feet and his shoes shined treacle black. 'Our dad has a last for shoes in the house. He could've built them up for you half an inch more. That would have got you in.' They both laughed.

Muriel changed the subject. She knew he would be disappointed not to get into the police force. It was a steady job, and they were hard to come by. 'Did you see the murals while you were in the town hall?' she said.

'The Muriels? She's standing right in front of me,' he joked.

'Don't be daft, I mean the paintings in the grand hall. Which one was your favourite?'

Jim scanned his short-term memory. What had he noticed? He remembered his damp palms resting on his knees and how hard the bench was, but the walls in the grand hall had mostly been a blur of colour. He would have to tell her something else to impress her.

'There was one of a park, I think it was a park. It had a big tree in the middle and a boy sitting in it eating an apple.' Muriel frowned, trying to recall the painting from his description. Jim wiped his palms on his suit again and held his breath.

'Boy in a tree? Oh I know the one! There's a boy bending over to pick up a ball and a dog about to bite his bum!' She roared with laughter. It was a laugh that turned heads, that switched back under hats and umbrellas to see the source of the siren sound.

He smiled. 'I never noticed the dog.'

'I can tell you all about those paintings. The one with the boy and the dog is of a boy's school near where the cathedral is, but the trees are from somewhere else. Ford Madox Brown studied the trees on Platt Lane for that picture.'

'The Platt Lane near us? Ford who?'

Muriel shook her head and linked her arm through his. The tram home could wait. 'I've a lot to teach you, Jim.'

She guided him through the crowds to Piccadilly Gardens. The park was lined with packed benches, but they found one space by the bare rose bushes and huddled amongst the shop workers on their lunch break. Muriel interrogated him, although she already knew a little about him from her careful questioning of Mickey and Flo.

'How long have you been on Princess Road then?' she said.

'A few months, we moved from Old Trafford.'

Muriel smiled at the memory of the place. 'We were out that way when I was little.' And everywhere else, she thought. They had moved so often, it might be nice to settle for a bit. It looked like they would on the avenue opposite the park. She was glad of it. Her restless soul needed something steady for a while. Recently she'd felt more flighty than usual – she needed an anchor. She linked her arm through Jim's again and gave it a gentle squeeze. 'Have you got brothers or sisters then?'

'I've got the one sister, Isabella, but she lives in Canada now. We write to each other all the time,' he said.

Muriel paused. It sounded like too small a family and she was suspicious, but the little uncertainty was overruled by the scrap of information he'd given her about Canada. It was interesting, somewhere to visit if he had a sister out there, maybe somewhere to live. An idea sparked and she attempted to moderate the excitement in her voice before it ran away with her. 'Canada, really? Have you seen that film about Canada, *Rose Marie*? Nelson Eddy plays a Mountie. I like Nelson Eddy.'

'I like Jeanette MacDonald,' Jim said. He reached for her hand and she let her small fingers settle into his palm.

'Would you go to Canada, Jim?' she prompted.

'Maybe one day, but not now, I think. I need to find steady work and bring in some money for my family.' He swallowed. 'I've only found work four of the last ten months.' His grip tightened slightly. Muriel knew that was hard – men's pride couldn't take not working. Women worked all the time, in the home and out of it; it was a natural state for her. 'My mother would be devastated if I left for Canada. She was heartbroken when Isabella went, never quite got over it,' he said.

Muriel thought she would. You get over loss, you cope, you manage. She'd seen her mother do it after she lost the baby, although she was never quite the same. She'd known families have children leave and thought of the wonderful Ford Madox Brown painting she'd just found in the city art gallery, on loan from The Walker in Liverpool. The Last of England it was called. It showed a couple huddled in a boat, hands clutched, determined to leave it all behind. The painting shone bright in a gold porthole frame, as if she was looking through the window of a ship. That couple would have left their family. It wasn't impossible. She half listened to Jim, distracted by ideas that were taking seed.

'We've moved house nineteen times since I was born,' he said. 'Maybe it's time I settled down.'

She watched the rose stems nodding, tight buds too soon for blooming. Maybe it was time he settled down with her. 'Nineteen times? Blimey, that's almost more times than I've had hot dinners.'

Her scarf had slipped and Jim bent to kiss her on her new smart curls. The fresh perm lotion stung his lips. Muriel tilted her head and let him kiss her properly, budded her lips to his and pressed her petal soft mouth against him. She felt suddenly dizzy with intense feeling and pulled away. Stared up at him defiantly in the public gardens. She didn't care who saw them.

'Can I take you out sometime, Muriel Cook?' he asked.

'You can take me out next Friday – there's a dance at The Ritz.'

*

When the following Friday came round Muriel was ready for The Ritz. She had begged and borrowed to make a new dress. A bias-cut stripe crêpe, flipping out at mid-calf with a contrast collar and a belt. That made three dresses in her collection, not including the swaps she could get from Joyce and Flo. Jim had promised to meet her there. She was a little disappointed that he wasn't coming to the house to pick her up. The more sophisticated venues were a tram ride away in the city centre, saved for weekends and special occasions. It would have been nice to be escorted on the journey, but Jim had said he would need to get his ticket at the door. She already had hers. She had been the first in the queue, as eager as she had been outside Handforth's, waiting for her tappers.

Muriel felt tense as she sat on the tram seat, sandwiched between Flo, Joyce and Rose, the sweat blooming in her armpits, her ticket clutched and crumpled in one gloved hand. The Ritz ballroom was a cut above, full-scale grand, a palace that met Muriel's strong appetite for life, where the band leaders had served their apprenticeships in cosmopolitan New York.

The girls walked the short distance from the tram stop and marvelled at the smart staff in uniform that took their coats and hats, the opulence of the entrance hall under an illuminated globe that sparked shatters of light onto a fountain below. Muriel peeled a glove off and leant over to test the water, barely touching the surface before Flo dragged her away.

'Leave that, this is a decent place, please be sensible.'

Muriel felt anything but sensible. She felt like a fizzed-up Vimto, her skin charged with excitement.

She followed Flo's shoulders through the double doors into the ballroom where hundreds of couples skimmed over a sprung dance floor in a whirl of whispering rayon. Puffs of Je Reviens and exotic Shalimar drifted up her nose, sweeter than the dive dance hall aroma of sweat and beer. There were linen-draped tables with fresh blooms in vases and crystal ashtrays clustered around the dance floor. The girls made their way to an empty table and Muriel sat tentatively on the gilt-backed chair, placed her clutch bag at her feet and scanned the crowd for Jim. She would have spotted his fair head, he was tall for the era, but he wasn't leaning at the bar with the other non-dancers or lined up in front of the stage watching the band. She looked above the Tuscan columns to balconies of gilt and cream. He was not there either, nor among the dancing couples with arms round shoulders, openly holding hands in the place for romance and escape. It was unlikely he would be dancing anyway, she knew he wasn't keen, but she had plans to change that. It might be hard to find him amongst the crowd. He would have to find her, and until then she decided she would need to make her own entertainments.

Joyce stumbled towards her friend, placing a wide-brimmed glass on the cloth. 'Make it last, Muriel. I can only afford the one – that took all of last week's wages,' she said, tapping her finger-waved curls.

Muriel sipped the cloudy liquid. It buzzed down her throat and made her eyes sting. 'Thank you, what is it?' she said.

'Gin something, I don't fancy it, I'm having a cup of tea.' Joyce fanned her face with the dance programme. 'Flamin' hot, isn't it? Oh Muriel, turn round, look at the stage now!'

Muriel looked. The stage was slowly turning. One band set disappearing into the dark as another emerged, fresh behind their golden music stands.

'It must be change-over time. You'll get one lot playing for half an hour, then the second band is up. Let's hope they play some jazz,' Muriel said, sharing her limited knowledge to educate her friend.

She'd spotted the dark sax player – jazz looked possible. She just needed to find the right partner. There were a few talented characters, but she couldn't ask a man to dance unless she was out there with Joyce and they played a 'buzz off' number. A tap on Joyce's shoulder and an excuse-me dance would be an improvement. Not that Joyce was bad, but she only came up to Muriel's chin, and it made an awkward pairing.

She noticed someone lingering by their table. A smart fella with slicked-back hair and round glasses hovered by her shoulder and extended his hand.

'May I have this dance?'

Muriel didn't need to be asked twice. She was up in a flash and off, quickstepping across the floor, spinning a heel and clicking out as if she were Eleanor Powell in *George White's Scandals*. Her dance partner could barely keep up with her. His pinstripe jacket shifted open and she could see patches of sweat on his shirt below.

'You're some dancer,' he panted, leading her back to her seat. 'Have you thought about giving lessons?'

She flipped her curls. 'I've got a job, I don't do that sort of thing, thank you.'

He fluttered his hands. 'Oh no, dear, I meant professionally. I work for Mecca management. We're always looking for dancers to instruct our less willing clients at The Raby. Do you know it? The dance instruction brings more people through the doors than the actual dances and you'd be paid, of course.'

She drained the last of her gin. She didn't fancy wrestling drunks on a Saturday night, but maybe dance lessons happened when the main hall was closed. 'Paid? How much? I'm not one of those sixpenny dancers for hire by the dance, you know, hanging around by the bar, or wherever they can get free cigarettes.'

The man took a seat. Muriel could see Joyce and Flo

watching her with interest, listening keenly through their exhales of smoke.

'Heavens, no,' he said. 'It's a respectable establishment. You would be paid decently for one class a week, if you could fit that around your other commitments.'

Muriel thought about the ten-hour shifts standing on the production line. Could her restless legs take stamping out more dances? They were strong from work and cycling: she thought she could do it. Extra money would mean money to buy fabric and lipstick. She'd have more dresses to make and she could spend the surplus on the flicks. She'd be doing something she loved. Maybe Jim could be one of her customers too.

'Would there be free cigarettes?' she asked.

'If you participated in the exhibition dances, yes.'

Muriel paused. 'All right then, can I start next week?'

He left her with his card and a date and Flo sneered at her sister's newfound fortune.

'I suppose this means dancing skills are more important than looks now, does it?'

Muriel shrugged. She wasn't going to let Flo get to her. Anyway, there was another man waiting, his hand extended in invitation. She looked up into a familiar face. The photographer Jack had grown a pencil moustache and looked even more like Clark Gable. Her stomach tightened.

'Well, hello, Miss Demure, could I have a dance with you?' Jack asked.

Muriel shook her head. 'No, thank you, I'm waiting for someone.'

Jack looked at the river of dancers flowing past. 'I don't see Fred Astaire in here tonight and there are none too many people queued up for your services, so perhaps I could take you out on the floor?' His eyes roamed over her dress and he leant in. He stank of old pipe tobacco. 'I've seen the prints from Crumpsall's, Muriel. You're quite something, you know. I still think you look better without the overalls though. Perhaps we could take some more pictures of you in that lovely dress, or without it?'

Muriel dabbed at the sweat on her top lip. Joyce was right, it was hot. There was a faint smell of nylon heating, the friction from upper thigh stockings rubbing together. She pressed out her cigarette and half rose in her seat. As a dance partner he would have to do, there was no one else. She caught a glimpse of Mickey by the stage and sat down again with a bump that let the hem of her dress kiss the floor. If Mickey was there, Jim had to be.

'I'll decline, thank you, but my sister Flo might give you a dance,' she said.

Jack's smile slid a little, but Flo beamed and held out her hand. 'I would be delighted,' she said.

Muriel watched her sister and her partner muddy into the crowd and lit herself another cigarette, grateful for a lucky escape. She started at the scrape of a chair behind her.

'Good decision, Muriel. I didn't like the look of him,' Jim said.

She blew smoke out of the side of her lips and turned a warm smile on her new partner. 'Neither did I.'

June 1935

Muriel kept the dance job a secret from her father and coerced her mother into her familiar role of co-conspirator.

Her mother was none too pleased. 'There'll be ructions if he finds out,' Edna said, following her daughter as she pushed her bike round the side of the house, her skirt tucked up and her dance shoes already in her bag.

Muriel wobbled against the apple tree her father had planted and its white blossom scattered her head like confetti. She bestowed a rare kiss on her mother's worn cheek, one kiss from her soft lips. 'But you won't tell him, will you, Mum? Thank you.'

Edna touched the damp spot on her skin as her daughter's kiss dried. Kisses were not allowed beyond immediate family. Her husband wouldn't even allow his relatives to kiss her hello. She watched her daughter belt away on her new Raleigh, three whole pounds' worth, paid back at a shilling a month. 'Well you'd best keep away from his tram route, love, just in case,' she called.

Muriel veered down the road to the left and took a back street that was free of tram tracks. She pulled up at Cowan's and parked her bike round the side of the building. Cowan's wasn't as good as The Ritz, it wasn't even as good as Raby's, but it was a start. She was sure her talent and ambition would take her to the city centre palaces soon enough. Jim appeared as she was about to open the fire escape door. She smiled and kissed him, pleased there would be time for her to press her body along his and lead him round the sprung floor before her official lessons began. He was in uniform, had joined the Royal Army Service Corps the week before.

Muriel touched the rough wool of his sleeve. 'My, you do look smart in uniform, Jim.' She winked at him. 'You're my hero.'

'You know it's only the territorials, Muriel. It's a little bit of extra cash, mind, just less than two bob a day, and if the war comes, as everyone says it will, I'll be transferred to the regulars.'

Muriel pulled him onto the dance floor and counted out his foxtrot steps, hastening her swift feet pattering beside his heavy boots. She knew Jim couldn't match her immersion in the rhythms and beats that guided her, and deliberately sped up, aggrieved he had mentioned war. They were all so keen to join up, her brothers and friends. She didn't want to lose Jim, just when she had found him.

He let go. 'That's enough now! I can't keep up. It feels like you'd fly off, Muriel, if I didn't hold you down,' he panted.

Muriel stepped back as the music started again. She had other, paying, dance clients waiting for her. 'Why don't you watch for a bit, Jim? You might learn something,' she suggested, and pushed him towards the bar, where Mickey had taken up residence. Jim would have to resign himself to the role of spectator. Muriel could sense his discomfort. She knew that as they had grown closer Jim had begun to feel he had some ownership of her.

She picked a partner furthest from the bar, a plump boy in a green sweater his mother had most likely knitted, with feet almost as clumsy as Jim's. The boy sweated so much his hands slipped continuously from her grip. They kept to the sides of the room and used the other couples as a shield, so Jim couldn't look daggers with jealous eyes, but she could see Mickey tilting his head so he could keep her in his eyeline.

'Is Mickey Evans your boyfriend?' the boy asked, stepping on her feet once again. 'I know him.'

'Everyone knows Mickey,' she sighed. 'No, he's not my boyfriend.' Not for the want of trying or opportunity.

At least Mickey could dance. They'd jigged around back yards as children and she'd danced with him at Raby's before she was with Jim, and on one occasion at Crumpsall's social club, after she knew Jim. But she'd kept that secret. Mickey had turned up at her workplace social club bevvied with one of the icing girls. He dropped her like a sack of flour when he saw Muriel. He'd asked her to dance instead. Muriel had not hesitated long before she agreed. After all, he was the closest thing to Jim and Jim wasn't there. Mickey bought her her first gin fizz. After she had drunk enough of them for her head to start swimming, Mickey had offered to escort her home. She left her bike locked to the biscuit factory railings and walked alongside him as the streets flexed under her feet. That was how she fell against him, that was why he propped her against a lamp post. That was why she didn't resist his cold hands creeping under her slip and his wet mouth that pressed itself against hers.

He would have gone further if a passing policeman hadn't asked, 'You all right there, miss?' She pushed Mickey away and threw up into a bush. She didn't know if he'd told Jim anything about it. She hadn't. Perhaps Mickey was saving the secret, polishing it carefully to let slip at the best opportunity. She steered her partner away from Mickey's leering looks and gripped her red talons into his green jumper, stepping heavily on his feet.

'Ouch! It's usually me who steps on your toes, Miss Cook,' he said.

'Then you need to be closer, so I don't tread on you,' she answered, waltzing across the room towards the bar in plain sight of Jim.

'Too close together, Miss Cook,' warned the chaperone as she danced past.

'My boyfriend is the one next to Mickey, the one in uniform,' she said.

Her partner craned his mottled neck to look Jim up and down. 'I'm joining up too,' he said.

She danced him past the bar again. Muriel wanted to push Jim, to test his devotion, which she knew to be steady. 'Men and war, it's all you want,' she said. Jim gave a half-wave and a heart-melting smile. 'Well, maybe not all you want,' Muriel conceded. Perhaps she did not need to test him anymore. Perhaps he was devoted enough for the steadiest thing she knew of, marriage.

Her friend Joyce had married in the spring. It was an inevitable step with a baby on the way. Muriel had taken regular trips to church with Joyce prior to the ceremony, where Joyce prayed fervently, her bump straining against the polka dot crêpe.

'Forgive me, Father, for I have sinned. Give me the strength for the baby, give me the strength I need.' Muriel sat next to Joyce's urgent mumblings. Her mind tugged in too many directions, she couldn't gather it up and fold it like the bed sheets anymore. On the one side she had Jim, steady and loved, with the prospect of marriage and all that brought with it, on the other, dance and giddy freedom. Perhaps it was time to turn the giddiness down like the dial on the wireless, but she liked life loud.

She picked up a Bible and caressed its transparent pages. 'Forgive me, for I know not what I do,' she muttered in echo to Joyce's prayers. Charcoal black words on white pages burned into her mind. 'Sin,' they whispered. 'Sin, sin, sin.' Shadows bloomed between the specks on the pages. The nave tickled with cool breezes in the Moss Side heat. Her thighs were sticky with it, fire blooming between them. She thought briefly of Jim, then pulled her thoughts back to her surroundings and the clean pews, cold on her bare legs, the salve words of the sermon as the vicar droned about sin. She found a little quiet peace at St Crispin's, among the hymn sheets. The stained-glass windows rippled their colours across her skin, and she whispered to Joyce, 'Makes me want a barley sugar.'

Her friend sniffed. 'What are you going on about?'

Muriel shrugged to the windows. 'Don't you think they look like boiled sweets, Joyce? All those colours, like soft melting sweets on your tongue?'

Finally it was her sister who blew the lid on her secret dance lessons. Flo had taken her new husband to Cowan's. She endeavoured to get him lessons that would move him a little faster than an elephant from Belle Vue Zoo. But she hadn't expected her sister to be the teacher. Muriel hadn't expected her sister to be glaring at her across the hall with an unremarkable man with a vacant smile who gave her the creeps. Flo had settled, she was sure of it. She wouldn't settle; there must be more to marriage than that.

Flo drew her aside. 'I can't believe you're still out dancing when our dad told you not to. Does he know you're teaching here?'

Muriel shook her off. 'Why should he? It's nothing to do with him.'

'It's everything to do with him while you're still living under his roof, Muriel, you know that! What does Jim think?' she said.

Muriel coloured. 'He doesn't mind, really he doesn't. He knows I need the work, how I love dancing. Anyway, he goes out with Mickey all the time. Why shouldn't I go out too?'

Florence looked at the queue of men forming for their instruction with her sister, jiggling their hands in their pockets and running fingers through oiled hair. Most were looking hungrily at Muriel's legs.

'He's a man, Muriel, of course he minds. You should be thinking about your responsibilities now you two have been courting this long. He'll be asking you to marry him next.'

Muriel's stomach flipped. She still wasn't sure what she thought about that.

'Now you've found your mate, I wouldn't have thought you needed to go out hunting anymore,' her sister continued.

Muriel railed against her. 'Dancing is not hunting, Flo. Anyway, apart from the teaching here, when I go out dancing I only dance with Joyce, you know that. You make it sound like I'm some floozy, dancing with every man that asks me.'

Her sister smiled slyly. 'Remember the biscuit factory do? You were dancing with every man that asked, and especially that Mickey Evans. I heard you were teaching those boys in packing more than a few steps too.'

Muriel jutted out her chin and glared at Flo. She would swing for her one of these days, scrap with her like they used to when they were kids, all teeth, hair and eyes, sticking her nose in where it wasn't wanted, she could push her headlong into the potted pansies outside the front door.

'Shut up, Flo, at least I got myself a man who could dance.' She snatched the hand of Flo's husband and led him out onto the dance floor.

Her sister called after them, 'You should stick with that Jim, he's a safe bet, and leave other people's men alone.'

Muriel intended to stick to Jim like icing on a bun and meld and melt him to her ambition.

They were rarely alone as a couple. Most evenings out they were surrounded by others, even deep in the dark at the cinema, sharing a packet of pastilles where Flo had advised Muriel to carry a hatpin in her bag.

'In case his hands come straying towards places they shouldn't,' she said.

Muriel ignored her advice. 'What if I don't mind where his hands go?' she said, delighted that she had shocked her sister with her answer.

She had learned about sex from Flo, but it seemed her older sister was describing something else entirely from

Muriel's experience. Flo described a slow, sedate waltz, pedestrian in its obligation. There for procreation and not for pleasure. Muriel's experience was more like the tango, fierce and urgent. She longed for Jim's touch during the Pathé News at the cinema. His fingers sliding under cotton to the tops of her stockings while the flickering shadows on the silver screen foretold the spectre of war.

She could smell it, war, the fear bubbled and belched in the air like smoke from the chimneys of Manchester. It sharpened their senses, made each urge more urgent. Her potassium bright passion lit, flared fierce and quick and took its chances where it could, blazing behind closed bedroom doors when they found themselves in the rarity of an empty house, simmered on warm days through long cycle rides to Rudyard Lake. Jim pushed her up the hill through the Cheshire countryside and they abandoned their bikes behind a hedge, crushing the wild garlic. The sharp smell mingling with musk and crushed grass, making stains that smeared her petticoats.

Muriel made Jim oblige her other passions dutifully. She practically dragged him up the stone steps of the city art gallery, around the balcony and to the third gallery along where she stopped and directed his attention across the room. Her little painting was tucked in the corner of a night blue wall, shining like the hot June sun in its burnished frame.

She pushed him in front of the circular picture. 'This is the one I told you about, Jim, it's one of my favourites, The Last of England, painted by Ford Madox Brown who painted the town hall murals, remember? What do you think of it?'

Jim studied the canvas, the couple that melded to each other in the prow of a small boat on a stormy sea, their faces calmly set. What was he supposed to think? He traced his finger round the golden frame. 'They're a golden couple, like us.' It was true, friends and family had described them thus with envy and affection. He looked at the picture again, the man swaddled in a brown moleskin coat sitting alongside his wife (he presumed she was his wife), one hand custodial across her palm. Muriel saw it was the woman who cupped her husband's hand, who supported him, resolute and determined. She dominated the picture, drew all eyes to her perfect face and budding mouth. 'She even looks like you,' Jim said.

'No, she's too beautiful.'

Jim turned his adoring eyes on his girl. 'No one could look as beautiful as you look today, Muriel.'

She settled one smile on him for the compliment and peered back into the painting, more interested in studying the teeming life that went on behind the couple. The bellicose drunks, a child biting an apple, a boy in a striped sailor's top. The depiction of the scraps and remnants of the lives they were leaving behind.

'The painting could just as easily be of your Isabella, leaving England.'

Jim laughed. 'Except she didn't leave that long ago!' He pointed to a tiny pink hand clutched against the woman's chest. 'Is that a hand under her shawl?'

'She's got a baby tucked under there. They're leaving to make a new life,' Muriel said.

Dust motes were suspended in the hushed gallery, they drifted over the velvet banquettes and polished benches.

Jim kneeled between the stanchions and held up a hand. 'Would you make a new life with me, Edith Muriel Cook?'

Muriel held her elation in check as she glanced back at The Last of England and the woman's resigned face. That's what women did, didn't they? Married those they loved. She was sure she loved Jim, but was marriage what she wanted? It was an inevitable step, a career choice for her, for family and friends. She was young though, only seventeen. Yet Jim was a good man and she was in a better situation than others like Flo. Flo had settled and she had already decided she and Jim would be more than that. She would make it so.

She dithered just for a moment before she gave her answer. 'If you take me to Canada with you, yes, Jim, I will marry you.'

*

Muriel and Jim couldn't get married as soon as they would have liked, there wasn't the money. Two years went by while they looked for work and saved. Jim found a position as a painter and decorator with an established firm with better prospects and Muriel got Joyce's mother-in-law to find her a place at a dressmaker's in town.

She worked alongside five other women in a small fusty room above a gown shop on Oxford Street. Mornings, she rattled to work through the early morning fog, alighting near the Palace Theatre, and passing The Koh-i-noor. She paused, entranced by the exotic aroma of toasted turmeric, as a woman came out of its side door, wrapped in swathes of saffron and blue silk that escaped the folds of a bulky coat. She was disguised against the Manchester cold. Muriel ascended the steps to her workplace and hung her own coat, with its new astrakhan collar, beside her colleagues' smoke-infused winter clothes. The small room smelled of women. Six of them sat crowded at close tables with their machines, making a sweet and fetid mix of Lily of the Valley and Pond's cold cream. Muriel took her place at her own table and threaded the bobbin with swift fingers, her feet splayed on the treadle as she wafted a draught up her rayon dress and began work on the precious silk.

An older woman who had taken Muriel under her wing glanced up from her machine. 'Have you put your hand cream on, Muriel? Keep your hands soft and your nails short, girl, don't want to be snagging that stuff, the customers wouldn't like it.'

Muriel took her mentor's advice seriously and slathered another layer of Pond's into her skin. She pointed out of the window to the street below, where a flock of bobbing hats was entering the shop. 'Like those ladies, you mean, Margaret? The lucky things, bet there's no tram rides for them. They get dropped off and picked up in black cabs every week.'

Muriel envied their money and leisure, their time for tea with friends in town, wafting through art galleries and exhibitions, past paintings they barely cared about. Muriel had little time left for leisure herself between working and courting. 'And we're stuck up here making their gowns to order because they can afford it, not off the peg from Affleck and Brown's,' she said.

Margaret stood by her shoulder and watched Muriel's talented fingers stitch tiny notes that sang across the cream silk. 'And how many Affleck and Brown dresses you got?' She patted the Singer sewing machine. 'Bet you make your own too.' Muriel nodded. She did, when she could afford the fabric. Margaret grasped the wheel from Muriel, taking her rhythm down to a rhumba. 'Push the pedal nice and slow and you'll get the machine to make just one stitch. If you push the pedal fast and get a good rhythm going, something else happens down there.' She pointed under her own skirt and flashed the top of a stocking on porridge-coloured skin. 'You know what I mean?'

Muriel laughed. 'Margie, there'll be no fun for me today. I've got five day dresses to finish before teatime.'

She thought about the woman she had seen coming out of the restaurant with silk wrapped round her body and asked Margaret about it.

Her friend lit an illicit cigarette and blew the smoke through the open sash window. 'That's Mrs Patel, she wears saris. Wraps it around her body and tucks it in without pins or stitches. Buggered if I know how it stays in place – it must be bloody freezing in the winter.'

Muriel bent to her work. She'd sacrifice cold to wear silk as exotic as that, she thought. The workroom door opened, and Mrs Belmont stepped inside. All the girls stopped work. It was rare to get a visit from the owner. Usually the assistants checked their work once a week; Mrs Belmont and her waspish suits stayed downstairs.

She scanned the room. 'Muriel? Where's that girl?' Muriel leaned out from behind her machine. What had she done wrong now? 'Come with me,' Mrs Belmont instructed.

'Now, Mrs Belmont?'

'Right now, leave that for Margaret to finish.'

Muriel brushed the threads from her dress and primped her hair. She descended the back stairs into the well-lit shop where a gaggle of women sat sipping tea from china cups. Mrs Belmont pulled a bewildered Muriel into the centre of the room for inspection.

'Mrs Green? Would you say this girl was about the same size as your daughter?'

Muriel fidgeted, her feet sinking in the deep carpet, watched by an older lady in a plum-coloured hat.

'She's not as tall, but near enough.'

'Lovely,' Mrs Belmont announced and guided Muriel into a curtained room at the back of the shop. 'You'll find a gown in there, dear. Pop it on, would you, and when you come out stand on the podium for us.'

Muriel draped the cool silk over her shoulders and curved her arms over her head, relieved she had flexible arms that could zip a dress up without help, and a clean slip on. She stayed a moment before she opened the curtain, enjoying her reflection in the mirror. She looked so glamorous, just like a film star, just like Jim said. She touched the silk reverently between her finger and thumb, its drape as rich as whipped cream. She was finally dressed in some finery as grand as Granny Cowburn's. Perhaps Mrs Belmont had seen something in her, recognised her class and seen her model potential. Perhaps Mrs Belmont would let her keep a dress like this ... She stepped back into the shop and Mrs Belmont gave her instructions. 'Come and stand by the column, dear, lean against it.'

Muriel did as she was asked. She imagined she was waiting for the hand of Fred Astaire, languorous against the pillar in the bias-cut gown that pooled around her feet.

Muriel would have made it shorter at the front for dancing, with a draped train to give it weight and movement when she spun.

She had watched the wealthy women at The Ritz. They didn't dance like she did, all sparks and flashes, they barely moved in their long gowns and glided like swans on snow. Mrs Belmont took some photographs with a Box Brownie as Muriel kept up her pose like a Greek goddess. Muriel smiled beatifically. She imagined she could wear the dress to The Ritz, once her dance job had graduated to taking her there. She would outshine the other girls like Cinderella at the ball.

The ladies smiled approval, or did they smirk behind their soft leather gloves? She thought she caught something. Her confidence wobbled. Maybe they were making fun of her. Suddenly feeling out of her depth she froze, drenched in shame. She wasn't good enough. How could she have thought she was?

Mrs Belmont interrupted her thoughts. 'Thank you, girl, you can go and take it off now, and don't snag it, please, it's going to Mrs Green.'

Muriel was catatonic at her employer's words. She stood staring at the women, who stared into their empty teacups.

'Muriel, take it off now and get back to work,' Mrs Belmont said.

Muriel tried not to cry. She bit her lip so hard that blood threatened to drip and stain the spotless silk.

Mrs Belmont guided her from the podium, a little softer than before. 'You did well, I could let you have a copy of the photograph when it's developed.'

Muriel shuffled back to the workroom in her own dress, flushed with humiliation and feeling foolish that she believed a girl like her could wear a silk dress. She rattled her machine into life again. Her hands were as soft as the next woman's – they wouldn't have snagged anything. With her next pay packet, Mrs Belmont gave her an extra bolt of rayon to make her own wedding dress. As she tore open the brown envelope containing her shillings of pay, she saw a copy of her photograph. Mrs Belmont had kept her word. Muriel put it in a wooden frame on her bedside table.

*

Marriage would have to be sooner rather than later: there was a war coming and Jim thought he might get called up to the regulars. Muriel promised to take a trip out to his house and make plans. She sat on the top deck of the number 53 one spring Sunday after Easter, and watched the city melt into blossom-laden trees and the open fields of Cheshire. Jim met her at the bus stop.

'My, girl, you look smart,' he said, appreciative of another new perm and the dress she had made for the occasion, cotton lawn sprigged with blue forget-me-nots. Muriel washed her only pair of lace gloves especially. She took in the pretty streets of Sale, dancing with fresh-budded birch trees.

'I'd like to live somewhere like this, Jim. It's lovely.' She knew there was little likelihood of that. They couldn't afford a place of their own yet and would have to live with family. That family would be hers.

He bent to kiss her red lips and took her hand. 'Just

wait till you see the house, we've a garden front and back. I've been growing flowers, beans, potatoes, beetroot and lettuce. If you stand at the end of the lawn you can see the trains passing to Liverpool and Wales.'

She took a deep breath of the clean air. Plant the seed, watch it grow, she thought. 'Liverpool? I like the gallery there. It's where the ships leave for America with all the emigrants, isn't it?'

'They do, they sail to Canada. Our Isabella sailed from there.' He pulled her to the canal path, pointed out the places where he'd worked for a local firm, building up the banks. 'It was poor pay for men, but better than drawing the dole. I would have liked to have taken a holiday like our Mickey did. Maybe I'll save enough to take you to Scotland someday.'

She giggled and leaned against him, running her finger over his top lip. 'Maybe you can take me further than that, Jim. You growing a moustache up there? Think it'll make you look like a tough guy?' she teased.

He kissed her again and brushed her face powder from his collar as the canal shifted in the breeze, the water shimmering late day ripples. Muriel stopped to brush her shoes against the grass, shine them up, as Jim checked the success of a nearby fisherman whose head had lifted at the pulse of Muriel's sweet cologne. She smiled down at them as they chatted, then grew impatient and drew Jim away from his conversation.

'That chap's been out of work the past three months,' Jim said, leading her along the canal path. 'I don't know, it's a puzzle, Muriel, trying to get a regular job round these parts. But the last time Isabella wrote back she told me there was still work to be had in Canada.'

Muriel's heart faltered. She squeezed his hand. 'Did she? And what did you tell her, Jim?'

'I wrote back and said it would hardly be British to go off and leave you here.'

Muriel dropped his hand like a scald and boiled up the screaming fury lurking under still waters. She unleashed a sudden screech that would have shamed harpies.

'You wouldn't leave me, you bleedin' idiot! You'd take me with you. You'd better bloody take me with you, Jim Burns!'

Jim was stunned by her outburst. He placed his hands on her shoulders and tried his soft, non-tough-guy voice. 'Muriel, calm down, I would never leave you. I'd take you with me if I could, after we were married, but it would break my mother's heart.'

Let it break, thought Muriel as she pranced off ahead of him. She can't own him anymore, he's mine. Jim trotted behind her until her temper cooled and they stopped for a fish and chip supper, with extra scraps for Jim's mother, Moira, as a peace offering.

Jim crackled the latch door on the back kitchen as his hard-faced mother came out of the pantry, untying her housecoat. She might have been making an effort to change for tea, but she did not comment on Muriel's fresh appearance. There was no recognition or kind comment on Muriel's dress, or her carefully curled hair. Muriel paused by the door, waiting for the invitation to sit down. It didn't come until Jim's father came into the kitchen.

He made the effort to smile. 'Why don't you make a brew, Moira, and I'll get the bread laid out so we can buttie up this feast,' he suggested.

Muriel felt drenched in darkness – their kitchen was

dull compared to Princess Road. A fine film of grey grease coated the enamel sink and the pantry door was stained with fingerprints the size of blackbird's eggs. Moira's most probably. The woman had unusually large hands for such a small frame.

They sat and ate, the silence broken only by their munching of the crackling scraps. Muriel had never known a family eat in silence before. She poked at her food. She felt as though she was shrinking, insignificant, under her future mother-in-law's inspection. Moira had never engaged her willingly in conversation, and only spoke to her son's girlfriend when necessary. That would have to change, she would have to speak to her a little more if she was to be the daughter-in-law. She left her chips to congeal and pushed the plate away, took a deep breath and dived in as swiftly as Flo in her swimming gala days.

'Has Jim told you we're going to be married?' she said. The kitchen tap dripped into the sink. No one said a thing. Muriel let the silence expand like overstretched knicker elastic and then pinged it back. 'We'd agreed he would be the one to tell you, but I thought I'd jump in and share our happy news.'

Jim spiked his brows together beside her. 'Muriel comes from a big family – she has to shout to be heard. It's hard for her to be patient with good news,' he said.

Muriel was unimpressed with his explanation. 'Why wait?' she said. She held Moira's stare.

'Is there a bairn on the way? Can't see why else you would want to marry the girl,' Moira said.

Muriel held her tongue against the barb and the kitchen fell into a charged silence again. Jim's father bestowed a weak smile. She left it a minute or two before she took action. 'Well I'm glad you're happy. And no, there's no baby. Jim asked me to marry him because he loves me, don't you?'

She startled her fiancée into a response. 'Of course I do,' he said.

'Then as nobody seems to be going to congratulate us, I think it's time I was going. Walk me to the bus, would you?'

Jim wiped his mouth and followed her out of the house. He contained himself until they were nearly at the bus stop. 'I would have told her,' he said.

'Why beat about the bush? I did it for you.' She pecked him on the cheek and flashed her return ticket at the driver, rattled up to the top deck and watched Jim turn away beneath the trees. She noticed he was just starting to go bald.

It was dark by the time she got home. She pushed through the front door, knowing everyone else would be in the kitchen. She didn't want to face the contrast between the two houses just yet.

She sat quietly in a parlour chair until Rose discovered her, crying. 'What's the matter with you?'

'Jim asked me to marry him,' Muriel said.

Her younger sister flopped on the floor beside her chair. 'I know, everyone knows that.'

'His mother didn't.'

'Oh, didn't she like it?'

Muriel blew her nose. 'Not much, she didn't say.'

Rose looked worried. 'You're not going to change your mind, are you? You promised you'd make me a bridesmaid's dress.'

Muriel sighed. Licking the salt tears out of her face powder, she pushed herself out of the chair and clicked the parlour radio on, pushed the volume up. 'Shall we dance, Rose? You were getting the foxtrot steps just right last time I taught you.'

Rose bounded to her feet. 'Can I be the man this time, can I lead?'

Muriel posed her sister's fine bone-china arms. 'No, follow me.'

*

She knew she wouldn't need to wait long before she saw Jim again. The next day was Monday, his usual day for a visit. He'd be back. Sure enough he pulled up on his bike just before teatime and she led him into the parlour. She had primed the rest of the family and they left them to it, listening quietly from the kitchen for the sparks to fly.

Muriel had been boiling up to a fight all day. At breakfast she had smashed a plate. She said she dropped it by accident, but Rose saw her fling it across the lino. She'd left for work earlier than usual and got there in record time, her feet pedalling furiously past the park. She'd not wanted a cup of tea as soon as she got in and had spent longer than usual unwrapping her headscarf and brushing out her curls. She'd turned the radio on in the front room, louder than usual, swinging her leg over her knee, but not getting up and dancing around the furniture like she normally did. Clarence left her to it. Where he would normally reprimand her, he sensed her mood and thought he would leave her future husband to challenge her.

Muriel turned the volume down on the radio and confronted Jim. 'You took your time.'

Jim stood his ground, removing his bicycle clips slowly. 'I came over as soon as I could.'

Muriel planted her hands on her hips. 'I don't know how you put up with that mother of yours, she's so mean all the time.'

He sat down, resigned already. 'Mother and I have had a falling out. She's never wanted me to get married since Isabella went away, and she insulted you. She said I had to give up living at home, or give up you, and you're the finest girl in the world, Muriel, I won't do that.' He reached up and pulled her to his lap.

Muriel pushed all the sparks and red-hot anger deep down inside her for another day. She held him tight and watched the fire flames waver in the grate, straightened his collar.

'Well done, Jim, I'm proud of you for sticking up for me at last. Why don't you come and live here? Flo's got a spare bed for us, and my mother and father won't mind. You know my dad likes you. This parlour can be our own room once we're married.'

*

They were married on 1 July 1939, a small ceremony at St Crispin's, with Rose and Flo as Muriel's bridesmaids and Mickey as Jim's best man. His parents didn't come, the rest of Muriel's family did. They stood outside their new home for their one wedding picture. Muriel sheltered under Jim's arm, her head tilted against him like a baby bird, in her new dress, a fresh rose corsage pinned above her breast. Jim smiled in his slightly crumpled suit. They both squinted against the bright sun, uncertain of their new life ahead.

August 1939

A letter dropped into the hall of Princess Road shortly after the wedding, scuttered across the linoleum, the envelope creased from travel and marked with the grease of handling. Edna picked it up and took a cursory glance at the postmark. She passed it immediately to Jim who was sitting at the crowded kitchen table with his white painters' overalls half off.

Muriel put down her porridge spoon and watched her new husband carefully as he read the contents. She had written to his Isabella just before she married Jim. Had composed a secret letter in her lunch break, the pencil balanced on her lap as she ate her cheese and pickle sandwiches in Piccadilly Gardens. She was thrilled with her artfulness, her words dripping onto the page like pepper specks of intrigue. She hadn't told Jim about the letter and satisfied her conscience that she was only doing the job of introducing herself. He hadn't gone out of his way to do it, and if she emphasised to Isabella how hard things had been for them in England, the lack of work, the crowded living conditions, she might at least get some sympathy, if nothing more.

A slip of paper escaped the envelope and fluttered to the chequered floor. It landed on black, a winning space. Muriel snatched it up and examined it.

'Jim! This is a cheque. Bloody hell, it's for a lot of money too! It's from the Bank of Canada.' She felt the familiar tingle of excitement where money or gifts were concerned and was disappointed when Jim refolded the letter and took the cheque off her, slipping it back into the envelope without comment. 'What's it for?' she pressed. 'Is it from your sister?'

Jim pushed his chair back, leaving his breakfast unfinished. 'It's something I need to think about, love. There's no need for you to worry about it.' He bent and kissed her on the forehead, wet lips leaving a smudge in her powder. 'I'm off to work now, I'll see you later.'

She stared at his retreating shoulders. They were married now, shouldn't they share any worries, the bad news and good? She fixed her eyes on the corner of the envelope tucked on the shelf, already curling in the kitchen steam, rose quickly and snatched her coat from the hook on the kitchen door. With one swift movement she swung the coat over her shoulders and picked the letter from its hiding place. She ran down the hall and along the street for the 53 bus. Twenty minutes into the city centre to the dressmaker's would give her time to read it and put it back before Jim got home for tea.

Muriel's hands trembled as she took it from her pocket and unfolded the secret on the top deck. It was from Jim's sister, Isabella, as she had suspected. It seemed Isabella's husband, Hillis, had recently come into a small inheritance and his wife had persuaded him to part with a portion of it and invite her brother and his new bride for a visit. Muriel's stomach flipped at the opportunity she had longed for. She wiped the condensation from the cool window and watched the Manchester buildings melt below the drizzle into wide lakes, crisp mountains and oceans of forest. She imagined Jim in a Mountie uniform, the brim of his hat tipped over his wide forehead as he began to sing. The jangle of the bus bell brought her back to life and she read on.

'I thought it would be too much to ask Mother to come, even though there was money enough for fares ...' Muriel's heart tightened. She couldn't have her dream turned into a nightmare by that woman. She read the next lines anxiously. ' ... but she has not replied, although I sent a telegram, so I'm sending you the cheque. It's enough for two third-class tickets for yourself and Muriel, and a train fare from New Brunswick. God grant it won't be too long before we see you again, Jim, please come.' Muriel was beside herself with pleasure. Here was a chance to push away the melancholy that had grown around her. Here was hope, with its bright sparks in the dark. She must persuade Jim.

When she got home, she washed and perfumed her work-worn skin and waited for her husband to return. He left the letter untouched on the shelf. She traced a painted nail over the hard line of his jaw as they lay in bed, the heat of summer burning behind the parlour curtains.

'What was in the letter?'

Jim raised himself on his elbows above the crumpled sheets and studied his wife. 'I think you know full well. You've read it, haven't you?'

There was no use feigning innocence, Jim saw the truth of her. 'We're married, Jim – we should share news, good and bad. It is good news, isn't it? We should go,' she said.

'There's a war coming, Muriel, surely. I'll be called up.'

'There's no war yet and I know you're keen to do your bit, but you've other duties first, Jim. You're forever telling me about Isabella, how much you miss her – you must be eager to see her again and didn't you write you hoped she would meet me one day?'

He sighed. 'I suppose we could take the chance and go now, before I'm transferred to the regulars.'

Muriel thought there was the possibility they could sit the war out in Canada. She could keep Jim out of danger at least, she could do nothing for her eager brothers. She kept these thoughts to herself, changed the subject to work, and the lack of it.

'Jim, this money gives you a breather from looking for work for a bit. We could use a bit of it for a honeymoon, couldn't we? We'll never get a chance like this again. Please, let's go,' she said.

'It's so far, Muriel. We can't afford to fly.'

'We won't fly – your sister did it by sea, didn't she? I'm sure Margaret at work knows someone who sailed to Canada last month. I could find out from her. I could sort the paperwork if you pay for it.'

It took another hour before her husband caved, assured by his excited wife that it would all be all right. She looked over his shoulder as he wrote a note to take to the telegraph office, and dictated the telegram to his sister. 'We would love to come, what an adventure!' They told Muriel's family that night while Edna re-set the fire she had laid. She'd been feeling the chill on late summer evenings.

'I'll write, Mum, I promise. We've got return tickets anyway,' Muriel said.

Edna didn't meet her daughter's eye, but spent the next morning cutting Muriel's old Whit Week dress into squares to make a collection of hand-embroidered handkerchiefs with the intertwined initials 'M&J' to add to her daughter's packing. Muriel washed and packed every single item of clothing they owned into a borrowed trunk. Her possessions filled two thirds of it; Jim's suit, two pairs of shoes, two good white shirts, two waistcoats and a fob watch the rest. He tried to explain his sister lived in a remote place, and there would be no need for Muriel's best dresses, or her dance shoes, but she would have none of it. To Muriel, Canada was another America. A technicolour world with all mod cons and conveniences on tap like cold Coke. There would be dance halls, she was sure of it, she had seen the movies.

*

They set sail on the SS *Athenia*, waving from the crowded deck to the remnants of her family on the Liverpool dockside. Her father had refused to see them off. He had told her not to go and it was the first time any of his daughters had shown him such bare-faced defiance. Muriel and Jim stood side by side like honorary cricket stumps, the distance between them born out of nervous worry for their future. She imagined herself the resolute woman in The Last of England and wrapped her chiffon scarf around her head like the shawled beauty in her favourite painting. It lifted in the stiff breeze and slapped Jim across the face. When the coast disappeared, Muriel reached for the hand of her husband, making an effort to brighten his glowering mood, and pulled him below deck.

'Thank God we're not in steerage. I hear they're packed in like cattle down there, and get served their food from pails!' she said.

They shared a cabin in stacked bunk beds with another, older couple who were leaving England for good.

Muriel waited until Jim had left the room, then confided in the other wife. 'We have no intention of coming back ourselves.'

The woman's husband listened, unfolded and refolded his shirtsleeves as the women chatted. He never took his eyes off Muriel for the whole trip. He watched her strong legs flexing up to the top bunk and her dark curls bouncing during the after-dinner dances. He wasn't the only one. Other eager men pursued Muriel with her accomplished tango, until Jim thought he should have a word.

'Stop flirting with the other men, will you? You're bleedin' winding me up and you know it!'

She smiled, a sly curve. It was true, somehow it wasn't enough that she was the sole focus of his life. She craved the attention she had always craved since she was a child. 'I'm not doing it deliberately, you daft bugger, I can't help it,' she lied. She knew how to wriggle away from Jim's attempts at control and manipulate his love. 'Why shouldn't I dance? I need a partner, don't I? You won't provide.'

They disembarked in the port at New Brunswick into a hot Canadian summer, so much more sweltering than Manchester on its warmest days. Muriel had tried to keep her best dress, her wedding dress, for the meeting with the fabled Isabella, but had broken it out of the deepest layer of their trunk for the last dance onboard ship. It was slightly sweat-stained. Unable to wash it in the cabin, she attempted to remove the worst of the smudges in the top room of a boarding house near the docks. She scrubbed at her dress as best she could and hung it by the attic window where a cloud of midges descended in the night and speckled her pale arms with red bites.

'Serves you right for leaving the window open,' Jim sniped. He was still sore about her on-board flirting. She hoped he'd forgive her on the long train journey. She wanted to be presented to Isabella as a prize, not a compensation.

If their single night in a lumpy bed was bad enough, the train was little better.

'I bet when King George VI visited, the royal family didn't have to sit on hard wooden benches,' she complained, adjusting her crumpled dress. It had dried crunchy in the humid air and was still damp at the seams. She'd seen the footage of the royal visit on the Palace screen. 'Why couldn't we have gone second-class, Jim? It's such a long way to go like this.' Jim was too busy staring out of the window to answer.

The port of Saint John sprawled around the bay, spreading its tentacles into the surrounding countryside, shipyards and chimneys belched industry. It was just like Manchester, she thought, although the buildings were wooden and looked as though they might blow away in a stiff wind. The landscape disappointed her. Where were the mountains and lakes she had seen in the movies? The train was steam, a beast of a locomotive. At any moment she expected cowboys and Indians to come racing alongside, just like in the Saturday westerns. She curled her hair between her fingers. If Jim's sister had managed a trip like this, she would too. She would make the best of it, just like pioneers.

In the morning, Quyon station emerged out of the mist. One lonely wooden shingled building with its pitched roof leaning as if it couldn't make up its mind which way to reach for the patches of blue above. The train heaved to a halt and Muriel took Jim's hand to climb down trackside, her shoes sinking into the shale and dust. There was no sign of Isabella, no sign of anyone.

'It's a ghost town,' she said as Jim manhandled their case to the ground.

The train belched into life and pulled away. She watched it go with a sinking heart. She had not expected glittering cities, but she had expected remarkable landscapes. Jim disappeared inside the wooden shack, leaving Muriel standing alone in her travel-stained dress. The mist was clearing, and a sharp blue sky promised a hot day. She was sweating already. There was no shade by the track, so she dragged their trunk under a porch round the front of the building, spotting a dust ball approaching far along the road.

'Jim, someone's coming,' she called, and listened for the sound of an engine, a chevy at least, it should be.

It was not. It was a horse and cart that trotted neatly towards her. A woman in a plain cotton shift curled the reins over the seat and jumped down right in front of Muriel. She smiled, a slightly crooked, know-it-all smile, just like her brother's. Muriel felt a pang of jealousy prod beneath her ribs, the bubbling of a low self-worth, even though she was the one in the tailored dress, with modern hair and red lips. Isabella had not a scrap of make-up on her clear skin, her eyes were weather-worn sea glass, her hair plaited. She looked like something out of the last century. Muriel conceded that

Isabella could win in the looks department: she was a natural beauty. The thought wriggled and planted in her mind, haunted her. She'd never come second in a beauty contest before. It made her uncertain, doubtful even, as Isabella threw her arms wide and welcomed her in a fierce embrace.

'You must be Muriel. I am so pleased to meet you at last.' Muriel patted her sister-in-law's back weakly. Isabella dropped her arms and stepped back, looking around, attitude changing as quickly as a passing cloud in a gale.

'Where's my brother?'

Muriel knew in that instant that she wasn't important, as discarded as a lost handkerchief. 'He's here,' she muttered, as Jim tumbled from the station building and swept his sister into a fierce hug. They laughed into each other's necks with the intimacy of lovers. She might as well have not come at all. She watched them, excluded from their sibling bond.

Muriel climbed onto the back of the cart as Jim helped lash their trunk to the carriage. She had never heard her quiet husband chat so much as she bounced along behind. He told Isabella all about their journey, told his sister about his in-laws in Moss Side and they fell into conspiratorial whispers over their mother.

Finally, Isabella seemed to remember she had another passenger and craned her neck to ask her sister-in-law, 'How did you cope with the crossing, Muriel?'

'Fine,' Muriel breezed. 'Wasn't so long. Our ship holds the record for the fastest crossing, doesn't it? Just over six days, and there was a dance most nights, so I was happy.' She poked Jim in the shoulder. 'Unlike your miserable brother. He doesn't like dancing.'

Isabella laughed. 'Expect you don't find it manly, do you, Jim? Hillis is of the same mind.'

The cart lurched and Muriel gripped the edge of the leather bench seat and tried to think of herself on an adventure in this new land. She wondered what Isabella's husband would be like. A rough cowboy, she imagined. And their house? She hoped it would have a cool, long porch shaded with wisteria, just like in *Gone with the Wind*. She had read the book and about the film in magazines, showed Jim the picture of Vivien Leigh.

'You look just like her,' Jim said, 'big eyes and rosebud lips.' She'd make a good Scarlett, but as she surveyed the flat landscape and wooden farmhouses they passed in Quyon, it seemed no place for crinolines and silks.

By the time they pulled into Shawville Road, some way beyond Quebec, Muriel was melting. She was coated in dust and her midge bites were tickling beyond mercy. The house was nothing more than a wooden log cabin with planks lining the outside walls, a long porch along one side, but no wisteria, just a rocking chair.

'Welcome to our home.' Isabella announced proudly. 'I know it's not grand like the big houses on Princess Avenue, but it's all ours.'

Muriel supposed in Canada it was possible to have your own house, even if it was little more than a shack. Better than the succession of council-rented properties her family had. A gangly boy emerged from the barn and lifted their trunk from the back of the cart.

'Thank you, Allen, you can leave it on the porch till Hillis comes home. We'll find somewhere to put your things then,' Isabella said.

Muriel hoped for their own room. It looked unlikely. The boy tipped his hat and she smiled at him, turning on some of her Manchester charm. 'Is he one of yours, Isabella?'

Her sister-in-law laughed. 'Oh no, mine are much younger. I have a whole brood of them, like chicks. Allen is helping on the farm, haying has been kind of slow this year. You'd think you could get help, but there's war brewing, so we hired him. He's fifteen, too young for war. Sleeps in the stable.'

Muriel felt a reluctant respect growing for her sister-in-law. Her own home and servants. She regarded the boy: maybe he wasn't too young for war. Her own brother Harry had talked about joining up, and he was only fifteen. She hoped they wouldn't have to sleep in the stable too – the cabin looked tiny. Perhaps there were other outbuildings.

Jim jumped down from the cart and paced the yard, eager to explore. 'Do you have animals?' he asked.

'Turkeys, goslings and chickens in the back field, calves and pigs over there and a nice wee colt called Molly.'

Muriel noticed the Scottish inflection in Isabella's voice. Of course, the family had come from a rural place. Farming might be natural to them. She watched Jim. It would be natural to him too, given half the chance, but they were rooted in the city and its boundaries. Perhaps she could change that. Could she live on a farm? For a moment she indulged a pastoral fantasy, long skirts filled with fresh eggs collected that morning, early mornings and milking. She looked down at her neat dress and ruined shoes. No. There would be no space for dancing if they farmed. It might make Jim happy, but she needed more of an audience than chickens and pigs.

They stepped into the cabin. Dark after the bright of day, it was enveloped in the dust-burned smell of damp and woodsmoke. The air closed around Muriel. There was only one room, a beast of a wood-burning stove at the far end, its grey ceramic belly glowing, despite the heat outside. On a side wall was a drop-leaf table draped with a tablecloth embroidered with flowers and birds.

'I got that out specially for you. It was a wedding gift from our mother,' Isabella said. 'Jim tells me you make dresses, don't you?' She took Muriel's hand and Muriel felt the dry and calloused skin against her own. She should have brought her sister-in-law some Pond's cream. 'I wish I was as clever with my hands, best I can do is use them for milking.'

Hooks studded the wooden walls, hung with balls of twine, an enamel coffee pot, oil lamps, candles, a flask made from animal skin and many wicker baskets. No space was wasted. Isabella produced a cup and saucer and snatched the kettle from the stove to pour a pot of tea.

'Is it always so hot?' Muriel asked, flapping the collar of her dress. She was desperate for a wash and cool water. She hadn't seen a sink.

Her sister-in-law had noticed her discomfort. 'Summers are always steamy. I expect you'll be wanting to freshen up. There's a wash house out back, we bring water from the well. It freezes in winter, but these days it's just right.'

Muriel sipped her tea. Back to a wash house then, not even a yard for privacy and no stone flags to tap out her beats. 'Are there any dances in town?'

Jim glared at his outspoken wife. 'Muriel likes dancing,' he muttered, draining his tea.

Isabella poured him another mug. 'You wrote and told me that, Jim. It happens there is one dance while you're here. Perhaps you could show me a few steps before then, Muriel. I can't get Hillis dancing, like most of the men.'

'I'm sure we could get a few of them up to dance with us, especially after I've taught you the tango,' Muriel said.

Her cup was the only one taken from a dark wood dresser with drawers and cupboards. Two shelves above held the whole lives of the family. Wooden toys for the children, a sugar bowl, carvings of owls, one Staffordshire plate, and a few books. She read their spines: *Pilgrims of the Wild*, the Bible and a book on modern farming. There was a picture frame too, with a faded photo. 'Who's that?' she asked, as if she didn't know. The siblings were unmistakable.

Isabella picked it up and showed it to her brother. 'That's you and me, taken at that photography studio in Glasgow. We got the train there for the day especially, remember, Jim?'

Muriel noticed some tennis racquets leaning against the door and pushed her way back into the conversation. 'Do you have a tennis court out here?'

Jim snorted. 'They're snowshoes, you daft mare.'

Muriel bristled. How was she to know? She changed the subject. 'What is the winter like in Canada? Do you have snow?'

'There's snow out of the window as far as you can see, so deep it comes up to your waist! Last winter, the neighbours had to dig us out with their heavy horse. It hauled the logs that had fallen across our door, sank right up to its calves, but it did it. We were snowed in, would've starved if it hadn't been for the blueberries I'd stored. You must try some. I usually preserve and keep them for winter, but as it's a celebration we can break open a jar.'

She fetched a glass jar crammed with the spreading bruises of tiny berries and handed Muriel a spoon. She scooped a few out, bit down on them. They were sweet bursts that left a purple stain on her lips. Her eagerness to make a new life there was ebbing and she was desperately tired. She just wanted a wash and a sleep on a good bed – that seemed unlikely.

Isabella ladled some blueberries onto a plate. They rolled like pebbles in the palm. 'Have some more.'

Muriel felt slightly queasy. She'd eaten nothing since breakfast and the fruit acid was churning her stomach. She pushed the plate away as three boys, barefoot, in short trousers and cut-down shirts, tumbled through the door. Her sister-in-law lined them up for inspection and patted each boy's head in turn as she introduced them.

'This is Laird, who's six, Willard, five, and Jim, just four. Guess who he's named after?' She patted her brother's head too and he beamed, tugging at little Jim's shirt.

'Look at you all, fine young men. Muriel and I would be proud to have boys like you.'

Muriel twisted her lip, sour with the taste of blueberries, and poured another cup of tea. It was stewed.

The boys regarded the couple with vague interest and no words, before their mother told them to wash their hands for dinner and they tumbled back out of the cabin in a wrestle of shouts and cries, blocked by the legs of a huge shambles of a man who filled the doorway.

He cuffed their ears. 'Watch your manners, boys.'

'Jim, you remember Hillis?' Isabella said as she stretched up and pecked her husband on his beard.

Muriel shrank back. He looked like a bear, thick hair slicked back with sweat over dancing eyebrows. Hillis slapped Jim on the back and kissed Muriel's hand. For a moment she forgave him his sour smell; at least he had manners.

'Would you like a cup of tea?' she offered.

Hillis roared with a laugh that shook the small cabin. 'I don't drink tea, ma'am, but I have some cold beer in the ice house. How's that sound, Jim?'

Muriel shook her curls and pointed her chin. 'I'd be happy to have a beer with you too.'

Hillis raised an eyebrow at his wife for affirmation, and she nodded. 'Well, why not, it's a special occasion,' he said. 'I'll wash up and we'll sit on the porch – it's a fine evening.'

He returned, freshly laundered, wearing a clean white shirt and braces. Muriel was longing to change herself, but the promise of a cold drink, and a beer at that, was enough to stave it off a little longer.

They crouched on the porch in companionable silence by the light of a kerosene lamp and watched the sun sinking over the fields as the midges swarmed and June bugs clattered against the screen doors. Muriel stared into the night, a thick, deep dark as if she were sleeping under her father's coat back in Florence Street. She had never known a silence like it. It unnerved her. Perhaps there was a way to break it.

'Do you have a radio?'

Her sister-in-law smiled. 'We have, but I've not had much time to listen to it recently, I'm mostly mending or reading. The boys like to listen to the news broadcasts, but it's all war and I don't like to worry them with things they can't do anything about, they're too little.' She softened at Muriel's obvious disappointment. 'I can get Hillis to bring the radio out for you.'

He tuned it against the background noise of animals rustling through the dark and Muriel strained to pick up any of the music she loved through the crackling sounds of blue grass banjo until suddenly jazz notes burst loud and clear across the static. Her heart lifted until a news bulletin terminated the music. She felt a sudden, intense pandemonium in her head. She had thought out in the wilds they were in another world, untouched by the clamouring for war, but how could they really believe they were safe anywhere? Wrung-out with tiredness and disappointment, she was overcome with emotion she couldn't contain, and burst out sobbing, weeping fat, hot tears onto the porch boards.

Jim swept her up and held her tight. He made excuses. 'It's just she's so tired.'

Isabella guided them to their bed. A nest behind a curtain at one end of the cabin with a mattress on the floor. She thought it a little odd, that the self-contained girl from Manchester could switch from light to dark with one blink of her beautiful eyes.

*

All were up at break of day, Hillis out to farm, Isabella to milk the cow and feed the children. On Sunday Muriel was woken by the smell of pipe smoke and tobacco. She crawled out of their nest bed to find Hillis sitting at the table, perusing the Bible. He tapped his pipe and placed it back into a wooden rack the ends of which were carved with a small upright animal.

She ran her finger over the chunky markings on the rack. 'What are these meant to be?'

'They're Squirrels, an Algonquin fellow made it for me,' Hillis said.

'A what?'

'He's an Indian friend.'

Muriel's eyes widened. 'You have Indians here. Like in the westerns?' She glanced out of the window, expecting a row of horsemen to be on the horizon.

Hillis picked a different pipe from the rack and filled it with fresh tobacco. 'The Indians have been here a lot longer than us. There's a reservation now on the other side of town. That same friend showed me how to hunt when we first got here.'

Muriel looked up at the rifle, shotgun and revolver pinned to the wall in places of honour. 'Do you still hunt?'

He drew long on his pipe and squinted at her through the smoke. 'Come fall, sometimes, for the deer cull, but I prefer to grow plants now. Must keep the guns oiled and clean and be methodical about it though. I've showed the boys how to do that.'

She folded her arms. 'You let the boys play with guns, Hillis?'

'Not play, Muriel, they need to know how to use them. They might need them to frighten bears away.'

Muriel wasn't sure if Hillis was teasing her. She thought she saw a lemon twist of a smile at the corner of his mouth, but it was hard to tell through the pipe smoke. She pointed to a set of sheathed knives hanging from hooks on the ceiling. 'What about these, are they hunting knives?'

Hillis nodded. 'Skinning knives only used for bread and bacon now.' He laughed. 'Don't look so worried, we get our meat from the store, it's a ten-minute ride into town. We might not have a fridge yet, but it keeps well on the shelf below the edge of the well.' He pointed to the front yard. 'We are modernising in some ways. Something that will please you, Muriel, I take delivery of a truck next week. You and Bella can ride to the dance in the back.'

She smiled and unfolded her arms, eager to have the opportunity to show the natives a thing or two about dancing. It was a relief they wouldn't be turning up in a horse and cart. She pointed to the hide of an animal draped over a chair. 'And what's that?'

'Wolf.' Hillis winked. 'You ask lots of questions, don't you? Jim wrote us you were a curious creature.'

*

Muriel had found the tiny fold-down writing desk in the corner of the cabin one of the first mornings they had been there. She'd complained of a headache and pulled the quilt over her head, hiding from the early start in pale light, watching the rest of the family sliding about the small space in practised moves like ants dancing in formation. When they had left, she had begun a forensic investigation of everything in the cabin. Studying in detail the minutiae of Isabella's organised life. Trying to understand how her sister-in-law could cope without any space or time for herself. She had seen Jim's letters stacked neatly in a drawer of the writing desk and curiosity got the better of her. She had undone the twine and read her husband's words. He was generous in his praise of Muriel. She was pleased by that. He described her as a bright spark, a lively girl who he found it hard to keep up with sometimes. She imagined Jim riding alongside a train like the cowboys in her favourite westerns. She always wondered how they managed to keep up.

The cabin door opened and Isabella burst in with a basket of eggs. 'Ah, you're up, Muriel. Would you like some breakfast?' Isabella shook the eggs in her sister-in law's direction, ignoring the fact she was hurriedly stuffing Jim's letters back into the drawer.

'I was looking for some paper so I could write to my mother,' Muriel lied.

'I have a few sheets spare, and a little ink, there on the shelf.'

She busied herself at the stove while Muriel wrote to Edna, both of them pretending that Muriel hadn't been prying. Pangs of homesickness pulled as Muriel wrote her letter. She described how Jim had offered to help around the farm and she had been given some chores, that there was nothing else to do except look forward to the dance in the local town. The rest was work. Work like she had never known before, hard, physical work. Muriel thought she was strong, but running the farm required gargantuan effort. She and Jim had no time alone: how Isabella and Hillis had got to have three boys she didn't know. It wasn't the honeymoon she had expected, and the thought of living that life day in, day out, frazzled like bacon in a skillet. She surprised herself by missing the commotion of the city.

The only saviour was the landscape, or the promise of it. There were blue haze mountains on the horizon and if she used Hillis's binoculars, she could make out a ridge – perhaps a Mountie would be working up there in the pine forests. In the spirit of exploration, she suggested Jim take her walking. Isabella lent her boots and stuffed them with paper, so they did not slip – her own shoes were useless. She told them to head for a spot a few miles down-river, where the water was wide and shallow, and Hillis had a canoe tied up.

'You two honeymooners deserve some time alone,' she said.

Muriel was grateful to her for granting them space. Sure enough, after they had walked for an hour, they saw the canoe pulled up on the shingle and climbed in. Muriel paddled with her biscuit-factory-strong arms. Jim steered, until they reached a gravel beach and unpacked their bread and jam. She lay and listened to the water murmur over the sandy-bottomed river, tinkling like milk bottles over the rocks. It was the clearest, cleanest water she had seen, not like the murk of the ship canal. A feathered shadow glanced across her face and she looked up into the sun, shading her eyes with a jam-flecked hand. A great bird hovered high above, a great bird flying free, wheeling on currents of air. She wished she could set her mind loose like that. Recently there had been a thickness to her thinking.

'Could that be an eagle up there, Jim?' she asked.

He was distracted, amorous, given the opportunity to be alone with his new wife and fumbling with the buttons on her dress. Muriel kissed him and let her mind settle in that place where she would be more receptive to his passion. Prudence kept her in check. She was exposed by the river and the sense they were being watched. The eagle circled again. She pushed Jim away. 'Is it an eagle?' she insisted.

He answered into her ear, nuzzling her neck with small kisses. 'It might be an eagle. Isabella would know. She told me there were a pair nesting nearby.'

Muriel shaded her eyes again, watching the deep beat of the bird's great wings. It swivelled its head from side to side and looked down on her, right at her, she thought. A tremor of cold fear stirred in her belly. A slap sound shattered the silence like a rifle shot. Muriel pushed Jim off her and jumped to her feet.

'What the bloody hell was that?'

Jim pulled her back, unperturbed, the midges dancing round his head. 'It's probably beavers – Hillis told me they're on the river here. They crash their paddle tails on the water. No need to worry, they won't harm you.'

She sat next to him and rebuttoned her dress, suddenly feeling adrift in the wild. She had thought herself brave enough to cope with alien territory, but she was growing weary of the unknown and she longed for something to be sure of, something familiar to find her place.

*

It was the second week into their stay and the last days of August when the Shawville fair came round, and the promised dance. Muriel had no illusions it would be as grand as The Ritz. From what she had seen of the area so far, the dance would be at the lower end of the market.

She left her chores early, giving time to make the required impression, and poked the remnants of her Helena Rubenstein from her lipstick barrel, dotted it on her lips and smoothed her skin with Pond's. She found a way to tame the perm that had frazzled in the heat by warming the handle of an iron skillet on the stove. She crouched beside it, carefully wrapping strands of hair until they sprang back like seeds, much to her sister-in-law's consternation.

'Muriel, please don't burn yourself. Miss Verain in town would have done you finger waves for 25 cents.'

Muriel stubbed out her afternoon Woodbine on the grate and frowned at Isabella's limp hair. 'I know what I'm doing, thanks.' She pressed a spray of cologne behind each ear, causing a rash of sneezing in her nephews.

'I would have ragged it for you last night if you'd asked,' Isabella said, and shepherded her sons towards the door and away from Muriel's influence.

Muriel made Jim dress in his uniform. They had taken their turns at the well and dressed behind the curtain in the cabin before the rest of the family. Ready early, they waited on the porch. Muriel tapped Jim's top button, gave it a spit and polish with her mother's embroidered handkerchief.

'I want us to make the best impression, Jim,' she said as she attempted to pull him into a brief tango. Jim pulled away from her and sank into a rocking chair instead. Muriel welcomed the moon rise and shine its spotlight upon her. She continued to dance alone as moths fluttered in the lamplight like dusty jewels to decorate her performance. She lunged and spun a quickstep, tripped on the splintered boards and collapsed on Jim's lap.

'They won't have seen dancing like that around here. I bet there's no instructors for dance lessons. Now there's an idea, Jim, I could give lessons here.'

He laughed and pulled her closer. 'Don't think you'll be setting up a dance school here, Muriel, you'll have no flamin' time. Hitler's about to invade Poland. You know what that means, don't you?'

She wriggled away from him, petulant. He'd poured cold water on her ambition and idea.

'Don't spoil the evening with your talk of war.'

Jim wrestled her still, held her tight. 'I'm being serious, Muriel. I'll be called up soon, we'll have to go back.'

She kept still, let her outer shell harden. He couldn't still the volcanic flow inside. She let the words bubble out. 'I'm serious too, Jim. I could have my own dance school here within a year. You could get some work on those new suburbs Hillis says they're building on the edge of Quebec City. We could move there, get a house of our own. We could stay away from the war.'

'And if we stayed why would we want to live in a city? What's wrong with living out here with Isabella? I like the farm. I thought you liked the space.'

She touched his face. He'd shaved in cold water and nicked the skin. There was a tiny scab clotting on his jaw. How could she let him come to any harm in a war? 'There's no space for us here.'

The family rattled out of the cabin, interrupting their conversation. Hillis made good on his promise and drove a gunmetal grey 1937 Fargo truck up to fetch them. Jim was soon lost under the double fold of the engine, forgetting all talk of future plans in Canada. He had to be prised away as the boys whooped with delight and scrambled in the back of the truck while Muriel and Isabella took seats up front.

'Don't get your uniform dirty,' Muriel warned him.

It was a short drive to the clapperboard church hall, its white, wide steps shadowed in the shortening day. Someone had hung bunting over the front door. A cluster of bugs tangled against it. The boys jumped out of the back and ran off to play. Muriel slid out of the truck and watched them disappear around the side of the building, pleased there would be no children inside. Why have competition for attention? She manoeuvred herself in front of Isabella as they ascended the steps. Linked arms with Jim and pushed open the doors as if she were a new gunslinger come to town, swinging the saloon doors wide. No silence fell, no drinkers paused with glasses half raised to their mouths. But there was a ripple of interest from the clutches of dowdily dressed dancers.

Isabella stepped forward and prised Jim from Muriel before she could enjoy the attention fully. Isabella led him round the room and Muriel was forced to trail, momentarily, as Isabella introduced her brother with pride and his wife as an aside. Isabella knew everyone. Muriel pouted. The hall was as she expected, hung with limp paper chains and an unpolished, unsprung floor with a forlorn-looking band upon the small stage, but she was stirring up interest, and was soon garnering the most attention as she pranced behind.

After the introductions, the women peered past Jim to appreciate the dark-haired beauty who followed him. Muriel had pulled out her wedding dress and washed it by hand in a barrel by the barn, copying her mother's laundry skills from the back yard at Florence Street. There was no washboard to scrub the travel stains away, nor any decent soap to remove the faintest sour smell, but she found a handful of Indian strawberry flowers growing in Isabella's scrap of a garden and managed to make it fresh again.

Men turned in admiration as she swished past. The air was thick with heat and expectation. Muriel charmed the locals with compliments about the cut of a simple linen dress or the shine on a new pair of shoes. Her words came out warm, melting the air around them. She couldn't find much to compliment in their plainness but had decided to be gracious. She chastised herself for her judgement, she had never thought herself a snob and her mother would have clipped her ears for behaving like one, but her dress was modern compared to the sea of backwater clinging to the sides of the room. Her dress whispered of sophistication and city life. She had shined her dance shoes specially and tapped an impatient foot as the band finally began a hurdy-gurdy waltz.

'Dance with me, Jim,' she implored, tugging on his jacket. He looked panicked. She knew if he didn't agree he would soon have to give her up to another. It was his common choice.

He chose the bar, a better bet. 'I'll get us a drink first,' he said.

Muriel leaned against the stage and let him go, watching other dancing couples bump clumsily by. He came back with a dry whisky in a plain glass with a sliver of ice winking from its amber liquid. She fished the ice out and dropped it down the front of her dress, let it slide, melting, on her hot skin. She smiled up at Jim, challenging him with her provocative behaviour. 'Well, if you won't dance with me, Jim, I'll find someone who will.'

He lit a cigarette and offered her one, delaying her impulse. 'Have a smoke first.' It might put off the inevitable, although he had seen his wife dance as elegantly with a lit cigarette as she did without. Her hand turned delicately outwards so the ash would not fall on the toes of her dance shoes. 'Why don't you dance with Isabella instead? She asked for lessons.'

Muriel ignored his suggestion and strode over to where Hillis sat with several other farmers, their pipes clamped and shirts gaping, crop worries shared as news of imminent war threatened from Europe.

She leant suggestively over their table, the melted ice a snail trail in her cleavage, and cracked their conversation. 'Surely one of you gentlemen will dance with me?'

Hillis laughed. 'Somebody needs to keep this lady occupied.'

One of his neighbours acquiesced. He could not refuse the glamorous stranger whose laughter rang higher than the band. Another followed his example. One after another the farmers leapt up and took her hand, attempting dance moves they had no idea how to execute. Country dances were no training for elegant foxtrots, although they had energy for the bounce in the quickstep and followed her like eager puppies around the dance floor. She tamed their exuberance with swift steps and gentle nudges, tapping on toes that floundered next to her sparking feet.

Muriel had almost exhausted all possible male partners when Isabella cut in during the ladies' excuse-me. 'Do you have to dance with everyone except your husband?' she pressed.

'He won't dance, so yes I do,' Muriel answered, showing her sister-in-law the steps to a tango. She took the lead and imagined herself a colourful bird in the smoke-filled room, scattering sweat droplets of passion over the watching faces with a toss of the head and a turn of the ankle. She danced Isabella through the tempo, becoming a shining bright star in her own painting. Her mind filled with a music that morphed into a cacophony of noise and light.

A discordant pain pulsed above her left eyebrow. The bunting fluttered. As the room spun the sea of faces swam and she felt sick.

Jim grabbed her arm as she passed. 'That's enough flamboyance now, Muriel, people are staring.' His grip was tight.

'They're meant to stare, Jim,' she said and placed her hand on her stomach. It fluttered, light, just a tiny shadow. Had it suddenly grown dark or had she imagined it? It was very quiet. 'The music's stopped anyway,' she muttered.

She was right. The band had announced a break, and someone had replaced their music by turning the radio on. It crackled and spat into life. There was a spatter of brief, bright notes from a big band in the States and then they ceased. An announcer spoke. The church hall fell silent under a crescendo of hushes, someone turned the radio volume up full blast and a sombre voice cut through the stilled dancers. They listened to the broadcast.

'We interrupt this broadcast to bring an announcement from London. Earlier today the Prime Minister of Great Britain, Mr Neville Chamberlain, told the nation that following Germany's invasion of Poland, Britain is now at war with Germany. There will be a special meeting of the Canadian Parliament later this week. It is expected that Canada will follow.'

Muriel steadied herself against her husband. 'What does that mean?' she asked.

Jim hugged her close and kissed the top of her dark curls. 'We're at war, Muriel. It means I'll get called up and be transferred to the regulars. You'll be married to a soldier. You never know, I might even get to be a hero.'

Her soft skin itched against his epaulette as her hopes for a new life in Canada died and curled like the ashes of burned paper into the heavy air. Families huddled and hushed around them. The band packed up and left. Men slapped Jim's back as they passed and shook his hand. Muriel's attractions were forgotten. She stood in his shadow. Perhaps there would be something she could do in the war. She could join up and put herself amid the action. She placed a hand across her belly: there was something that might stop her.

October 1939

Shortly after their return from Canada they moved in with Jim's parents. Muriel unpacked their trunk on their first day in Hulme, while Jim sat fidgeting on the edge of the bed. They did have their own room at last. She fluttered her wedding dress loose, slipped it over a hanger inside the empty wardrobe.

'Your mother's got no cedar balls in here. I hope the moths won't get at my dress.' She ran a hand down the rayon. It hung limp: perhaps it was beyond hope. 'I'll have to make some new clothes. I need my sewing machine and that's at my mum's,' she said.

Jim lounged back and lit a cigarette. 'I could fetch that over here for you and my mother could help you make something.'

Muriel slammed the wardrobe door. She would rather have Hitler help her sew a new dress.

'Jim, I know we're here because you want to give her another chance, and granted, there is more room, but you're just feeling sorry for the woman. Maybe you appreciate how much she misses Isabella now because you miss her more having spent time with her. We could have stayed if you really wanted.'

He reached out and pulled her down next to him. 'While we've got the chance for a whole bed and a whole room to ourselves?' He laughed. 'It's all right here. Besides, we had to come back because of the war.'

There was tape on the window already. The marks of war were quick to bloom. His parents' tiny garden had been given over to vegetables and was too small for a shelter – they'd have to go to the town hall when the sirens sounded. It was a small compensation, but she couldn't see how they'd let them share a shelter with the murals. They'd be covered up for safety. She rolled away from him. The mattress sagged. Things would be all right with Jim as a buffer between his mother and herself, but he couldn't be there all the time, he had training manoeuvres. She had more allies at Princess Road in her own family, and there was more than the two of them to consider now.

'You're right Jim, things have changed. I'm expecting a baby.' His face ignited and he bounced off the bed, gathered her up and swung her round the small room so her heels caught the wall and she protested, laughing. 'Be careful, you big lummox, I need looking after now.'

He put her back on the bed like a china doll. 'I can look after you.'

Muriel set her jaw and began unpacking the rest of the clothes. 'But do we have to stay here?' she pleaded. 'Your mum will give me the worst chores. It's like she's testing me, and she ignores me when you're not here.'

She was reluctant to see him off to training the next morning and tightened the top button of his uniform at the door knowing that Moira would have cleared the unfinished porridge before she could return to the kitchen table and eat it.

'The blasted woman has probably kept my extra milk rations for herself,' she said.

Jim kissed her forehead. 'I'll bring you something back from the base,' he promised and disappeared up the road.

Moira gave her daughter-in-law a spade too short to spare her back from aches and pains and instructed her to dig over the vegetable patch in the back garden. She had been less than ecstatic at the news she was going to be a grandmother again and took every opportunity she had to remind Muriel that she could do nothing for the war effort.

'You're expected to stay at home,' she said, stepping between the rows of cabbages and pushing a copy of the *Manchester Evening News* under Muriel's nose. It was open at the pages and pages of categorised columns. 'Look, you're in the expectant mother category. Register, but stay at home, it says.' She pattered a half-bitten fingernail over the print.

Muriel read the notice; the article confirmed it. She felt like a burden. She put her spade down, straightened her back, picked up her coat and took a bus to Princess Road.

'I could be part of the war effort too, I could do a factory job. I had a bit of technical experience at the dressmaker's,' she complained to her parents as soon as she got in the front door.

'Fixing a sewing machine's not engineering, Muriel,' her father remarked. 'You ought to be grateful Moira's giving you bed and board. You're best staying there and resting with a baby on the way – that's how you do your bit for the war effort.'

Muriel glowered. She didn't want her own father siding with Moira. She'd find his sympathy instead. 'It's not my home and she won't let me rest,' she said. She could apply herself, given the chance, she could mend a puncture on her bike, more than her sisters could, and one of them had found work. 'Rose is operating lathes at that rifle factory on Ladysmith Road. If she can make rifle barrels, I can do just as well.'

By the time she returned to Hulme, Jim was back from training. He was less than pleased she wasn't there to meet him, even though he had succeeded in bringing extra milk rations with him. Muriel noticed Moira had decanted the milk into a jug. It looked like she'd used most of it for her afternoon tea.

'Where've you been, young lady? I could have done with some help with dinner,' his mother said, her back turned as she stirred a weak stew on the stove.

'What if there had been a raid? You'd have been out on your own, and Mother would have been alone,' Jim said.

Muriel slid into the seat next to him. 'I'm sure Moira could get to the nearest shelter faster without me waddling behind and holding her up. I was closer to the shelter at Mum's. Dad is putting an Anderson shelter in their back garden next week.' She lowered her voice and scrutinised her mother-in-law's hunched shoulders for twitches. She knew she would be listening. 'We'd be safer at Princess Road, Jim. It's nearer your base, and Rose is moving out, so we could have her old room.'

*

Muriel's appeals for safety wore Jim down and they were back at her parents' before the end of the month. Promoted to their own room upstairs where they slept under a second-hand candlewick from Flo. Muriel's Singer sewing machine nestled in the corner like a cat waiting to be stroked. She was happy to be back amongst allies. Even her father softened towards her with Jim's company. He promised to make them a crib, although Flo offered her a pram for the new baby.

'No thank you,' Muriel said. 'I've seen you hauling coal in it.'

Her sister sniffed. 'You'll find yourself doing the same a few years down the line, Lady Muck.'

'Don't think so, I've got a job back in the biscuit factory in Northenden. I can buy my own pram. I've made a new quilt and a matinee jacket for the baby already,' Muriel said.

'Them biscuits will be the next thing on ration – you'll be out of a job by Christmas,' Flo sniped.

Muriel coloured but she wouldn't let her sister's barbs puncture this time. Whose husband was it that was going to see active service? Not Flo's, who was too old for the war. He was a dolt, and she didn't like the way his arm crept round her thickening waist at every greeting.

'Don't be daft,' she said, riled. 'People need a treat, they'll always want biscuits, war or no war.' She wasn't sure of the truth of that. War had unsettled everything except the certainty of her impending motherhood. She clung to the hope of a new life like a life raft. It quelled the queasiness domesticity made.

*

She and Jim worked the small garden at the back of the house. The calls of children drifting from Alexandra Park as the tang of autumn stirred the air. Muriel moved her rake through the scatter of leaf snow and carefully poked around the freshly ruptured earth where the new Anderson shelter sprouted. She watched her husband pulling carrots from the thick clods and wondered if they had time to sneak in the shelter alone. Her impulse faded as quickly as a cloud crossing the sun. Jim brushed the soil from a carrot and handed it to her. She snapped it in two, biting hard on the sweet root.

'I'm being called up next week. They've finally moved me into the regulars. 502 Company, E.L. Division, Royal Army Service Corps,' he said, so proud he was almost standing to attention.

The numbers meant little to Muriel, but she knew Service Corps was supply. He'd be in a warehouse somewhere, not charging into battle. She swallowed the carrot. 'Got your wish then. Fixing tanks, is it?' she said.

'Might be active service yet. The division's moving to Northumberland under Northern Command. I'll get a rifle.'

She dropped the rest of the carrot and kissed him. There might be chance to sneak into the Anderson shelter yet. 'Well, if they're giving you a rifle.'

'Probably one between two. They're putting us in camps to start, but then we get billeted out with local families. Do you think there's any chance you can come and visit me? Maybe if Flo travels with you?'

She laid her hands over her swollen belly. 'I don't need Flo, I can make it on my own.' She'd go to make sure he was safe, make sure he was always hers, make sure he came back.

*

Muriel planned the visit for the first winter chill of November. She took a bus into the city past end terraces blown out with walls that hung like open wounds. The bleeding snapshots of domestic life. Withered wallpaper fluttered in the wind and shredded curtains hung at empty windows. A bouquet of flowers still blooming bright colours lay on the roadside, blasted onto the pavement from an upper room. The history of what was happening was imprinted on the crumbled walls and the people of the city. It had no less effect on Muriel. She should be used to it by now but it took all her resilience to float above.

Piccadilly Station was packed, thronged with a mess of soldiers and workers. She waltzed through the swirling mass, exhausting all her 'excuse me's until she gave up on politeness and shoved her way through like the rest. She clambered onto her train, watching from the carriage window as women shepherded small children into huddles, ready for evacuation. They stood on the platform, some wide-eyed and shell-shocked, others crying and clinging to their mothers, all clutching their gas masks in tidy cardboard boxes. Muriel drew her mask close and tucked her suitcase under the seat. She was taking up enough room for two, the size of her. She felt like a barrage balloon and her legs ached from holding up her weight. A woman smiled across the carriage in solidarity and Muriel rested an arm across her belly, wondering if her child would need a mask too. Would the war stretch on so long she'd have to evacuate her child? She decided then there would be no separating them: the two of them would be shipped out to the countryside together.

The train pulled out of the war-stained city through unremarkable suburbs and clattered on into the countryside. She was glad to get away and make her own small escape. Muriel managed to reapply her lipstick just before the train pulled in at the station, despite the restricted elbow room, and planted a red brand on her husband's cheek as he picked her from the carriage.

'Put me down, you great oaf, you'll crease my jacket up. It's crumpled enough after that journey – I've never seen a train so packed. Here, you can carry this for me, it weighs a ton.' She passed him her case and smiled at the man waiting beside him, a thin figure whose jacket hung as desolate as the shredded curtains from a bombed-out window.

Jim introduced him. 'Muriel, this is Jim Thain. He and his wife have been looking after me. You'll be staying with them while you're here.'

Muriel extended her hand. 'Another Jim? Fancy! Kind of you to have me. Thank you for taking care of my husband.'

The other Jim took her soft hand in his bony one and cracked a smile. 'It's no trouble, pet, we've all got to do our bit. I've got the car out the front. Let's get you home and off your feet, they must be sore in those shoes.' He looked at her feet. She'd worn her dancing shoes, the best ones she had left.

The last time Muriel had been in a car was months ago, travelling in Hillis's truck across the flat lands of Canada back to the station. She reflected on how much had changed as she studied the narrow streets. It was a short journey through the town alongside a grimy beach where the sea lay cold and still. Still, it was the sea, it was space, and the air was cleaner than home, she thought. She lifted her tidy shoes over the Thains' thick stone doorstep and stepped straight from the street into the parlour. There was a fire blazing and a pot of tea already stewing on the table.

A small, round woman with a generous smile bustled forward, tugging at her too-tight cardigan. 'Muriel, I am so pleased to meet you. Your Jim has told us all about you and you're just as beautiful as he said. So glamorous too, just like a film star, isn't she, Jim?'

Muriel dipped her head in acquiescence and warmed to the compliment. She liked Minnie, who let her have the best seat by the fire and enquired how her pregnancy was going.

'I'm tired all the time,' Muriel complained.

Minnie nodded. 'That's to be expected. Are you taking the extra milk rations? It's hard, I know, so hard as Jim isn't at home either. You must miss him so.'

Muriel glanced at Jim. She did and she didn't. Life was full of friends and there had been other distractions, only some of which he knew about. She missed him at night though. She often stretched her feet into the dip where his body imprinted.

'It will be worth it, Muriel – children are a blessing,' Minnie continued. 'We've a daughter, Nancy, who's much the same age as you, and our Alan, well he was a professional footballer before the war. He's fighting out in

Greece now. You can have his room.' Minnie looked away and into the fire.

Muriel knew that look. Saying her son's name out loud, saying where he was, was like a charm to bring him home. How many women believed the war was down to fate or God? She was becoming just like them.

Their daughter Nancy came over after tea. As skinny as her father, but with a little more bend to her body and a light step. Muriel watched her closely with Jim, but Nancy didn't seem interested in flirting. She was more interested in hearing about the dances in Manchester from his wife.

'Theatres and dance halls closed after they announced the war – that made everyone gloomy. People complained so much they opened them again!' Muriel said.

'Really?' Nancy said. 'They stayed open round here, but there's just the one, over in Ashington.'

Muriel squeezed her hand. 'Fancy having only one dance hall to choose from. There's no men at all to dance with anyway, not even out of uniform.' She glanced at Jim. 'But the girls at the biscuit factory told me the Yanks will be over soon, maybe in a few months. They'll be willing dancers.'

Jim grunted and finished his drop of whisky by the fire. 'I best be off now.' He leaned across and kissed his wife. Muriel saw the look on Nancy's face, a longing maybe. She kissed him back harder. He drew away. 'Steady now, I'll see you tomorrow.'

She got up to show him to the door, put a hand on his sleeve as she spoke in a stage whisper. 'I thought we were staying here.'

He dropped his voice below hers. 'The billet extends to meals and company only. There's no room anyway – Alan's bed is a single.'

'We could manage?' she suggested.

'Not tonight, Muriel. Nancy will keep you company.' Another kiss and he was gone into the sharp night, whistling up the street.

Muriel folded her arms across her chest. What was she meant to do? She went up to unpack her few things in Alan's empty room. Her small childhood Bible fell from her case and clattered across the boards. She picked it up and heaved herself onto her knees at the side of the bed, opened the book and prayed over the flicker-flatter of words. It was a comfort. She muttered words and incantations and asked God to protect Jim, to keep him safe from temptation. That Nancy was a bit of a looker. By the time she reached 'Amen' the girl was there, as if summoned, standing by the bedroom door and fluttering two scarves from her fingers.

'I thought you might like to take a walk, get some sea air,' Nancy said. She flourished a packet of cigarettes too as she helped Muriel to her feet.

They wrapped their heads in the scarves against the chill and cut through the dark back streets to the beach. It was quiet in the town, so close to the coast and so close to Europe across the fierce North Sea. Nancy passed her a cigarette.

'Aren't you worried that Jim will get sent out there? I know I would be if he were my husband, worried sick.'

Muriel drew her cardigan over her belly, shucked off her shoes and allowed the cold sand to caress her feet. Jim was the one certainty in her life. Solid, dependable Jim. How could anything happen to him? Her feet sank into the sand. She was anchored to the earth, safe in this place, where Jim was safe too, leaden with the child growing inside her, their roots growing into a new family. Nancy was no threat. She pulled her feet out of the sand and shook them, tipped onto her toes as she dusted the granules from her skin and slipped her shoes back on.

'Jim will be all right,' she said, peering over Nancy's shoulder at the dark shadow of the houses behind. 'I don't suppose there's anywhere with music or dancing?' How she missed dancing.

Nancy laughed at the suggestion. 'No, but there's a pub back there with a snug. Do you fancy a quiet gin?'

*

Jim was back in Manchester for Christmas leave. It was a cautious festive feast, rabbit for dinner, with veg from the garden.

Jim's face fell. 'I know no one's having turkey this year, but you could have told me, I would have got a chicken off Mickey,' he said.

Muriel poked at the dry, dark meat on her plate. It would be like Mickey to provide in times of scarcity, he never seemed to go without. 'Last time I saw a chicken was at our wedding meal,' she said.

By the new year Jim's company had transferred to Southern Command and moved to Wiltshire, too far for her to visit in her advanced state of pregnancy. She weathered the winter, the baby keeping her awake at night, one foot straining against its restricted space, protesting, pushing against her stomach. Muriel touched the tiny imprint and marvelled at it.

'I know how you feel,' she said. 'House is packed, isn't it? And work's manic, they're closing next week to make it into a munitions factory. You and I will be out of a job, little one. They won't let a lady in my condition work in munitions.'

She heaved herself out of a warm bed and dressed in the dark, set her hair under a scarf, and squashed her feet into boots as she made to leave, wriggling her toes. At least she knew there was some glamour hiding under her thick socks: she had persuaded Harry to paint her toenails with a bright red gloss the night before.

The lamps of Alexandra Park were extinguished in the blackout. When she opened the door on the choking February fog, the morning was thick and stew-like. She planned a short walk before the rest of the house was up, to buy herself some time before work. She was too big to cycle now and had to leave earlier to catch the tram. The silhouette of her father's apple tree was barely visible in the small front garden as she groped along the path, almost bumping straight into a figure that moved beyond it.

'Who's that?'

'It's me, Muriel,' a familiar voice said, his wool uniform steaming. Jim's pack was slung over one shoulder and he was carrying no rifle or ammunition.

Muriel stumbled in her boots, surprised and immediately disappointed. She had planned to go to a dance Friday with her youngest sister Rose. Even though she would have only been tapping her shoes on the sidelines – no one wanted to lindy hop with a pregnant woman. She bit down on her guilt at her disappointment, gathered herself and launched at her husband, hugging him as close as she could manage with the bump between them and mumbling into his smoke-smelling shoulder.

'Jim! What are you doing here?'

He disentangled himself and waved a letter at her. 'I've been discharged.'

She followed his shuffle into the house. She would be late for work. 'There's still tea in the pot,' she said. 'What does that mean then, "discharged"?' Jim rinsed a mug. He didn't meet her eye and passed her his letter instead. She read carefully, trying to make sense of the words. 'It says medical discharge.'

'It looks like my ears are blown pretty bad, perforated, the doctor says. There's nothing to be done.'

Muriel chewed on a nail and primped her curls. She'd heard doctors say there was nothing to be done before. When her mother lost the baby all those years ago. She hadn't had another. She ran a hand over her belly, trying to keep a rush of battling emotions in check. 'There must be something you could do.'

'I could go back to the reserves, but there's not much I can do there,' Jim said.

She sat down. She was sorry for him, genuinely sorry. He was no longer a soldier and like her he could not help with the war effort. They were both limited by medical conditions. She was sorry for herself too: she would no longer have a husband in uniform to boast about. She swallowed it all down with the cold tea and resolved to see what fate would deal.

*

Clarence got Jim a job on the docks, which didn't please Muriel. She heard the bombs falling on the ship canal and worried while he was there. 'What would I do as a widow with a baby?' she asked.

'I would have been in more danger if I was fighting abroad, and you weren't worried about that, were you?' he snapped.

She had the sense not to press any further. Her husband was a placid man, but his hackles were raised with his wounded pride. He was right, but the docks were too close to home – she felt he'd brought danger right in their front door. When he was stationed away there was some distance to it. She could try to push it to the back of her mind. She upped her nightly prayers from well-worn Bible pages and prayed there would be something better. There was. Jim disturbed her one afternoon when she was taking a rare nap, bursting into the bedroom.

'I've got a new job, Muriel! Porter at the local hospital. I'll be working where you'll have the baby, I'll be right on hand.'

She turned over in the bed, heavy and adrift, feigning sleep.

June 1940

The baby was born in the early summer of 1940, when the war was in full swing. It was a daughter, who they named Annie, with hair as red as a match spark. The birth was a battle all of its own for Muriel. It was hours of pain and blood, edge blunted by large inhalations of Entonox that helped her float away from the scene but not beyond the sound of distant sirens and birdsong from the open window. Until a small, furious wail called her back to consciousness. Annie's birth left her mother stunned by a force of pain and raw physical energy that settled like the shadows of her childhood, breaking like waves on the shore of a defeated body and mind. She became a functioning automaton with legs no good for dancing and a heart full of love for her child. A love that wandered and drifted in fear.

Her father Clarence had kept his promise and made a wooden crib, but it wasn't quite ready in time, so Annie spent her first two months in Muriel's emptied bottom drawer, squeezed beside their bed. She was a quiet baby in a subdued house. Her infrequent crying barely disturbed the restrained tension: the family had more to worry about.

Harry was too young to be called up when the war began, much to Muriel's relief, although he'd tried. They put him in the Home Guard until he was sixteen. He ran down to the recruitment office on Oxford Road the morning of his sixteenth birthday and lined up for the physical.

'As long as you're breathing you pass,' they told him. He requested the Navy. A month went by with no news until a letter arrived. They had put him in a colliery.

'Country's run on coal,' his father said. 'Can't churn it out fast enough. I hear there's near on 500,000 men needed to work in the coal mines, be good to do your bit, Harry.'

Muriel felt her brother's disappointment. She missed him when he was sent to Lime Colliery at Haydock and was happy when he was transferred to Bradford Colliery in Manchester, which meant he could live at home. He could keep her company and take Annie off her hands when she'd suffered too many sleepless nights with a baby.

'It's about two lengths of Blackpool Tower down underground, Muriel, no lights or hard helmets. It's doing my eyes in, sis,' Harry told her.

She shuddered, and rocked her daughter, sympathetic to her poor brother being kept in the dark. She couldn't bear it. It would drive her mad. How could a body survive without light and air?

*

Late December 1940 showed her they couldn't. The bombs fell like rain for two days. Two days when she didn't see the light, huddled in a shelter with her baby, Rose and her father and mother, counting the minutes, then counting the hours as best she could, sick with worry, pinching Annie to her breast in a damp corner and willing her milk to flow. The baby sucked as if it knew it was a limited supply. When the all-clear sounded she crept back into the light like a startled bird, flapping and pecking through the rubble and dust, trying to find familiar landmarks that marked her way home. The very top of Princess Road had gone, the tip swallowed by a huge crater. Muriel pulled her scarf around the baby's head – she did not want Annie to see the lost shoes she had spotted amongst the rubble. One blasted and balanced in a shattered window frame, the other balanced across the one remaining wall of the house. She'd known a young girl with red dance shoes just like that.

Jim was waiting outside, crouched beneath her father's apple tree. He stood and took Annie silently, swaddled her in her blanket. Muriel didn't ask him how he was or where he had had to spend the night. She peeled a loose fingernail from his trembling hands.

'Watch you don't scratch her with that,' she said.

He rocked the baby close, like he was about to tell her a bedtime story or sing a lullaby. 'You're all right, you're all right,' he muttered like a charm.

Muriel prised Annie away, trying to keep her own hands from shaking. 'You're all right too, Jim.'

He rubbed his hands across his face. 'I walked home this morning when it was still dark, Muriel. The air was full of sparks, I saw the doors of the cathedral opened out.'

She corrected him. 'They don't open out, they open in,' she said.

'Not this time,' he said. 'Free Trade Hall, Royal Exchange, the courts, Victoria Station, all bombed.'

'What about the town hall?' she asked.

He looked at her, blank. 'They say there's more than three hundred dead and you're worried about your murals.'

She hugged Annie and scuttled into the house, guilty. 'She needs feeding.'

*

Muriel had taken the pram offered by Flo. It proved useful even after Annie didn't need it anymore and could walk. Harry took it to the depot and filled it with coal. Muriel led her toddler through Alexandra Park on clear days when she knew it was safe enough and they stopped by the bandstand.

'I used to dance here, Annie,' she said, skipping up the steps and waltzing her daughter in her arms below the wrought-iron roof. She had saved enough money from the biscuit factory to buy herself her own radio, tuned it to music whenever she could and balanced her daughter on her feet in their bedroom, showing her dance steps in the tiny space of floor between their bed and the front window. Pulling her daughter back up when she slumped like a bag of coal on the floor.

'Come on, Annie, you must learn to dance, Annie. Dancing's all we've got,' she said and hefted her to her shoulder as the rain fell, folded herself around her to protect her from all the madness outside.

It was months before Muriel went out dancing again. She got Rose to look after Annie and took Margaret to see another Lancashire lass with the same first name, Muriel Higson. She was playing with her all-female orchestra at

The Ritz. She still didn't tell Jim – he was always out with Mickey playing pool. She felt it was about time she had some fun too. It was a risk, but she reasoned life was all about risks and she hadn't taken enough of them since she had had the baby. In the Moss Side blitz the warnings had sounded constantly, and then the incendiaries wouldn't drop, creating a degree of complacency that Muriel herself was not immune to. Still, she tried not to let Margaret's scare stories rattle her as they walked down Deansgate arm in arm.

'Did you hear about the dance hall in Cheetham that was hit? Poor dance leader was decapitated, his head flew clean off when a bomb fell through the roof!' Margaret said.

Muriel pulled her jacket round her shoulders. 'The Ritz shelter is twenty foot underground, Margaret. We'll be all right there tonight.'

They joined the end of a line that snaked round the building, a line almost exclusively female, sibilant with female voices and pulsing with wafts of cologne and coal tar soap.

'All these girls, they're just out Yank hunting, you know,' Margaret sniffed.

Muriel brightened, her face reflecting the hope of the rest of the line. 'Will there be GIs inside then?' she said.

'Expect so. There's no restrictions on coloured troops either.'

Muriel's heart quickened again. She was eager to dance with them if there were. New, wild and daring dances she'd seen last time she'd been to the cinema as she watched wide-eyed at the pure fury of the dancers in *Hellzapoppin'*.

They blew the staid waltz and foxtrot out of the window. When they finally made it inside, Muriel saw the crystal chandeliers had been taken down for safety and the fountain in the foyer drained. There was still some glamour to the place, a shine and spark that emanated from its customers and the satin sway of the band on stage.

Muriel yelled to Margaret over the music, cradling her glass of gin. 'This lot are better than The Saints from Ashton-under-Lyne, aren't they? It's heavenly. Thanks for coming with me, Margaret, it's made me feel a sight more cheerful.' She giggled as if to prove it. 'Jim would go barmy if he found out I was here. He would never have let me come if I'd asked him, but I've got a right to enjoy the simple things in life, haven't I? Not being able to dance, it's left a big hole in my life. You understand that, don't you?'

Margaret hugged her briefly and gestured to the dance floor. 'We all know how much you love dancing, Muriel, so go on, get in there, my knees won't take the pace.'

Muriel hesitated a moment. The room was boiling with a mass of jumping bodies, new colours and creeds, a new world. She watched for a while until she thought she had memorised the fast jitterbug steps and then tentatively stepped into the melee. She was snatched and pulled into the throng before she could draw breath, and spun, flying over a shoulder, landing upside down and dizzy, laughing, free as the girl in the back yard.

She spotted a familiar figure through the hustle, watching, and, as always, propped up at the bar. Mickey Evans grew like fungi through the cracks of her life, turning up everywhere and always at the wrong time.

He grabbed her arm as she spun past and pulled her away from the crowd. His breath was stained with rum. 'What you dancing with them for?' he sneered, gesturing to the black American soldiers.

Muriel shook him off. He had no right to touch her. 'I can dance with who I like, Mickey,' she snapped.

'Really? Can you? Does Jim know you're here then?' he said. Their faces were so close she could see the convex of the sweat drops on his forehead quivering.

A piercing wail, pulling a primeval reaction faster than any of Annie's cries, split the air. The band stopped playing and an air-raid warden waddled onto the stage. Muriel could see him panting from the back of the room. He grabbed the microphone and a screech of feedback subdued the crowd. 'Please, everyone, make your way down to the cellar, ladies and gents. No one's allowed out now, only in.'

As if to reiterate his point, the ballroom doors flapped open and two women staggered forward, a mother and daughter by the looks of them, one holding the other up, both covered in debris. The mother's hair was full of dried plaster, her best coat torn, and there were smears of blood across her daughter's face.

Muriel made her escape from Mickey, snatched a glass of discarded gin and pulled Margaret towards the cellar steps. 'Who would want to go out there?' she said.

When she got back to Princess Road, Jim was already there. Sent home early, he'd arrived to find his wife missing, with no one admitting they knew where she was. By the time Muriel arrived home, sweat-stained and dust-spattered, he was frantic with worry and gave her no chance to explain herself as her drew her to the privacy of their room.

'I need a word with you.' Many words followed, a fountain of accusations and blame rattling the blackout tape loose on the window pane. She let Jim rant a while before she snatched at the curtains and threw them wide, dividing the night, hung on to them, her arms stretched taut and white, the black window a proscenium arch beyond which an invisible audience waited. She burst into loud and insistent song, making her rendition of 'Ballin' the Jack' as an insult to her ill-tempered James. He tried to raise his voice above hers. In the other room Edna stoked the fire and pretended she couldn't hear the cacophony between husband and wife. If only her daughter just did as she was told. She'd always been a wilful girl; seemed even a war couldn't change that.

Muriel let her song shrivel into a whisper. She gave a heave of her shoulders and started to weep quietly.

'You can't go out and leave Annie motherless, Muriel, you're my wife, I forbid you to go out again!' Jim yelled.

Muriel pulled her dress up over her shoulders, still damp under the arms from her exertions, and dropped it on the floor in a puddle. She spun on him in her white slip like a mad spirit shadow, spitting fire, framed in the window pane. She looked like an angel about to take flight. 'If you want me to stay your wife, Jim, don't you tell me what to do, don't you dare!'

*

Muriel sipped her scalding-hot tea from her favourite cup. There was a fine grey trace above the meniscus of the strong brew, a line that split between the delicate, hand-painted flowers on the outside of the china and her hand which trembled slightly as she sipped. When the cup slipped, she made no effort to save it and it crashed upon the lino, shattering hot brown liquid all up her bare legs. She bit her lip against the sudden scald, leaving her mother to silently pick up the white bone remnants and quickly mop.

Edna kissed her daughter's head. 'Good job Harry's taken Annie out – she could have been right under your feet.'

Muriel unclenched her fingers and expelled a whistle of air. She inhaled a damp breath from the Monday, laundry-day room and brushed the stains of tea on her skirt. 'That was my best cup,' she said.

It was a weekend and Jim worked shifts. She'd enjoyed the longest lie-in she could get away with in their empty bed and decided to tidy her dresser when Harry volunteered to take Annie for a walk. He told her they were going on a treasure hunt. Muriel knew what he was hunting. He'd done the same last week. He'd put Annie's coat on and her new wellies without any socks, and an Easter bonnet Muriel had made, and dragged the poor child down Claremont Road to Wilmslow, along to Platt Fields, through the park to Platt Lane. They stopped at every shop that might have had cigarettes. Annie's bonnet blew off in the park and Harry raced after it. Her feet were bleeding by the time they got home. Muriel was furious and boxed her brother's ears.

'All that way and in every shop looking for cigarettes, and there's none to be had anyway, Harry, you gormless lad,' she'd said.

'Annie never complained, we had an adventure, didn't we, girl?' Harry answered and ruffled her daughter's red curls.

'The daft child would probably follow you anywhere,' Muriel said. She'd only let Harry take her out again when she had socks on, and he had the pushchair as a back-up.

Muriel had found a disused shoe box with some postcards and a photograph in her dresser and taken them into the kitchen to sort. She ran her fingers around a faded postcard, flipped it over and reread the back, 'The Last of England, Manchester Art Gallery.' The gallery was closed, and she didn't know where they had stored the paintings. She picked up the photograph underneath it.

Her mother interrupted. 'You should get that photograph framed before it gets damaged,' she said. 'It should remind you of what you've got.'

The photograph was a black-and-white print of herself and the baby. One pearl earring peeked from Muriel's dark curls. The shine had gone on those pearls now. It was the last time her beauty would be captured so. She would rather frame the postcard of her favourite painting and put that on the wall.

She glared at her mother's back bent over the sink. Her broad shoulders stooped more nowadays. Dancing light kaleidoscope-flickered through the branches of the apple tree outside and pushed through the trellis of blackout tape across the window.

'What have I got then, Mother? Tell me, I'm sure you will.' She spat the words out, formed from a bitterness at the war that was meant to be over by the first Christmas. Her feelings were in good company: the whole land was littered with broken promises and dreams.

Edna wrung another bundle of white nappies to peg out on the line and scooped a few more from the bucket by her feet. 'You've a healthy baby for a start, maybe another on the way.' The smell from the bucket turned Muriel's stomach sour. She touched her hand to the thin cotton of the dress over her belly. Not again, she thought. It was too soon. She watched her mother inspect one washed white square and plunge it back into the murk and flubber suds of the sink and scrub again. 'Don't you think your Annie should be out of these now – she's past two.'

Muriel lit another cigarette. The tin ashtray was overflowing and it was only 10 a.m. 'It's just for nights, Mum,' she said. She couldn't be doing taking her daughter from the bedroom to the downstairs toilet in the pitch black. What if a bomb came without warning?

The family had become delicate sleepers, perched on a wire, a hair trigger springing them awake at the slightest noise; nerves were shredded. Muriel once thought herself safe in their family home on Princess Road. She wondered if anywhere would ever feel safe again.

It was as if Edna read her daughter's thoughts. 'The top of Meadow Street was blasted last night. Joyce's mother was under the stairs, daft mare. Her Bill never put their Anderson shelter up, so the whole place came down on top of her. I don't know how they got out alive.'

Muriel studied her photograph again and wound a thick curl around one finger. 'I ought to go and see Joyce sometime.' She'd passed her friend a few months ago on Deansgate, her head down as she pushed a pram, powder caked below her right eye, and she hadn't stopped to chat. Muriel had seen the violence of war mutate into violence at home when the men returned. Joyce's husband had been at Dunkirk: who knows what horrors he had seen.

It had been her mother's idea to get the commemorative photograph taken. The family clubbed together and made the sitting a Christmas present. Muriel waited months before she would go. She wanted to feel more of her old self, to gather the scraps of the woman she had been that had fluttered loose on the wind. Inside the photography studio it was cold, despite the spring warmth. Annie was six months old and Muriel had wrapped her in a shawl passed on from one of Flo's brood. Edna went with them and took herself off for a cup of tea at the café down the street while Muriel climbed the stairs on Tib Street.

'Come in with me, Mum,' she'd asked. 'There's safety in numbers.'

'You don't need me,' her mother said.

'But what if something happens to you, Mum?' She didn't want to say a bomb, but they both understood the threat. Muriel couldn't think what she would do if she had left her mother sipping tea when something came screaming out of the sky. Edna had slipped away anyway, reassuring her daughter all would be well.

She recognised the photographer straight away. He didn't have his moustache anymore, but he still had that sly twist to his smile. James Prince did not recognise her. He'd moved on from factory girls, and she was respectable now, a mother. Her movie star looks just about holding on. She had spent at least an hour applying her lipstick so it was line perfect on her pout, grinding her teeth underneath it, jaw set. And when it came to the taking of the photograph, she had looked away from the camera.

'Let's have a smile,' the photographer said, and finding no warmth forthcoming tried another tack. 'Well, do wistful instead, think of something nice. Maybe a good roast for tea, swerve the ration for a change.' He clicked the shutter. 'I could get you some beef if you like, a nice rump?'

She ignored the innuendo and made herself an ice queen, a Greta Garbo lost in Ancoats. She made her eyes blank and pulled her curls out, so they bounced on her shoulders. She had pushed her best fake pearl earrings through her lobes and one shone, peeking from behind a sweep of hair, like a bright star of hope. Her jacket was crumpled from holding Annie so close on the tram, its buttons straining below a bust full of mother's milk. She'd adjusted it so it gathered like loose handkerchiefs over her chest, over a best dress printed with blooming pansies. It was the first one she made after giving birth, from fabric Jim had bought, straining her tired eyes in reduced light over the Singer in the box room. The dress was a little too small still, it pinched. Her body had changed, it was softer, with blurred edges and an empty pouch on her belly where the baby had grown.

Annie lay on a crocheted blanket in front of her mother, gripping the wool in her small fist. She started as the photographer pressed his flash. Muriel stayed calm, detached from the infant lying before her like an offering on a plate. When the picture was developed, it struck her who she looked like. She had the same resigned and distant look as the woman in her favourite painting, The Last of England.

Muriel considered her mother's suggestion about the picture frame as she sat in the kitchen. It would mean a trip to town. The tram lines were out at the top of the road. Perhaps she could cycle. If she was careful of bomb craters – they should be easy to see in daylight. She'd heard Mickey had fallen into a bomb crater on Solway Road last week. Probably out boozing after blackout, she thought. He'd come back from Dunkirk burned. Not too badly, not as badly as some she'd seen, faces turned into wax. Mickey's burns were mostly on his hands and arms. But it was bad enough that he was not to be called up again, and he had to wear woollen gloves in the heat of summer to cover the scars. He'd complained that no girl was interested in him now. Muriel doubted it was the injuries that kept them away, more the sense of self-pity he carried with him. Since their discharge, Mickey had been a more frequent a visitor than he used to be, knocking about with Jim every day. The rest of the family still loved him, Harry especially.

Muriel stood up. 'Mum, do you think you could look after Annie when Harry gets back with her? I think I will go into town and get a frame. I'll take my bike,' she said.

'The tyres'll need pumping up – can you wait for Harry?' Edna countered.

Muriel didn't want to wait. She wanted to get out of there before Mickey turned up again.

'I can do it myself, I'll get my jacket,' she said and ran up the stairs before she changed her mind. Her jacket hung between Jim's one suit and one other dress. As she pulled it out she dislodged her dance shoes from where they'd been hidden under a pile of baby clothes. She tucked them back out of sight.

*

Muriel cycled past the barrage balloons that floated, bloated and grey, above Alexandra Park. Their daylight whale shape reminding her the skies were mostly safe. She braked and stopped to watch with envy the women who were adjusting the tethered ropes.

Filled with a sudden rush of strength, she yelled through the railings, 'I could do that, you know! I could swing those ropes better than you and get those balloons to fly higher!'

The women went about their business, the shouts of a cycling shouting woman ignored.

Muriel hitched her skirt back up and pushed down on the pedals. She pushed on past the walls and pavements, crowding in and cracked. Pushed on beyond the cries of children, the baying packs of stray dogs, the bells and staggering buses. Pushed on as a hubbub of voices murmured in her mind, things her family had said, an insistent babble that captured her thoughts and twisted them into unquiet mutterings. She shouted at them too, 'Do shut up!' as she cut across Moss Lane, startling a small dog that wheeled and nipped at her ankles. She wobbled at the crossroads: one way to the city centre, the other to the new estates on the outskirts of Manchester. Muriel rode her bike in circles. She could make a run for it and head away from the city towards Wythenshawe. A car backfired as her skirt unravelled and caught on the pedal. She staggered and breached the bike, toppling with it sideways into an unmarked bomb crater.

Figures hurried towards her. Beyond their blurred outlines, she spotted a small shape that feathered and flickered in the corner of her eye. A chicken strutted proudly by. Muriel abandoned her bike and ignored her scuffed knees and the outstretched hands of concerned citizens. Pushing past, she clambered over the rubble and limped behind the bird, coaxing and cooing at it until her hands were near enough to close around its neck. One quick twist and its life was gone. She put its limp body in her bicycle basket.

'Are you sure you're all right, love?' someone asked.

'I'm fine, thank you, just heading home,' she answered, covering the coveted chicken as she turned the bike towards Princess Road.

*

Muriel threw the chicken on the kitchen table. Harry looked up, startled away from his game of peekaboo with his little niece. His sister's hair was wild and her eyes were sparking.

'There you are! No eggs, but a chicken. The chicken before the egg,' she said and snatched her daughter up to her hip. 'Chick, chick, chick, chick, chicken, lay a little egg for me. Chick, chick, chick, chick, chicken, I want one for my tea, I haven't had an egg since Easter, and now it's half past three, oh, chick, chick, chick, chick, chicken, lay a little egg for me,' she sang. Annie whimpered, part delighted, part uncertain of her mother's change of mood.

Harry prised her away. 'Steady now, Muriel, you're frightening her.'

Muriel dropped her hands to her side. Her dress was still half tucked in her knickers and there was blood trickling from her grazed knee, warm and unclotted. 'I'd have a cup of tea, but I broke my cup,' she muttered, staring at the floor.

'Well, we'll get you another one,' Harry said.

Muriel grabbed the back of the chair: the kitchen was closing in on her. 'No, no thank you, I'll get a glass of water instead. I've got a belting headache. Watch Annie, will you, while I go and have a lie down?'

Harry laughed. 'In the middle of the day? It's a good job Mum's gone out, she'd nag you for being lazy.'

Muriel ignored Harry and climbed the stairs, one foot in front of the other, heavy with worry. She lay quietly on the clean bedspread and let herself go under the grip of a fierce and blackening pain. Her head felt grasped by large hands that squeezed hard enough to crack open her skull; she saw warm white war-dust flashes of light, stark as gull feathers over the shadowed walls. Her tongue thickened and her left eyelid drooped as the migraine paralysis crept down to her cheek.

February 1947

The noise, speed and clattering train wreck of war ceased. For Muriel, its hangover lasted well into the decade. Returning home late one night, she found her father in the front room, waiting to pronounce judgement from behind his newspaper pulpit. He barely rustled his copy of the *Mirror* before his sermon began.

'Now you're a mother don't you think it's time you behaved like one? No one wants to see you gadding about when you should be home looking after your daughter and Jim.'

She skirted his armchair and shucked off her dance shoes to warm her toes on the settle, the fire died down to a steady glow. Primping her hair, she laid a hand across her belly. She hadn't told anyone there was another child on the way yet.

'You remind me every day that it's your house and your rules, Dad. You're narky with Annie too, just like you were with me.'

Clarence balled the paper up and threw it to the floor. 'Well, if you don't like it then you should get your own place like your sister, shouldn't you?'

She opened her mouth to protest, but the words shrivelled on her tongue. At least she knew where she got her temper from. She and her father had locked horns all her life – she wasn't giving way now. Jim was the one who was meant to find them somewhere else to live. That was what Flo's husband had done, but Jim had his feet too far under his in-laws' table to try. Muriel found it hard enough to breathe with the three of them sleeping in the parlour, her brothers and parents upstairs and the rest of the family forever visiting. She'd go mad if they didn't get their own space soon.

*

Muriel was enveloped in lethargy as the new baby grew. It turned her light moods into sombre tunes as she sat in the kitchen knitting, fingers clacking between the bright yellow yarn. She couldn't get near her beloved Singer and had to settle for Flo's cast-off maternity dresses. At least Jim brought her tea in bed most mornings, and occasionally toast, until the family accused him of mollycoddling her. Muriel's dancing days stopped again as she waited for the baby to be born. The frustration pent up and expelled in an affirmatory roar during its quick birth in Wythenshawe Hospital. There she rested amongst the bouquets and bright sheets with her new baby boy, Billy, swaddled in a waffle blanket, and kissed his milky forehead.

'I promise I will give you more love, Billy, you and Annie,' she said. Yet it was a hard practice in a family that behaved as if it were still on ration.

When Billy was a few months old and Muriel had regained some of her senses, she developed a plan of escape.

She told the family she was going to visit Florence. Muriel had not hidden the fact she coveted her sister's new home with its neat kitchen and butler sink. She knew if she had one like it, she could make it even more of a palace. She took the bus to the city and went to the housing offices that were newly situated in her beloved town hall. Sad that this time she would have to bypass her beloved murals. She climbed the steps with a new rhythm and purpose to her walk, Billy hanging from one hip and Annie swinging from her other hand like a forgotten Christmas tree bauble. Muriel shoved her way to the front of the queue and stamped her feet in impatient beats until the thin-lipped woman in glasses looked up from behind the pane of glass.

'You have to take a ticket and wait your turn like everyone else, madam,' the woman said and the queue grumbled its agreement.

Muriel stared the clerk down as she yanked Annie's arm and shifted Billy to her other hip. 'What am I meant to take the ticket with? My teeth? This is an emergency. I need to see someone now.' She tipped forward until her head rested on the glass between them, and beat a dull thud with her forehead in time with her stamping feet. A flamenco of frustration. Muriel felt it hurt a little, but it had quietened the clamouring voices in her head, so she kept on doing it. Billy began to cry and people stared. She was making a scene, but she kept on.

The clerk stood up. 'Please stop that, madam, you'll do yourself an injury.'

Muriel paused a moment. There was a bruise blooming on her forehead. She replied with a chant in time to the tap of her feet, her voice shrill. 'I – can't – sleep, I – can't – move,

I – can't – cope – anymore. Please – help – me. Something bad is going to happen if I don't get out of there. I can feel it. I – CAN'T COPE!' she screamed.

The clerk scuttled away to find help.

Muriel was led firmly to a small side room that smelled of vinegar, someone's leftover fish and chip lunch folded in the wastepaper basket.

The supervisor was sympathetic, her soft hands resting on top of Muriel's tightly clenched fists. 'You must understand, Mrs Burns, there's a long waiting list for housing.'

Cold tears leaked train tracks down Muriel's powdered cheeks. 'But I must have more space, the children need more space, we're living on top of one another like ants and it's so noisy there, they never stop talking. I didn't mind before, but I want them to be quiet now,' she whispered.

The supervisor looked down at her papers. 'More points are given for those in essential services. Is your husband in essential services?'

The tears were dripping from Muriel's nose now. 'He's a painter and decorator for Mayle and Silburn. His company is painting the new hospital at Northenden. A hospital is an essential service, isn't it?'

The supervisor looked at the children. 'And you have two children … families with two children or more take a step towards the top of the list. Northenden is close, but we prefer to place people who are working in Wythenshawe, if that's where you want to be housed?'

'Yes, my sister lives there already. Does it have to be my husband who works in the Wythenshawe district? Could it be me instead?'

'Either you or your husband, but why would you want to work with two little ones to look after?'

Muriel ignored the second part; she was cheered a little by the first. She could find work anywhere.

*

Muriel took the 54 bus out of the city the next day, along the narrow streets as they stretched out their limbs into the wide avenues of Wythenshawe. She pressed her lips together, smudging the pink of her new lipstick and blanching her top lip. Annie wiped a space on the top-deck window, her view obscured by a fug of cigarette smoke and smears of hair oil on the glass.

'Don't touch!' her mother warned, snatching her hand away. She took a long inhalation of her cigarette and settled Billy beside her. 'You can ring the bell though if you want. Go on, do it now.' Annie's arm reached up, as elastic as the branches of the young trees that brushed the bus. The stop bell clanged and they rattled down the stairs to alight at the junction of Bromley and Altrincham Road, right next to the Sharston Pub.

Its modern, metal-framed windows were smeared with the light drizzle that was beginning to fall. Muriel dug deep in her handbag for her scarf, and remembered it was on the pulley maid at home because it was wash day: she'd have to face the manager with frizzy hair. The children's appearance needed improvement too, and from the smell emanating from him, Billy needed a fresh nappy. Finding the front door closed she walked round to the back where there were two huge horses sighing in their shafts on a dray cart. The shires reminded her of the farm horse Isabella had in Canada. She nuzzled the leathered nose of one and let Annie pat its caramel flank.

'Do you want to feed them?' The man's voice made her jump. His face was dark, his hair as black as treacle toffee, curled close to his head like hers, and his eyes were hidden behind thick glasses. She flushed a little as he passed a sugar lump to Annie.

'Here you go, red, try this, hold your hand flat now.' The horse bent and snuffled the crystals from her daughter's outstretched hand.

'It tickles,' she giggled.

Muriel shifted Billy to the other hip and pushed herself a little closer to the man. 'Have you got one for me?'

He flourished another cube between finger and thumb like treasure. 'I think you're sweet enough, aren't you?'

Muriel lowered her eyes to his polished shoes. She was used to getting compliments, but the opportunity to receive them had dwindled. Jim gave her crumbs now and again, but she had taken to looking in the mirror and reminding herself she was still attractive.

The man wiped his hand on his apron and held it out to shake. 'My name's William, this is Fred.' He slapped the horse's flank.

'My brother's called William, but we call him Billy,' Annie said, brazen behind her mother's skirts.

Muriel gathered her close and reached out her free hand to shake. 'Muriel Burns, pleased to meet you. Are you the manager? I heard you might have some work going.' She gestured over his shoulder to the three-storey building behind. 'Big place, isn't it?'

'Five bars and a snug for the ladies – we're run off our feet,' he said. 'I need deliverymen and barmen. I suppose I could offer you a cleaning job, but that's not really right for a refined lady like you.'

Muriel turned up her smile and shifted Billy again. She would need to change him soon before the horse manure couldn't disguise his smell any longer. 'It's kind of you to say so, but I'm perfectly capable of getting my hands dirty. Needs must.'

*

Muriel started within the week. She enrolled her mother to watch the children while she was there. She had been at The Sharston a month when there was a hammering on the front door ten minutes before opening time. Muriel shot the bolts and stuck her head out. One customer waited. Mickey Evans looked like he'd been sleeping on someone's floor. Stubble covered his chin and his mouth was pursed, hatch-marked with cigarette creases. His hands were gloveless and yellow nicotine stains glowed on his burned skin. His breath smelled of alcohol.

'What are you doing here?' she hissed.

He swayed past her and into the dark of the snug. 'I'm here for a drink. It is a pub, isn't it?'

She pulled her stockings up through her skirt and scuttled after him. 'You're so nowty when you've had a drink, Mickey.'

He spun on her, hands wide like bleached starfish in the unlit gloom of the snug. 'I've not had one yet. Surely my best mate's wife will get me one?'

She shook her head. 'We're not open and I'm not allowed to serve.'

'Go on, Muriel, you'll be open in ten minutes. Get me a drink and I'll prove you wrong. I won't be nowty, I'll be charm itself.' She shrugged and fetched him a warm glass of water from the sink. He grimaced. 'It tastes like you poisoned it. Have you got anything stronger?'

She noticed his Panther motorbike parked on the pavement outside. 'You can't drink if you're riding your motorbike. What you doing out this way? It's not your local.'

He pushed the glass away. 'I just came for a ride and to get out of the house. It's hard being a grown man and living with your mother.'

Muriel had seen Mrs Evans at the market the month before. She was upset, talked about her son taking off with a married woman. 'I thought you'd moved in with that woman on Beaumont Street,' she said.

'That didn't work out.'

Muriel carried on cleaning. 'Her husband came back from the Navy, did he? I expect you'll be calling at ours all the time for Jim's company, or off with Harry on your bikes.' Harry followed 'Uncle Mickey' wherever his hare-brained plans took them.

Mickey shrugged. 'Give over mithering, Muriel, and get me that drink.'

She felt a tremble of excitement and the flash of temptation Mickey's company always brought, everyone was susceptible to it, and glanced at the toffee-bright shine of the motorbike chassis, pushed a duster round his elbows, an idea budding. 'I'll get you a drink, Mickey, if next time you come calling you take me out with you as well.'

'Jim would never allow that,' he said quickly.

'He wouldn't know, would he?' she answered. She'd guessed Mickey's desire for a drink might temporarily dissolve his loyalty. She would find a way to explain a trip out to Jim another time.

*

The following week Muriel told Flo she had to go to a church meeting and left the children with her sister before she had the chance to protest. She ran round the corner and hitched herself onto the pillion of her brother's Panther. It was the first time she'd been on a motorbike. Her father had banned the girls from going anywhere near such a machine. Indecent, he called it. She folded her arms around her brother's waist, yelling in his ear as they sped down the ring road, her hands freezing.

'Is this the right way to hold on?' she said.

Harry yelled back against the wind, 'Hold tight, you'll be fine. Safer on the back of Mickey's bike, though, it's bigger.'

Somewhere round the outskirts of Chester they stopped for a cup of tea and caught up with Mickey Evans. 'We thought we'd ride out to Meifod,' he said.

'Where's that?' Muriel asked.

'A village just inside North Wales, past Welshpool.'

She hesitated. Wales meant she might not make it back to Princess Road before Jim got in from work. 'It's too far,' she said.

Mickey offered her his spare helmet. 'If we go now we'll be back before it's dark. Come on, Muriel, what are you frightened of?'

She glared at him. Always there with a challenge, Mickey bloody Evans. She swung a leg over the smooth leather of his pillion and the piping pushed into the soft flesh of her thighs where it would chafe. She could endure it. She folded her hands into the pockets of his leather jacket as they shot down the A-road towards Wales. She yelled in his ear, 'Don't go too fast, I don't want to come off.'

'You won't, just hold tight, I'm a safe driver.'

'But what about all the other drivers?'

'There's hardly any cars on this road – we'll be there in no time.'

It felt disloyal to lean her body against Mickey. Her father was right, it was indecent, with her legs spread behind him. She'd known Mickey longer than she'd been a mother, longer than she had been a wife. There had once been the promise of something more, but she had taken the road that led to Jim. She convinced herself that Mickey was a reminder of her youth and freedom, nothing more. As they climbed between a pelt of green-backed hills into Wales, she found it harder to convince herself of that thought. They leaned into a curve that took them hurtling past dry-stone walls and a blur of white and black houses and stopped at The King's Head to park the bikes. Muriel waited in the pub garden and let Mickey bring her a half of stout. She gulped the metallic liquid to calm her quickening nerves. It was so quiet. The sharp Welsh air cleaned her city lungs and tickled out the nicotine clogging her throat. She let her head fall back under the flickering willows, drinking in the silence, until Mickey fractured the spell.

'The landlord told me there's a cottage coming up for sale down by the river. I'm thinking of buying it,' he announced.

Muriel stared at Mickey with his drawn face and half-burned neck. He was tied to the city with every sinew, they all were. She'd never known anyone move away, thought it impossible since her own plans for Canada were crushed.

'You'll never leave Manchester,' she said.

He drained his pint. 'I might ... let's go and have a look, shall we?' When he offered his hand, she took it, and followed him down a lane until he stopped by a cottage at the end of a row with a blue door.

'The place next door is already up for sale – you and Jim could move in there.' Mickey laughed.

Muriel looked up at the patchwork walls, the tiny windows and smoking chimney. It looked like something from a biscuit factory tin. She hadn't thought places like that were real. Perhaps he was serious.

Harry caught them up, eager as a puppy. 'I heard the first cuckoo here when we rode out in spring,' he said.

Muriel could see the attraction.

They climbed a pinch stile to the river and she stopped to watch the ripples on the fast-flowing water. It might even be warm enough to dip Billy's chubby toes in without him screaming. Would do him some good, the fresh air. He'd been a sickly child, one thing after another with his ears and a nose that ran constantly. And Annie was a girl with a fondness for nature, already tending plants in the garden with a knowledge and care she must have inherited from her father. Annie liked to explore, had been discovered putting halfpennies on the railway track to try and flatten them into pennies. Jim had taken his belt off for that, but he didn't use it. He wasn't a man for corporal punishment. Muriel thought their little family could be happy there, under the big skies and glowering hills. It would be a fresh start. She might even be happy too.

She rolled off her stockings and waded into the water below the willows, the taste of stout still on her tongue. The cold numbed her skin, and her garters flapped against her thighs. She knew Mickey was watching from the riverbank. But he was wrong if he thought she wanted him; she wanted this. She lifted her head to the autumn sun. She wanted the freedom to paddle in water whenever her feet were hot or tired in this sweet-smelling space.

Mickey put out his cigarette and called to her. 'We should get back, Muriel, before it gets dark.'

Dusk had settled over the rooves of Princess Avenue as Mickey cut his engine and dropped Muriel around the corner. Harry drove his bike up the side of the house and waited for his sister. They entered the back door together to find their father was waiting by the pantry in the kitchen with his sleeves rolled up, ready for a fight.

'Where the bloody hell have you two been all this time?' He grabbed Harry before Muriel had a chance to answer and boxed his ears. 'You should know better, taking your sister out when she should be at home looking after the nippers.'

She pushed her way between her father's gentle fists and her brother's soft head. 'All right, Dad, stop it now! I asked Mickey to take me, it's not Harry's fault. Daft ha'p'orth would follow Mickey over a cliff if he asked him to.'

By the time Jim came in from work Muriel had been delivered of her children by an irate Flo and had managed to calm her father down. She put Annie and Billy either side of her in the armchair as if they had been settled there for hours. She read to them from the illustrated Bible, its pictures reminding her of her favourite paintings, old friends she had not seen for so long, like so many friends she had let drift because of marriage. Jim bent to kiss his family curled in the chair and Muriel ducked her head away from the smell of white spirit on his overalls. She knew she smelled of country lanes, birdsong and cigarettes.

'How's your day been?' he asked.

She shrugged, turning the pages. 'All right. Dad's maddling at me though, just because we had a ride out.'

Jim picked his son up and swung him high. 'Did you have a ride out on the bus, Billy?'

Muriel pushed her daughter from the chair. It was best to tell him now. 'Go on, Annie, take Billy and get ready for bed. We didn't go on the bus, Jim, we took the bikes. Flo looked after the kids,' she said.

'Bikes? Where'd you go?'

'Meifod,' she said.

'Wales? That's a bloody long way to cycle, Muriel.'

'It's only a couple of hours on a motorbike,' she rattled, barely drawing breath, letting her words hang, explaining before they could seep into his brain. 'It's a lovely place, Meifod. You've been before, haven't you? Mickey's looking to buy a place there. It was his idea,' she lied. 'Jim, we could move out there with him, couldn't we? It would be good for the children.' She batted her ideas at him as if she were taking the first serve at a tennis club.

He didn't respond to her rally. His face had already turned puce with contained rage. 'You went off with my best mate for a little holiday, while I was at work earning a living?'

Muriel tugged a cushion in front of her. The upholstery wasn't much defence. If she'd got home earlier and had more time she would have sorted her hair out and put some lipstick on. 'You're out with Mickey all the time as it is. What am I meant to do? Stay at home and stew?' she said.

'You're meant to be looking after the kids.'

She leapt up and faced him. 'I can't be forever in this bloody house! It's driving me mad,' she shouted. 'Why can't we move to Wales, Jim? God knows we need the space, there's no room for us here.' She gestured around the parlour, catching her reflection in the mirror that hung across the mantel. Her face was weather-blown. There was something else there now: lines, granted, a few, but the bloom had fallen from her beauty, the shine faded from her eyes, at least it had when she looked at her husband. She knew it, tried to hide it and something flickered between them. A distance she couldn't quite measure. Muriel had ideas he could never keep up with.

'It's too far, don't be daft,' he said.

'It's not so far if we had a car. It's only a couple of hours or less by road.'

'How can we afford a car?' Jim asked.

Her temple pulsed. 'Maybe if you weren't just a painter and decorator, we could afford it.'

He ignored the barb, defeated again. Shook his head. 'I don't understand you, Muriel. You've got a nice home here, why can't you be happy with that?'

She screamed and pushed away from him, storming into the kitchen.

Their row had pushed the rest of the family into corners and outside into the garden – it wasn't their business to interfere. Only her brother Leslie was left at the table when Muriel entered the room. His eyes like saucers in the evening light. He was silent, smoking and fiddling with the handle of the mangle. Muriel snatched up the empty plate in front of him and threw it across the room. It smashed into the sink, sending fragments flying against the window.

That brought Harry from his hiding place. He wrapped his arms around his sister, rocking her. 'Steady there, Moo,' he said.

Muriel fell back into him, letting the tears of frustration stream down her face. She had no energy left to protest at his use of the nickname she usually despised. 'I've had enough of it, Harry.'

'Enough of what?'

'Everything.'

September 1953

The Burnses made it to the top of the housing list and were placed in a house on the Wythenshawe Estate before Christmas. Solid and square at the end of an avenue with grass verges and trees, it had a main bedroom, a back bedroom for Annie and a box room for Billy. They had a room each. So many rooms to furnish now that Muriel had a house to make into her own palace. Furniture was hard to come by. They had struggled to squeeze Aunt May's sideboard through the back door, and it sat dominating the small front room. Jim collected dockets at work for utility pieces, twenty-four units for two wardrobes, one in the main bedroom, one in Annie's.

Yet Wythenshawe was not the paradise Muriel had envisioned. She missed the doorstep gossip of the city streets and it was strange being alone after the crowded company of family. She had yearned for light, and Wythenshawe, with its wide avenues and patches of green garden, had given her that. Her front bay window sparkled as she polished each pane to perfection daily, but the domestic routine kept her a captive. The kitchen became her enchanted room, her place of escape, its steaming kettle clouding the air and feeding her fantasies.

She sat at the new Formica table and wrote in her housekeeping book, watching the garden birds beyond the window as she flipped over the page from columns of pencil-drawn figures to scrawl angrily across a new blank page: 'I feel like a flippin' slave.' She tore the page out in frustration and threw it in the bin with the potato peelings. Her nerves were worn down by a sickly child who was often screaming, and the frustration of chores undone. The washing line had snapped that morning and spread her smalls over their tiny borders like late-blooming pansies. She was tired all the time and the fizz spark of passion well dimmed for her husband. Most of her female friends had disappeared into marriage, motherhood and sometimes work. There was no one to chat to.

It would have to be her sister Flo who heard her complaints, although she could only bear her sanctimonious judgements in small doses. She twisted Flo's arm and made her go to the Wednesday afternoon matinee at The Forum where Muriel sat fidgeting in the stall seats, while Flo settled beside her.

'What's the matter with you?' her sister asked.

'This bloody girdle's too tight,' Muriel said, wriggling her fingers below the waistband of her skirt to release the hooks pressing into her flesh. Life for me is as tight as this girdle, she thought. The titles rolled above them. 'Give us a cigarette, Flo,' she said. It had been a choice between affording to go to the pictures and smoke last weekend.

'Fancy you'll have to give up going to the pictures then,' Jim had said. Muriel would never do that. She settled down to watch the movie, wishing it was a technicolour glare to brighten her day, letting her thoughts flirt with the wish for a big drama in her life. She had wanted to see *From Here to Eternity* for weeks. 'Soppy stuff,' Jim had declared when he'd seen the previews of Burt Lancaster rolling in the surf with Deborah Kerr. Muriel thought it had looked stirring, romantic.

Flo rummaged in her handbag and emerged triumphant with a clutch of barley sugars in her fist. 'Want one? They'll be selling sweets here before we know it, now sugar rationing's ended.'

Muriel accepted the offering in place of the cigarette she had asked for. It would have to do. 'I was going to wait until the interval and have an ice cream,' she said.

'You flush or something?' Flo asked. Muriel rattled the boiled sweet across her front teeth and ignored her. 'Are you sure this will be finished before the children get back from school?' Flo continued.

'I told Annie to pick up Billy on her way home,' Muriel said.

'Will she remember?'

'Of course. She's a good girl, responsible.'

'Unlike her mother,' Flo commented.

Muriel swivelled round in her seat to challenge her sister. Their murmured conversation was drawing shushes and tuts from the sparse audience.

'What's that meant to mean?' she hissed.

'Well, you've left Annie on her own before, haven't you? She looked after Billy when he was just a tiny baby.'

'I left them once, Flo, once, and it was years ago, only for ten minutes when I was desperate to get to the shops.

Billy was asleep, it was the only chance I had. Would you have had them starve instead?' It wasn't quite the truth. She would never have let the children starve; there was always a little food in the house. They had been at the tail end of their time at Princess Road and Muriel was at the end of her tether. The continuous cries of her fractious baby had made her desperate for peace, just a morsel of it. She had rocked, soothed and fed Billy until she could think of nothing else except gripe water. The last bottle rattled empty on the pantry shelf, so she had buttoned her coat and told Annie not to shift from the parlour as she tapped her way towards the shops. Annie had perched on the edge of the bed, sat on her hands, frightened to move lest she wake her sleeping brother. When the sirens went off, she leapt up and cradled him close. She sat with her back to the front door and prayed. By the time Muriel got back she was shaking with fear, it took half an hour to calm her down.

'The war had finished, the sirens were miles away and they were in no danger,' Muriel said. She watched the actors lean across the screen and whispered to her sister, 'Jim used to say I looked like a movie star.' He hadn't said any such thing for a long time.

'You've always behaved as if you were living in a movie,' Flo said.

Muriel didn't dignify her sister's barb with an answer. She rummaged in her handbag and brought out her powder compact, flipped it open and tried to find her reflection in the dim movie light. She checked her face with a more critical eye these days; she saw a thickening jaw, pores that were large and open across the soft skin of her nose, hair that frizzed because she'd neglected the salon in favour of cheaper home perms. Her looks had been an embellishment, like a painting Ford Madox Brown had created. Those thick layers of paint expressing the feelings she could not, unless she could dance, and there were few chances to do that. She saw something of herself in those paintings that not even her dancing feet could express, a lurking wildness, a vivacity that she had once had.

There was a truth to her beauty once; now she felt it was fast disappearing. She relied on her own artistry with powder and make-up she could barely afford, but something else lurked beneath the Max Factor: she seemed to be melting into a different person, a nobody, disappearing into the characterless mass of homogenous houses, the same streets, the same sky, the same concrete kerbs, the same grass verges. She clipped her compact shut and dropped it back into the depths of her bag and placed it at her feet.

They boarded the bus home and the whole way out of the city Muriel noticed the mothers bouncing along the street pushing prams and shepherding gaggles of children out of the school gates. She floated above them, watching through milky sunshine. Her sister's comments niggled into her guilt like bees in a tulip. Perhaps she should have been there to meet Billy from school like all the other women.

'Do you think I'm a good mother?' she asked Flo.

'I think you're like Frank Sinatra in the film we've just seen, absent without leave!'

It was true, she had been tied up in her own thoughts. Annie was thirteen and nearly a woman. She was letting her go with wafer crumbs of independence, sending her to the library with lists for new books, getting her to bring Billy home from school and make the tea of thick slices of bread and jam. She'd shown her how to bake, how to wash and how to sew, passing on what feminine skills she had. She knew she would have to have 'the talk' with her sometime. It wasn't something she wanted to discuss with her daughter. It was something cloistered in the dark, in the privacy of their marital bed when Jim was smelling of beer and she was too tired to argue.

Flo kept on, labouring the point. 'You don't know how lucky you are. Your husband takes you out now and then to the pub, doesn't he?'

'When he's not out with Mickey,' Muriel said. Why should she sit nicely in the snug at The Sharston, when she could play darts and cards as well as the rest of them? All this anger, she thought, and tucked her hands under her coat. She was so angry all the time these days. The sparks she had felt as a child were now a constant burn at the back of her throat. She had to turn it in, tuck it down like her bedsheets with neat housewife corners.

*

Another Monday morning and Muriel rose before seven to prepare Jim's breakfast. He liked his porridge thick, with a crust of sugar. When he came into the kitchen, he was already dressed in his work outfit, splattered with varying shades of cream paint.

Muriel looked disparagingly at his overalls. 'When are you going to paint our house, Jim? This kitchen's dead dingy. If you stayed in a bit more instead of going up the pool hall all the time with Mickey, you could make our place nice and fresh.'

Jim picked up his tin of cheese and pickle sandwiches and moved into the front room. Muriel followed, as close to his elbow as a seed burr latched to a jumper. His trouser legs were rolled up and flakes of magnolia threatened to float to the floor. She twitched at the threat. 'Why are you wearing your overalls in here? You'll get paint on the rug.'

Jim preened in her new mirror, combed his fair hair, transparent at the back. 'I go out the front way to work or do you want me to leave by the back door now?'

She pouted next to him. 'Yes and maybe you should come in that way too.'

Jim laughed and pinched her snub nose. 'I don't think the neighbours care what I look like, Edith Muriel. A working man needs the right clothes.'

'But I mind,' she grumbled, tugging at her housecoat, her domestic overalls. Her day would be as busy as his, she often told him so, listing the chores she'd completed at the end of the day as he hid behind his paper: turning down beds, opening windows, washing up, dusting and tidying, cleaning the grate and laying the fire for the evening and peeling the veg. All unpaid work. 'It's Monday too, I've got everything to do, plus the laundry.'

Jim cleared his throat and drew deep on his Woodbine. 'I'll save you the bother of making tea then and bring us home fish and chips.'

Muriel brightened. That was a treat and she allowed him a rare hug, like she meant it. 'Thank you, that would be smashing, I'll get some bread and butter in.'

He kissed her lightly on the forehead and shuffled out of the front door.

*

By the time five o'clock came the light was stealing away from the last of the summer. Muriel had washed her hair at four and put it in curlers, making a bit of an effort for a shared chip supper. She sat on the edge of the sofa, kirby grips between her teeth, re-plaiting Annie's hair as it dried in front of the fire. She had tuned the radio to the Light Programme and was enjoying the dulcet tones of Nat King Cole and Dean Martin, getting her daughter to join in with Doris Day as she sang the *Calamity Jane* refrain. '"Just blew in from the windy city…"'

The front door went and Jim rolled in, flustered. He was scratching at the skin on his neck.

'Can you get this paint off the back of me, love? I'm running late. I promised a few of the boys a game of pool tonight. Reckon I can beat the lot of them.' He grinned.

Muriel stared at the red welts appearing on his pale skin. 'Where's the fish and chips then?'

Jim dumped a canvas sack on the floor, but his offering was not food. He kicked the sack and released a roll of butter-coloured balls across the living-room rug. 'Mayle and Silburn said I could keep all the balls I collected from the guttering on the tennis club. Annie, you can use them for under over on the back wall.' His daughter wrenched her hair from her mother's fingers and filled her arms with new toys.

'And what am I expected to feed the kids? They can't eat tennis balls. Are they going to have to have bread and jam again?' Muriel snapped.

Jim dug in his pockets and pulled out some coins. 'There's two bob there. You can leave them for a few minutes, can't you? Nip up to that new chip shop in the precinct.'

She snatched the balls from Annie and stuffed them back in the sack and she shoved it in the sideboard behind a half-empty bottle of Bell's whisky. She caught her reflection in the mirror. 'I am not going out with my hair in curlers.' She was talking to herself; her husband's reflected image had slipped behind the skirts of the painted crinoline lady. When Muriel turned round, he had disappeared. She swore quietly and picked her scarf from the hook in the hallway, wrapped it around the curler spikes that bit into her scalp, put her coat on and gave Annie her instructions. 'Do not answer the door, stay away from the fire and keep the radio on. I'll only be five minutes.'

It was raining by the time she headed back home. Fat lashings of rain that licked at her face and wriggled her headscarf free at the back, rolling cold drops down the nape of her neck and soaking the chip paper that flapped free from her coat. Fast, swift rain that soon polished the roads and formed puddles. A car nudged the kerb and splashed her legs and the clean stockings she'd slipped on. Muriel tucked her chin down and ran the last ten yards.

She unwrapped the paper from the cooling food. 'Eat out of the paper, I'm not getting the plates out. Annie, pour out some milk for you and Billy.'

Annie checked the pantry. 'We haven't got any, Mum.'

Muriel clenched her fists, making small half-moon indents in her palms with her chipped nails. 'Now you tell me, I could have got it from the shop. Well I'm buggered if I'm going out again, you'll just have to have warm Vimto. Put the kettle on.'

Annie smiled. That was what she was after anyway. The children delved for their tea from the folds in the paper as Muriel picked up the scraps of batter between her fingers and licked the salt from her thumb. She swallowed her food down with her hurt. Jim would have her cold back as a welcome in bed when he got home.

She sensed it before she heard the knock. It was a dread, pungent as the smell of rain, seeping into their small house with a pinch of cold as her chips cooled. When the sharp rap at the front door came, she ignored it. If it was family, they would come round the back and let themselves in; anyone else, she was not interested. The second knock was more insistent. She pushed herself up, her legs leaden and reluctant, and forced herself to the front door. Two policemen waited on the step. The younger one was about the same age as their Harry, with heavy eyebrows and a face so red it looked like someone had slapped him. The other was older, pale and measured with eyes that had seen it all before. Muriel clutched the door frame, seized with the impulse to slam the door, and pretend they weren't there. Nothing good could ever come of letting the police into a house, she knew that.

The older one removed his helmet and tucked it under his arm. 'We're sorry to disturb you, madam. Are you Mrs Burns?' She nodded her head imperceptibly and wished she wasn't. 'I'm Sergeant Fields, this is Constable Poke. Could we come in?'

Muriel knew they were going to tell her a truth she would not want to believe. She felt it already, had drifted away, detached from her blurry figure in the tiny hall.

The policemen slid past her uninvited. Her breath quickened as she followed them into the front room and a vicelike pain spread behind her left temple: the beginning of another migraine.

'Would you like to sit down, Mrs Burns?' Sergeant Fields asked.

She perched on the edge of the sofa and folded her hands together to stop them shaking. It was never good news when they asked you to sit down. The sergeant stood in front of the fire, steam curling from his trousers as Constable Poke sat down beside her.

'Have you got someone who could come in and look after the children, Mrs Burns?' the sergeant asked. He frowned with such concern his eyebrows met in the middle, making a black smudge across his forehead. It would look funny if he weren't so serious, she thought. Annie stuck her head around the kitchen door, a chip cooling in her clenched fingers. Her mother waved her away.

'Annie can look after herself, Billy too if she needs to,' she said.

'You might want to call someone anyway,' the sergeant said.

Muriel was confused. They didn't have a telephone. 'Why?' she asked.

The sergeant flipped open his notebook so he didn't have to look at her when he told her. 'There's been an accident, Mrs Burns, a motorbike accident. Mickey Evans pulled out of a side alley into Princess Road and was hit by a milk truck.' He paused and wiped his forehead. 'There's more motorbikes than trucks on the road these days.'

Muriel quelled her sense of relief. 'What's that got to do with me?'

'Your husband ... Jim, is it?' She nodded, battling the cold fear that was drowning her. The policeman continued, 'Your husband was riding pillion. He was thrown off. The truck ran over his right leg. They got an ambulance out and it took him straight to hospital, but he's pretty beat up.'

Muriel felt the numbness spreading through her fingers and down her legs. Her mind flashed back to her cold hands folded inside Mickey's leather jacket pockets as they leant around the corners on the country lanes racing towards Wales. Was this her punishment for going with him? Should it have been her? Muriel stared at the sideboard. The crinoline lady hovered above it in her mirror, inscrutable. She wanted Jim to be leaning against it like he was that morning, combing his hair. She could start the day all over again and undo this horror. 'Please, God, please, God,' she muttered, trying to find a path out of her limbo. Jim had to live, he would be all right, they could not be parted like this.

She was unaware she was rocking until her daughter took her hand. 'Mum, you've gone white – do you want me to get Auntie Flo? Who do you want me to get?'

Muriel didn't know. Who would she tell? She'd have to send a telegram to Isabella in an ominous yellow envelope. She was overtaken by helplessness, suddenly wanted her own mother, someone to hold her and tell her it would be all right. She looked at Annie's serious face. Her good girl, her sensible, grown-up girl. She took a deep breath, it would have to be Flo. Muriel would have to go to the hospital on her own and prove to herself that Jim was fine.

She stood up and the room rocked. 'Which hospital has he gone to?'

'Withington, the new one. He's got the best doctors there,' Poke said.

She shot the young constable a sharp look. Didn't he know doctors made home calls and delivered babies? No one went to hospital unless it was very bad, and then didn't come out again.

The sergeant steadied her arm with his big hands, warm hands, like Jim's. 'I can take you there if you like.'

Muriel leaned against him. 'Annie, there's coins for the phone box at the end of the street in the biscuit tin in the kitchen. Take Billy with you and ring Flo. Come straight back, mind.' She glanced at the red-faced Poke. 'Can you stay with them till my sister gets here? I'll get my coat.'

October 1953

The night Jim had his accident Muriel had arrived at the hospital as if in a dream. She walked through a temple of bright and polished white on white. White walls, ceilings and corridors, where the nurses flitted like angel hosts. She a serious interloper whose loud shoes hushed on the thick vinyl floor. There were still mud splashes up her calves, she had no lipstick on, and had hustled her unkempt hair under her scarf. There had been no time to make herself presentable: what would Jim think of the state she was in? Her coat smelled of the fish and chip tea, a vinegar tang that muddled with the disinfectant making her sneeze and causing a passing nurse to frown. She was a blistering infection breaking into their neat world.

Finally, they came to a ward at the end of a corridor. Five beds were packed together, the patients sleeping, swaddled in their hospital sheets like babies in a maternity ward. A green screen shielded the sixth bed in the window corner. Sergeant Fields marched between the beds, Muriel compelled to follow, her stomach sinking through her legs and pooling in her shoes. He pulled aside the screen and a young nurse leaped from a chair beside the bed. For an instant Muriel thought she had disturbed lovers canoodling by the street-lit window.

The nurse fluttered a hand to her meringue hat and gestured to the chair she had recently vacated. 'Mrs Burns? Please sit down. Jim's very sleepy at the moment. The doctors gave him a ton of morphine to dull the pain, but I'm sure he'll know you're here. You can talk to him, he'll hear you.'

Muriel regarded the young nurse, her smooth skin and soft smile. Everyone wanted her to sit, as if it was better for her, easier to take bad news when she was sitting down. Perhaps they thought her legs might give way ... she wasn't that old, yet. She looked at her husband asleep in the bed. His lower limbs were hidden by a frame that lifted the covering blanket into a tent. 'They said a truck ran over his legs, flattened them. How are they?' she said.

The nurse exchanged glances with the sergeant. 'The doctors said his right leg is shattered below the knee. They're going to operate and pin it. They're very good, I'm sure it will heal, Mrs Burns. His hip's fractured too, but that can heal. Ribs and arms are bruised, bruises fade.'

Muriel rested her hands on her trembling knees. All this healing, she should have brought her Bible. She could have read and recited the words. There was power in the incantations of scripture, wasn't there? She forced herself to look at her husband. His lantern jaw softened, hair invisible on his forehead, pale lips and skin the colour of old paint. It didn't look like her Jim. Perhaps it was not. They had brought her here by mistake and sat her next to a stranger. This was not the man she married.

She took his hand, soft skin still warm, and turned it over, staring at the map of blue veins on his wrist, and imagined the red blood pushing through. She tightened her grip, pushing sharp nails into his palm.

'Why do you go and spend all your time with that idiot Mickey when you could have taken me out instead? We could have gone dancing, Jim, dancing. We could have gone to The Ritz, I haven't been there for years. I could have taught you how to dance properly after all this time – it's just practice, Jim. We could have danced under the chandeliers.' She dropped the hand and curled in upon herself, rocking, holding in the tears of rage. 'You should have let me take you dancing, you stupid, stupid bugger.' Hot tears got the better of her and ran freely down her face.

The nurse hovered. 'I'm so very sorry, Mrs Burns. Can I get you anything?'

Muriel looked up. 'It'll be all right, it'll be all right,' she muttered. 'When Jim gets out of here, I'm going to teach him how to dance.'

*

She visited daily the first week. A week in which she felt half in, half out of the world, moving between home and hospital like a somnambulist. She was patient and waited for him to wake, praying that he would do so, so she could shout at him. She did read him the Bible, and on less angry days, the interior design articles in *Woman* magazine. She read him everything ... anything to let him know she was there. Rain pelted the hospital each day as she strained to read in the grey light and reached over to divert the bedside lamp that was shining a halo over Jim's head.

On the Friday his eyelids fluttered and parched lips parted. 'Muriel ...' he said.

She bent and kissed his forehead. His perspiration tasted of stale chips. 'Jim. How are you feeling?' He coughed. She held a glass to his lips, and when he gulped the water, scolded him. 'Sip it, or you'll have the nurse over telling me off.' He sank back into the pillows. 'You're all right, you're going to be all right, Jim.' She was unsure if she was saying this for his benefit or hers. 'The doctors have operated on your leg and it's healing well.' She willed this to be true. They had told her the operation was long, but they had pinned what they could. With time they hoped he would recover, although he would always have a limp, and there was the risk of infection. Jim looked completely lost. She reached for his hand, trying to understand his bewilderment. He'd set off that evening on an ordinary night out with his mate. Now he was stranded in a hospital bed, helpless. He had never been helpless before.

'What happened to Mickey?'

Muriel withdrew her hand. 'Oh, don't you worry about him, he's going to be fine. Always comes up smelling of roses.' She turned to watch the rain blurring the hospital window and crossed her cardigan over her chest, fiddling with its small leather buttons.

'He was going dead slow, just pulled out onto Brownley Road, and the truck hit us straight on. I didn't see it, Muriel, just felt a dead thud over my leg.'

Muriel winced and thought of her pillion-passenger ride, flashing through Welsh lanes. By rights it should have been she who flew off back then, not Jim, crawling out of a gate at five miles an hour and knocked flat by a milk truck.

'You were just round the corner from home,' she said.

*

Jim was bound in plaster up to his chest like a mummy in a cheap B-movie horror. The doctors told her it was to keep everything in place, but Muriel wondered if her husband would ever be whole again. Daily visits were no longer allowed once he was awake. She was limited to Tuesdays, Thursdays and Sundays. She never missed a visiting day where she kept vigil by his bedside and listened to the doctors talk over her head. When she asked questions, they placated with promises. They promised he would be discharged by the end of the month. The month went by. Come November she was exhausted with it all and began to think the doctors were all thoughtless beings who treated her like a child. They were plotting against her. They stood in front of her by his bedside and talked about him as if he wasn't there. They talked about Muriel as if she wasn't there too.

'They're robots,' she told Annie, 'with their pens and clipboards and stethoscope prods. Marching in and out of the ward like they own the place and dispensing orders.' Like the ants in the pantry, she thought, incessant, organised, persistent. There was only one doctor she liked, with curly hair and tempting dark skin who always remembered her name, unlike the others. A Dr Hopton. He skirted the spaces between the bedpans and trolleys with such a light step she considered he would be good at the quickstep.

One morning she was sitting next to Jim's bed, another chapter of *Reader's Digest* finished and frost melting on the window, when Dr Hopton asked her into his office. He offered her a cigarette, Senior Service, she noted. She noticed a shaving nick on his right cheek too. He was still young – probably needed more practice with a razor.

'Mrs Burns ... may I call you Muriel?' he asked. She nodded. First-name terms: it must be bad news. 'I'm Charles.' He paused as a nurse rattled in a trolley with a teapot and two cups. He poured one and waited for the nurse to leave then pushed the cup across the desk. She wanted to ask for sugar but couldn't see a sugar bowl. Charles blew on his tea and rattled out words that made ripples on the liquid. 'Muriel, your husband has suddenly developed an infection in his left leg, the damaged leg, and it's a nasty one. We've been trying to fight it, but I'm very, very sorry, there's nothing more we can do to save the leg. We're going to have to amputate, and quickly. As his next of kin, I need you to sign the form – I've got it with me.' He pushed a sheet of white paper across the desk. 'We need to do it today.'

She stared at the form on the table: a leg for a life. She'd seen men come back from the war missing an arm, a leg, a mind, swinging on crutches through Albert Square on parade days, their palms blistered from the handles. Jim had never fought, and he was still whole. Why take some of him away?

'What will you do?' she mumbled.

'We'll take the leg off below the hip, leaving some thigh to attach a prosthetic.' She had no idea what he was talking about. 'A false leg,' he clarified. 'He'll be able to walk with a false leg.'

He won't be able to dance, though, she thought.

Muriel was silent the whole way when Harry drove her home. She spoke as his car pulled up beside the privet hedge. 'What a Christmas present for the children this is. Their father is never going to be the same again.' She was struck with a sudden urge to run down the cul-de-sac and across the stream, through the wide avenues and out into the countryside, to go feral and never come back.

Harry stayed her arm. 'I'll fetch the kids, shall I, and take them to Flo's? Bring our mum back to sit with you for a while. How's that sound?'

She waited until they had all gone until she climbed into her wardrobe and cried, weeping for an hour in the dark until her stomach clenched. She heaved and dashed across the landing to the shiny bathroom, where she vomited up all love and hope. Her tears dried, stinging and wrinkling the fine skin below her eyes with their harsh salt, and she wandered from the house into the sharp night, down to the culvert where she sat on the edge of the stream in her slippers watching the planes from Ringway blinking by the stars on their travels. Away and out of Manchester. A dark thought gripped her mind: if Jim died during the operation, she could leave too. She pinched her arms hard for thinking such awful thoughts.

She finally trailed home to her anxious mother and an empty bed with a dip that reminded her where her husband was and what he would wake up to. She slept till morning.

Her mother was stirring a thick pan of porridge over the gas. 'This has caught, Muriel. I can't work your newfangled cooker. I would have made eggs, but you haven't any in. The kids stayed over at Flo's. They'll get a better breakfast there. Have some of this anyway, it'll do you good.'

Muriel stared at the congealing mess as it was ladled into her bowl, the spoon rigid in the thick porridge. Black, burned flecks peppered the surface and wriggled like ants as she stirred. 'I can't eat this, Mum, it's got ants in it.'

Her mother peered into the bowl. 'Don't be daft. Those black specks are only burned bits. Come on, you have to eat something. Shall I put a bit of sugar on it for you?'

Muriel folded her arms like a petulant child. Her family couldn't bear waste. Her mother would watch until she'd eaten the lot.

The impasse was broken by the arrival of Harry who brought thick sliced bacon wrapped in greaseproof, and without a fuss started to make them all bacon butties for lunch, narrating his morning as he fried.

'I've been up to Withington to check how Jim is. They wouldn't let me see him, but one of the nurses told me the operation went well. He'll be awake by this afternoon, so I'll take you to see him then, if you feel up to it, Muriel, you look awful.'

She felt awful. She pulled at her tangled hair, wanted to pull it off, pull her whole skin off and cast it aside like an old coat, keep scouring away at the layers until all that was left was a small girl, dancing her flighty feet in the back yard to make her little brother laugh. Her shoulders crumpled. 'I don't want to see him,' she sobbed.

'You need to pull yourself together for the sake of the children, love,' Edna said. 'You're not the only mother coping on her own, you know. You're not going to die.'

Muriel thought she might. She waited for Harry and her mother to leave before she turned the radio on in the front room. The music pushed at the walls and it was like a window opened. For a moment her fears were blown away. She turned it up loud, kicked off her slippers and balanced on the balls of her feet, singing beside Rosemary Clooney. '"Hey there, you with the stars in your eyes, love never made a fool of you, you used to be too wise."' She spun and crooned between the furniture, the dancing unleashing her expression until sweat streaked between her breasts and freckled her temples. She was unaware her performance had an audience. Billy stood at the kitchen door, watching, fresh home from school.

Muriel fell on him. 'Come and dance with me, Billy, stand on my feet and I'll teach you the waltz.'

'I've got my shoes on,' he protested.

'Well, take them off, come on.'

He pulled away from her embrace as she spun under the standard lamp. 'Oh you're just as bad as your dad – he won't dance with me either.'

'Dad can't dance with one leg,' he said.

The truth hit her like a punch in the stomach. She switched the radio off and gathered all her strength. 'How about you and I get the bus and go into Manchester, Billy? It's ages since I've been to the gallery.' She suddenly longed to see her pictures that showed with paint emotions she lacked the words for. If only she could paint herself, but her family would laugh if she tried. Especially her father. What had he said when as a girl she told him, bright-eyed, all about the town hall murals? He had sneered behind his paper. 'Ford Madox who? Stupid name. If you ask me all artists are mad, or homosexual, and all of them poor.' She'd laughed: what did he know?

She snatched her son's hand up. 'Come on, Billy, let's go!' she pleaded.

He glanced hopefully at the mantel clock. It was after four. 'Won't it be closed by the time we get there?'

Muriel sat down. She knew she was putting off the inevitable. 'On Saturday then. We can go after we've visited your dad.'

*

Muriel knew her way to the ward. The whole family did. The white corridors, clanking drips and trolleys were as familiar as home. Annie marched ahead, confident and at ease with the medical surroundings. Billy held his mother's hand, his soft skin pricked with perspiration. Muriel measured her steps, pretending to protect her children from the catastrophe in ward nine, a husband and father reduced; it was more like the children were shielding her.

Jim was suspended in his end bed amongst a web of slings, ropes and pulleys. He looked like a puppet. A white coat hovered nearby adjusting buckles and straps and convincing Muriel of her belief that the doctors and nurses were controlling him.

'What are they doing?' she asked Annie, battling to keep the panic out of her voice.

Her daughter answered, calm as always, 'It's physiotherapy, Mum. It will help to get him strong enough to get out of bed. I read an article about it in *Reader's Digest*.'

Muriel watched, uncertain if she should interrupt a medical procedure.

But the doctor had noticed them, or the session had come to an end. She released Jim from his cradle and lowered him back to the bed, ticked a few notes on her clipboard and left him to his family.

Annie and Billy embraced their father. Muriel hung back. She knew he would be disappointed in her. She had not been there immediately after his operation. She had not been the first face he saw when he came round from the anaesthetic. She kissed him on the forehead anyway and tried not to look down the bed at the missing covered limb, the elephant in the room.

'How are you, Jim?' she said.

He managed a weak smile. 'Bearing up, but I'll be glad to get out of this place and come home. Even though they do a good rhubarb crumble.' He winked at Annie, who was partial to rhubarb. 'Reminds me, how are the roses doing?'

Muriel sat down, her hands pushed under her thighs in an effort to quell the panic blooming as the roses had in their front border. The roses were wilted, their green leaves blackened and struck by blight. The garden was a shared world of father and daughter. Muriel had not been part of it. She hoped Annie wouldn't tell him about the roses.

'Uncle Harry's been helping look after them,' her daughter said.

'Has he mulched some manure round the roots? They need feeding this time of year.'

Muriel made her contribution. 'Well he put something down there last week that stank.' She glanced down the bed. Jim wouldn't be gardening any time soon. She would never get used to this; she didn't expect the children would either. Their father had gone from a strong, dependable man to an invalid overnight.

The visiting bell rang all too soon and they left with kisses and promises of another visit on Tuesday and went on into the city. It had been a while since Muriel had been into Manchester. It had recovered well after the war. Jewellers' windows sparkled, there were fresh pasties in the bakers' and a sense of vibrancy about the streets. She noticed Annie's clothes as she sat beside her on the tram. Her daughter was wearing a neat dress she had made herself. She had inherited her mother's skills. Muriel regarded her own dour outfit and the skirt that tickled her thickened calves. She felt a sudden squeeze of envy at her daughter's youth. Her children herded her from the tram and through the crowds as though she were a lost lamb in their care.

Once inside the promised destination of the art gallery Muriel brightened. She remembered the paintings and narrated the stories of each of her favourites to her children. No one said anything about the visit to their father. Annie tried to share her mother's enthusiasm and lost herself in the stories behind beautiful watercolours. Billy trailed behind, kicking his toes against the polished benches. His mother didn't seem to notice, but a room steward frowned at him.

They meandered from room to room until Muriel came upon a small drawing hidden in a burnished frame in a blue room behind a gallery door. She stopped. There was something familiar about it, but she could not remember seeing it before. Perhaps it had been in storage during the war. She peered at the label. It said it was by Ford Madox Brown. She felt a spark of excitement as she realised why it was familiar to her. She had read the story in the tissue-paper pages of her Bible many times.

'It's a drawing from the Old Testament!' she exclaimed and pressed her finger over the glass protecting the pencil sketch. 'It's about Joseph. His brothers have brought his coat back to show his father. The brothers pretended he had been killed, but really they had sold him as a slave.'

Annie moved her mother's hand back from the frame and checked the room steward wasn't watching. He was busy lecturing Billy. 'I don't think you're allowed to touch it, Mum. Be careful.'

Muriel shook her off. 'Of course I'm allowed to touch it. I'm not going to hurt it.'

She was sharp and her words startled her daughter, who decided to distract her mother before she lost her temper. It was quick to rise these days. 'Why did Joseph's brothers sell him into slavery?' she asked.

Muriel frowned, irritated she did not know the answer immediately – she knew all her Bible stories. Lately her mind had been emptying of its memory as quickly as a coal scuttle in winter. 'It was jealousy, I think. Joseph was his father's favourite. Oh, what was his father's name?' She fiddled with the hem of her coat. If only she had brought her other handbag with the gold clasp, a nub of lipstick and her small Bible, although she had scored many passages so heavily their words were obscured. She should have been able to commit them to her fractured memory by now; she had recited them under her breath often enough. Recounting the words like charms to keep the bad luck away. She should have known that never worked. A rush of sudden connections pulsated through her head and her voice rose, not quite a shout, but getting there. Loud enough that the other people in the gallery turned and stared.

'Jacob! That's it. That was Joseph's father. That's another Bible story, Jacob and the angel. There's something about a hip in that one,' she said. 'That Jacob wrestled with an angel.' Annie tugged at her mother's sleeve like a terrier, but it was too late, Muriel's voice had reached a crescendo. 'Jacob could not be overpowered! He wrestled all night. "Let me go for it is daybreak,"' she yelled.

The room steward switched his attention from Billy to the loud woman in the corner and trotted over. 'Are you all right, madam?' he asked.

'Don't shout, Mum,' Billy said.

Annie tried another tactic. 'Shall we go and get a cup of tea in the café now?'

Her mother's mood dipped below the gilt frames, suddenly subdued again. 'He wrenched his hip,' she whispered. 'Jacob wrenched his hip when he wrestled with the angel. It made him lame, just like your dad.' She allowed herself to be led away.

*

Jim was not discharged from hospital. The doctors made false promises and gave false hope. He would be out next month, then the next, and the next, but something always got in the way. Months stretched into a year of uncertainty and struggle. His absence created a new daily routine and Muriel tried to imagine how life might be when he eventually returned.

'It will be like having a stranger in the house. An invalid lodger, like having another child to care for again,' she told Harry. 'I'll have to be his nurse and his wife.' They were sitting underneath the cherry tree in the front garden as it blossomed bright in spring, curled up between the roots that split the lawn Harry had been battling to mow. Muriel ran a hand over the shorn blades of grass. 'It's like Jim's hair after the barber's,' she said, slapped by a sickening fear that made her gasp. She hugged her knees, bare and bony through her rayon skirt, and moaned quietly. 'I'll have to take over the garden too. Jesus Christ! I might as well be a widow for all the use he'll be. Oh dear Lord Jesus, help me, help me, Lord.' She began to cry.

Harry tried to console her. 'Come on, Muriel. You'll be all right.'

She pushed him away. 'Yes, pull yourself together, Muriel,' she spat. A breeze shook a confetti of petals onto her head and she plucked them from her shoulders and pressed a bitten nail into each, making dark scars on the soft petal discs until she had a collection of wounded blossoms on her lap, like the May Queen all over again.

*

The day of Jim's discharge did arrive. Muriel whispered to her reflection in the dressing-table mirror that sunlit Monday, 'Which me is me now? Who am I?' She removed her curlers and applied the powder and sweet cologne that made up the wife, mother and housewife mask. She had aged rapidly that year. Still nearer thirty than forty, she looked older. Tea-brown shadows bloomed below her eyes, pouches formed, her hair frizzed and refused to behave. She pulled at it with her chromium-plated brush, one hundred strokes of increasing pressure, faster and faster until her scalp throbbed.

She pushed hard into the snagged knots and grey whispers, belting her head in a series of battering beats, willing the brush to draw blood. She threw it across the eiderdown and curled herself on the bed in a tight ball of anguish and screamed into the candlewick ridges. She kept on screaming in animal-like shrieks that brought Annie running. She was afraid to hug her mother in case her crouched form stretched out into a violent banshee. It was a possibility. She waited until there was a break between screams.

'Are you all right?' she asked and braved some soft strokes of reassurance on the boulder of her mother's back. 'Do you want me to fetch Harry?' Harry could calm Muriel when she was like this, or her gran could. Annie had sensed a madness seeping like sherry through a trifle sponge on her mother's side of the family. She'd closed her door firmly against it. If only everything could be how it had been before her father had his accident.

'Come on, Mum, you'll be scaring Billy. Pull yourself together. Dad will be home in an hour, and I have to go into work for a bit, so someone needs to open the door to them,' she said.

Muriel wrapped herself tighter. The house was ready for Jim's homecoming. She had cleaned and washed until her small palace sparkled. Harry had brought a bed that was squeezed into the front room, so Jim could shuffle to the toilet from there. Annie had made sandwiches and unearthed a bottle of whisky to sit beside the teapot with the promise of many visitors to welcome him back. Muriel did not want a party. What was there to celebrate? At Annie's insistence, she rose and washed her face, reapplied her make-up, descended the stairs and put on her bravest face.

Annie went to work and she was left alone, standing sentry at the bay window behind her clean nets, waiting for the charge of medics and her missing husband to break the safe haven of her home. The cream of the ambulance roof striped the green privet as it pulled up by the gate. Panic fluttered around her torso, sharp as the frost glittering on the front path. Everything would change. She would not go outside, could not face the neighbours who had come out to meet him. She could see the shimmer on Mrs Saxon's chiffon scarf, and Arthur, from number four, in his blue overalls. He must have swapped a shift to see the invalid return. She let the nets fall. 'Anyone would think he was royalty,' she said.

The ambulancemen bore Jim down the steep front path on a stretcher. He was still bound in plaster, a red waffle blanket draped over the space where his leg should have been.

'I best get the front door open before they batter through it,' Muriel muttered. They levered Jim upright and walked him, corner to corner like a wardrobe, Muriel leading the way, and manoeuvred him onto the bed that had pushed their sparse furniture into corners and crowded out the bay. Muriel had not been alone with her husband for well over a year, and hardly much before then. Their whole married life had been lived as part of a crowd, clustered amongst family, children and friends. It didn't seem right to be alone. It wasn't normal.

Jim was grateful to be home, ebullient and wide-eyed. 'You've got the room set up lovely, Muriel,' he said.

'Harry helped, he'll be round later, said he'd bring you a bottle of beer. Annie helped too, she'll be back soon,'

Muriel said, checking the clock on the mantel. Not soon enough – she needed her daughter's stoic company.

'That's great, and Mickey said he'd drop by too,' Jim said. He paused. 'If that's all right?'

She folded her hands behind her yellow dress and scratched at the skin above her wrists. 'I've got to nip out anyway. I'll go when he comes.'

She had told Jim she had not allowed Mickey Evans in the house while he was absent. It was not exactly true. What she could not tell him was that a year was a long time, and Mickey had been to the house many times. At first with Harry as his defence, when she had pushed him out the door each time he tried to come in. She had screamed like a banshee, bringing Mrs Saxon running to her front gate as Harry had bundled Mickey into the car and Muriel crumpled in the road, rocking and weeping, firing insults as they reversed. Her neighbour had helped her back into the kitchen. Mickey had tried under cover of darkness, on his own, but she had learned to check through the bay window first and recognised his bulk on the doorstep. She ignored his pleas for forgiveness through the letterbox.

He had finally surprised her one laundry day when she had the back door open to let the steam escape as she wrung out the sheets. He came in behind her. 'Muriel? It's me.'

She'd spun, petrified, entangled in the damp cotton, draped like a gallery sculpture. 'Get out.'

Mickey twirled his hat in his hands. His big hands with their scars shining shrouded by the puffs of steam from the washing that dangled from the pulley maid. Muriel had an urge to push his digits through the mangle, but she could not move.

He advanced. 'Let me talk to you, please. I'm so sorry, Muriel. It wasn't my fault. Please let me talk to you.' Mickey unwrapped her hand from the sheet and ran a finger down the lifeline across her palm. 'Jim won't be home for a long time ... it must be hard for you without a man in the house.'

Her smalls were hanging directly over his head, dripping dry. A drop rolled down his cheek, made it look like he was crying. Muriel stepped back towards the pantry, remembering what she'd read in Jim's copy of *Pears' Cyclopaedia*. 'South poles repel,' she said.

'What did you say?'

'South poles, two alike poles, repel. You repel me, Mickey Evans, you disgust me.' She was warming to her theme, unfreezing, finding her steam power. She reached to the stove and picked up the flat iron she had been heating, brandishing it towards him. 'You might have survived the burns you got at Dunkirk, you won't survive these burns. Get out of my house, bugger off!'

He backed away, shaking his head. 'You're mad, you know that?'

She did not care. He had not tried to come back again. Now Jim had invited him in to pierce the bubble she had made to repel Mickey Evans. She still blamed him entirely for the accident. She knew Jim did not.

Her husband began to barter and negotiate, a tactic that had long been a feature of their relationship. 'I've said it so many times, Muriel. It wasn't his fault,' he said.

Muriel would not meet his eye. She studied the pattern on her yellow dress. 'I can't stand the man, Jim. I don't want him in my house.'

'It's my house too, and he's my best friend. He would have visited as often as you while I was in hospital, if it wasn't for his work. Harry's still seeing him – why can't you forgive him?'

Muriel dropped the skirt she had bunched in her hands and sneered. She wished Jim would be quiet. She'd got used to the quiet in the front room, on the outside of her head quiet anyway. The fire flared and crackled in the unsettled pause between them. She quelled her temper and changed the subject. 'Do you want the telly on?' she said.

'Nowt on during the day, is there?'

'The radio then?'

'No, but a cup of tea would be nice.'

'I'll make one.' She didn't want to give him too much to drink. The nurses had cut a hole in his plaster for convenience and shown Muriel how to use the glass bottle he'd need. She would rather he did that himself. 'I'll have to empty it,' she said aloud.

'What?'

'The teapot, I'll empty the teapot.'

She filled the kettle like she had filled the silence in her house, by talking to herself and training a budgie she'd bought from Tibbs Lane to chatter back. It was meant for Annie's birthday, but Muriel had claimed it as her own. It was nattering at her in the kitchen, fluffing its soft green feathers and preening, its voice competing with her husband's.

'Why don't you bring the bird in here?' he called.

'I'll bring him in after. You need to rest now.' She laid the cup and saucer on a table by his bed and helped him to sit up a little. It was not easy. 'Bloody hell, Jim, help me out, you weigh a ton.'

He pushed himself up the bed with a free arm and the bed creaked alarmingly. 'It's the weight of this plaster. It'll be better when it comes off.'

'When's that then?'

'Dr Hopton told you, don't you remember? It's next week.' She didn't recall being given a date. She probably hadn't listened. Half of what the nurses and doctors told her went in one ear and out the other.

Jim held a dry hand up to her wet face. She hadn't realised she was crying. 'Come here,' he said. 'It'll be all right, Muriel, it will. It's good to be home at last.'

She felt she should say something in return, she should tell him it was good to have him home, but the lie clogged in her throat like clarty winter catarrh. She moved away from him and stood stock still in the middle of the front room, apart and adrift from the stranger in the bay. Her face bloomed above the pansies painted onto her mirror, and the crinoline lady turned her bonneted head away in judgement. She saw her own drooping dress, a figure sliding, her skin weary, dull and unpolished. Annie had made her the dress and she had worn it especially. She thought Jim would like its yellow roses. There were goosebumps on her arms, despite the fire's heat. The cotton was too thin for November.

Flo was the first of the family to arrive. She bustled into the front room with her shapeless husband in tow and turned all the lamps on. 'What you all sitting in the dark for? Muriel, draw the curtains, Jim will freeze.'

Muriel obliged, reluctantly, squeezing past Bert, avoiding the reach of his arms. She allowed her sister a peck on the cheek, but not her brother-in-law.

He satisfied himself with a hearty handshake from Jim.

'Bet you're bloody glad to be out of that place and home having a wife look after you, eh?' He winked.

Muriel retreated to the kitchen. She couldn't bear the implication. She would look after him, she had to, it was her duty, the family had told her that often enough, but she found it hard to imagine how far that duty might stretch while she was struggling to look after herself as she used to.

Harry was knocking on the door by five. They were well into a second pot of tea by then and the whisky was nearly empty. When Billy flew in from school he dropped his bags to run first to the box room and fetch his new guitar to show his father. By then there were twelve people squeezed into the front room, with nowhere to sit.

By six there were more neighbours than Muriel recognised, and her parents had arrived. She'd run out of glasses and dusted off some cups from the back of the kitchen cabinet, barely able to draw down its fold-out front for lack of room. She grabbed four of her best plates as well and cleared a space by the sink for buttering up. She hid herself in the pantry first for a bit on the pretence of looking for a tin of oxtail, corned beef or anything to feed the growing throng.

As she passed a plate of sandwiches round the front room, she spotted the bulk of Mickey through the bay, opening the front gate. She left the plate in her mother's hands and snatched her coat from the hall, making for the back door.

Muriel was on a carousel of moods, up one day and down the next, unaware that her sister Flo had noticed. Flo had seen the changes in Muriel flicker by the hour into a zoetrope of light and dark that had them all walking on thin ice. Muriel had always been a giddy kipper, and the family had indulged her creative side when she was young, tolerated her love of dance and art. Now all they saw was a woman with an unhinged mind and they were afraid of it.

Flo trailed after Muriel and blocked her escape route, proffering a cigarette. 'Are you going out?' she said.

Muriel thought up an excuse quickly. 'We've no more milk.'

'I could nip home and get some, save you the bother. No one wants tea anyway, Muriel.'

Her sister's lip trembled. Everyone was getting drunk. Someone had turned the radio on in the front room and someone had started to sing. They'd be dancing next, if they could find the space. Most of them ... the man lying in the bed in the bay wouldn't dance anymore. They needed a back yard with space for party dancing. A cold stone space for tapping feet, or a nearby dance hall. Muriel missed tap dancing; she didn't think her feet could move fast enough now. She glimpsed Mickey's head emerging round the kitchen door, his eyes more bloodshot than she remembered, and stepped back.

'No, I'll go. It's turning into a flamin' circus in here.'

Flo lit her cigarette. 'I'm surprised. You always liked a party. I thought you'd be glad Jim's back, get things back to normal.'

Muriel pushed away from her. Sweat was making her dress stick to the skin between her shoulder blades. She needed some fresh air. 'There's no normal anymore.'

*

With Jim back at home and his great hulk limping and thumping about downstairs, she slept lightly. Alert as a new mother for his movements, her nerves were set on edge by the soon familiar sounds as he bumped through the dark to the toilet behind the kitchen. She listened to the lift of the latch on the back door, the clang of the chain and finally, the flush of the cistern. At least she didn't have to get up and empty his sour-smelling bottle and wash it out in the same sink she washed her plates. Eventually the pattern of his night roaming became familiar and she gave herself permission to sleep, but sleep didn't come. She woke in the middle of the night, sweat-drenched with the worry. It would only be a matter of time before he would be advancing on her up those stairs. The worry was another brick stacked on a towering pile of worries that threatened to collapse at any moment.

After several weeks, he did make it to their bedroom. She couldn't bear to watch him undress and could not bring herself to look at his stump. He unstrapped the false leg and rested it in the corner by the window, so it peeked below the flowered curtains like a soldier standing to attention. It was like having another person in the room, watching while they slept, or tried to sleep. Jim caved in half the mattress with his weight as Muriel lay paralysed beside him, terrified to move unless she brushed against his leg, and when, in half-sleep, he stirred and shifted towards her with affection, she screamed.

'Get that thing away from me!' Her shouts startled Annie awake in the next room.

July 1956

Muriel had reluctantly adjusted to her husband's nightly presence. The redness of his stump had faded, the skin pearl white, reminding her of Mickey's burned hands. She ripped up his old vests and sewed them on her Singer, flat-seamed and soft to give some comfort against his metal leg. She still found it possible to carry out the practical tasks her everyday life demanded, even though her nerves were frayed. She needed something to fix upon, something to aim for that would provide a diversion from the weight of worry that hung upon her like a second-hand coat. Her days were split by nursing, washing, cooking and caring, her world shrunk to the rooms of her house, the parade of shops and her sister's house.

She was surprised how grateful she was to escape to Flo's when she could. Her sister had triumphed over her when they were young with her prowess at swimming. She took every opportunity to belittle Muriel's dance achievements and ambition. She was the first daughter to leave the family nest and rubbed Muriel's nose in the fact that she had her own home. The first to show off her husband, although he was hardly a catch. Their lifelong competitiveness had subsided since Flo's realisation of her younger sister's increasingly fragile state of mind. Muriel thought her sister was less acerbic with her barbs these days: she had softened like butter towards her.

Harry too. The little brother she had always cherished behaved more like an older brother than a younger sibling. He was the last of the family to leave home, remaining to look after an ailing father and mother. Kind and selfless, Harry married late, a quiet, timid girl who liked to stay home. They could not have children and he spent most of his time at Muriel's, fussing over his niece and nephew and his older sister, who needed looking after. He offered morsels of hope and light in her darkening life.

'We've got a few disabled men working on the switchboard at Ringway, war veterans. I reckon that's something Jim could do if he's interested,' he suggested.

'He's not a war veteran,' she said.

Harry tried again. 'What about up at the hospital? They've got a big switchboard there.'

Muriel pushed forward the idea when Jim came home. 'You used to work there – you could use your contacts,' she said, plating up a stew that had been simmering too long on the stove. She broke the thick skin wrinkled across it with a metal spoon. It would have been perfect to serve an hour before, but Jim had disappeared to the pool hall with Mickey just before the rest of the family sat down for dinner.

He poked at it, carried it into the front room and sat eating it in front of the television. Even though he knew his wife objected. 'The only contacts I have now are through this thing.' He tapped his leg and the metal rang like an out-of-tune piano. 'But the doctors and nurses I see at the hospital can't help me get a job.'

Muriel sat in her chair and glared over the room at him. She pulled a curtain across her lap. She had taken them down to loosen the hems now that Jim was back upstairs and no longer sleeping in the bay. If she had her way, they'd have new curtains, perhaps embroidered silk that brushed the floor like a ballgown. She bunched the fabric and used her bare teeth to sever the thread. She stared at the side of Jim's head as he fed food into his mouth and watched the black-and-white shadows jumping on their new television set.

'Don't be narky,' she said. 'Someone must know something. You need to be useful now you're mobile, Jim. It's no use getting under my feet at home.' Her husband had never been one for indolence before. He'd been driven by a need to find work even in the worst of times. She needed to be the driver now. 'If you're not going to work you should be after more compensation from the accident. We deserve it after everything we've been through. If you made a fuss, we could maybe get enough to visit your Isabella, go to Canada again.'

Jim flung his fork down. It wasn't the first time she had mentioned the compensation; it had become something of an obsession. 'I'm not making a fuss, Muriel. I don't want all and sundry prying into our business. Feels like taking charity and I'm not taking charity. Leave it,' he said.

She sank back into her sewing, bitter that he had used the money to buy a disabled car. All those years she had desired a car to take them places, and now they had a single seater on the new concrete drive that had been built specially to park the three-wheeler. A car with no space for a passenger.

*

When Harry came on his next visit, he suggested an outing for them all to Morecambe Bay and Muriel readily agreed. Annie took her into the city to buy a new cardigan for the occasion. Muriel had tried to knit one but had dropped so many stitches that the mustard-yellow wool had slipped from her lap and she had flung it across the room. She buttoned it against the summer chill when Harry pulled up in his second-hand Austin and folded herself into the seat behind her brother. There was no room behind Jim. He had to push the seat all the way back because of his leg. The bright window light was cooking the vinyl already and she could smell hot plastic and warm canine: the previous owners must have had a dog. Billy wanted a dog. He scrambled across her lap, sharp knees digging in and skinny legs hanging from his shorts.

'Careful,' she chastised, 'and shift over. I've got no room as it is. Harry, can you open your window? I feel a bit sick.'

'You'll be fine once we get going. A bit of fresh air will do you good,' Harry said.

Muriel settled her bag in the small space by her feet, worried that the barm cakes she'd made for the journey would overheat in the boot of the car, fat with margarine and sliced ham as they were. 'Could we put the food in the front by Jim? He's got room,' she said.

Harry revved the engine. 'I told you not to fuss about a picnic, Muriel – there's a café on the front, we can go there, my treat.'

She'd thought she'd rather have her own dried and floured bread, wrapped in tinfoil and a paper bag. She lit a cigarette and let the smoke curl out of the window, recalling happiness as a sharp sense of déjà vu that flashed light through the brambles of her dark moods. As they skirted the ring road and broke out onto the roads heading north, ash scattered her yellow cardigan and she wound the window up and settled on watching the scenery instead. She glanced at the back of Jim's head, fixed in bright conversation with her brother.

They were talking about Mickey. Jim had wanted him to come but Muriel made sure Billy came, so there wouldn't be room in the car. Her efforts to curtail her husband's friendship had been hopeless. She had as much chance of coming between them as of breaking up the newly formed NATO. No doubt they would be off to the pub together as soon as they got back – it was a Saturday night tradition. An almost every night tradition.

She could not get her mind to settle, it was riotous with worry. What if they got to the beach and Jim couldn't walk on the sand? What would people say? The neighbours knew not to stare, and the family had adjusted, but this was a new place. Her anxiety built until she felt sick and she wound the window down and pushed her head out towards the flashing fields, barely noticing the roaming horses or the scattered sheep that stared mournfully at the passing car.

She didn't notice how far she was leaning out until Billy pulled her back. 'Will you shut the window, Mum, it's freezing,' he said.

She did as he asked. Closed her eyes, twisted the leather buttons on her cardigan and reached for her son's hand, whispering, 'Do you think there'll be a lot of wounded war veterans in Morecambe, Billy? Let's tell people that's what happened to your dad, if anyone asks.' Jim could not object to that fantasy if it made him look a hero, a better man, she thought, twisting her buttons again until one came off and fell into her empty palm. She put it in her pocket. 'Don't make clothes like they used to,' she said.

The car drew up beside a long promenade and Harry pulled his seat forward to let Muriel out first. She found she could not move. Although he was leaning right into the back seat, Harry seemed very far away. The smell of warm vinyl was overpowering the scent of sea air that wafted into the car.

'Come on, Muriel, I need you to help me get Jim out,' Harry pleaded, his voice muffled and distant. 'Do you want a hand? Come on, love, just reach out a leg and I'll pull you up from there.'

She heard his voice shrink away from her until it became a hum of notes like the swaddled sounds of a silencer on a jazz trombone. He made no sense. She remained immobile and stared straight ahead through the windscreen.

'I'll do it,' Billy offered. He scrambled across his frozen mother.

She barely felt his sharp knees dig into her lap. She knew somehow that she was meant to help, was expected to. The nurses had shown her how to lever Jim upright without hurting her back or giving herself a hernia. It was always a strain, but she could do it. Except now she could not get out of the car. Her body had jammed, her legs leaden and useless. She could only watch as Harry and Billy helped Jim over to a bench. Billy ran back to the car and fetched a ball from the boot. He would never have a kick-about with his father again, she thought. She could see her husband staring out to sea. He'd be thinking she was just being awkward. He'd think her an embarrassment, wouldn't he? Sat there with the car door open for everyone to see her, when she had thought they would all be staring at him.

A dark shape grew at the edge of Muriel's vision. A shadow that came into focus as a horse and rider raced through the shallow surf. She watched them thunder past the parked car and shrink along the sand, until they were barely a speck at the far end of the long swathe of beach. It must be wonderful to move like that. She was frozen, turned to stone. Perhaps someone had put a spell on her. It would be the cruelest thing, to make a giddy girl dancing a heavy lump, wouldn't it? Make Muriel into a wallflower while she watched the dancers waltz past. Her eyes were burning. She could feel hot tears swiftly drying from her cheeks in the sea breeze.

A larger shadow fell across the open door, and Harry offered an outstretched hand. 'Come on now, girl, you can't stay there. Let's get you out – you love the beach.'

His words still sounded muffled, underwater, but this time she caught his meaning. She couldn't stay there. That would mean the curse had worked and she would never dance again. There would be none of that. She grasped her brother's outstretched hand and with a gargantuan effort heaved herself, inch by inch, out of her seat. Muriel lifted her leaden feet as she walked heavily under the open sky, an insignificant speck in front of the wide sea. She lowered herself as soon as she reached the sand and lay flat out. She closed her eyes, breathed shallow and fast, exhausted with it all. Terrified, as the stupor rapidly faded to be replaced by a galloping mania that made her heart race and her limbs twitch.

Muriel pushed herself upright again and stood up. She unlatched her garters and rolled her stockings down to let the cool air wrap around her thighs. She watched Billy mould a sandcastle by the water's edge as the wild wind off the Irish Sea cast her hair into tangles. She dragged herself over to her son and offered him her limp stockings. 'Billy, you could use these as a flag for your castle.'

Her son recoiled. 'No, Mum, please keep them.'

Muriel wiggled her toes in the damp sand as the weight dropped from her legs. She felt light enough to dance and held out her hand. 'Want to jump the waves with me then?' she asked.

Billy focused on his castle. 'No thanks, I'm going to find some shells to decorate this.'

Muriel lifted her skirt, leaving her slip showing, and she ran, skipping the waves like a child. 'Please yourself!' she yelled and balled her stockings into her hand and cast them into the waves. They floated away like translucent sea creatures, long jellyfish in the brine.

The beach steadily filled with families, wind breaks and buckets. By then Jim needed the toilet and Harry wanted a cup of tea at the café down the front. His sister was still dancing by the shore. It might be time to round her up. 'Put your shoes on, Muriel. Let's go and get some tea,' he said.

Muriel did as Harry asked. She trailed behind them in silence, limited to her own thoughts, the sand rubbing between her toes. She could barely walk in a straight line. While Jim thumped before his wife as if on a railway track, she meandered, letting the sounds of the sea play tunes in her head until she began to hum along, her mind as loose as her garters.

She let Harry steer her into the first café they came across. The only table available was right by the window. Harry wasn't sure if he wanted his sister's erratic behaviour on display like a shop dummy. He'd noticed several people already staring at her bare legs and wild hair. 'Shall we go somewhere else?' he suggested, but Jim was already halfway to the table.

'I need to sit down, Harry, this'll do fine,' he said.

Harry took Muriel's elbow and guided her firmly to the table. His sister sat down and looked about her in wonder. She blinked at a film poster that burned its colours down, colours as new and bright as fresh roses in June, glaring so bright they almost hurt her eyes. Her senses were overloaded by the clattering of company after the quiet space on the beach. She put her hands over her eyes.

'We could get you a milkshake, Billy, and I'm gasping for a cup of tea. That should put you right, Muriel,' Harry suggested.

She smiled at him vacantly behind her palms. 'I'd rather have a Vimto,' she mumbled.

'Have a cup of tea first, love,' Harry directed.

When the waitress set down the china, Muriel heard the sound so loudly that she snatched her hands away from her eyes and clamped them over her ears. The clattering, banging and breaking broke into her whirl of thoughts. She kept her hands there as the tea was poured. Then peeled them away to stir spoonful upon spoonful of sugar into her cup, rattling her spoon and adding her own noise to the din in her head. Clinking the spoon against the china until she thought she could break it, like the ball game her Annie had played in the street.

'Chipped, cracked, broken,' she recited.

Jim removed the sugar bowl she had dipped into several times. 'Stop it now, Muriel, that's enough,' he said.

She didn't think it was.

*

On the homeward journey Muriel's torpor returned. She wrapped her cardigan around her as her darkness settled like a blanket and turned herself inwards, let her mind bubble under the lid of quietening sleep. She did not look out of the window once. Billy pushed himself so far away from her on the back seat that he was plastered to his window. He thought the outside world looked so much safer than the atmosphere inside the car. Muriel was silent when Harry led her into the house and numb again as he set the fire.

'Muriel, love, are you all right?' he asked.

She stared into the flames. She would not look at Harry or her husband. If she did not look, they were not there, waiting to tell her off.

Jim watched his distant wife. 'It might be best if we left her alone for a bit, Harry. She's better on her own when she's like this. There's no reaching her. I promised Mickey I'd meet him at The Sharston tonight. Why don't you come too, as a thank-you for taking us out for the day,' he said.

Harry pushed his glasses up his nose. 'What about Muriel?' She still hadn't moved, or looked at either of them. Billy had shot into the kitchen to see his sister as soon as they got back.

'Annie's home,' Jim said.

Harry dropped his voice to a whisper. 'I don't know, Jim. I've seen our Leslie like this when he had his breakdown. She might be a danger to herself if we leave her.'

Jim had already swung his leg out of the front door. There was a half-warm pint with his name on it behind the bar, and he was thirsty. The Sharston was five minutes up the road if they drove. He folded his guilt away. 'Annie deals with her mother best of all of us when she's in a state like this. There's not much I can do and Muriel won't listen to me. Annie has the pub number and she'll call if there's trouble, but I'm sure there won't be.'

The sound of Billy playing his guitar finally roused Muriel. She felt the feeling returning to her limbs, to her leaden legs, and wriggled her fingers. She noticed the room around her as her mind paused in its break from the internal babble. There was a cup of tea cooling on the mantel that Annie must have left. She took one sour sip and went upstairs to run herself a bath, flicking the immersion switch off so the water quickly cooled and ran as clear and cold as the sea from the shiny steel taps. When she stepped in, she did so without flinching. The cold could not touch her. She sank halfway into the bath and sat, letting her mind tumble in half-formed thoughts until her skin puckered, and, finally feeling a chill, she emerged and wrapped a towel around her chicken-skin body, staring blankly at her reflection in the bathroom mirror.

She cast about her tidy black-and-white bathroom. There was something she needed. She picked up Jim's razor from a mug on the sink. He was as clean-shaven and soft-cheeked as the first time she had tried to get him to dance with her. She had pressed her powdered face to his and left her mark anyway, made them one whole. When she glanced into the bathroom mirror, only one half stared back. Muriel released the blade from the razor and walked, towel wrapped, into her bedroom. She laid the razor down next to the Bible and pulled out a drawer from her sewing box. Unfolded the pattern she'd kept from her wedding dress and spread it reverently across the bed. She dropped the towel and lay over the paper naked, her body spreading across the edges of the delicate paper as it crinkled and rustled beneath her weight. The afternoon light had a moonlight sheen to it as it trickled through the net curtains. The wind was getting up, tickling her bare skin through the open window. She was cold. She wrapped herself and the pattern in the eiderdown, the quills of chicken feathers poking into her upper arms. She rolled onto her side as she did most nights, away from Jim's pillow with its smell of Brylcreem and musk.

The razor glistened on her dresser. A ferment of rage possessed Muriel as she snatched it up, balanced it on her palm and staggered to her wardrobe. She flung open the door and pulled her clothes off the hangers: five blouses, four dresses, two skirts, three cardigans and a jumper, laid them all on the bed like outfits for a paper doll, ready to dress herself. She chose a white shirtwaister and stepped carefully into it without her underwear, leaving the top buttons undone. She hated her clothes, hated her skin, wanted to cut them away and make something new.

'Thank you, Mrs Belmont,' she sang. 'Thank you for sending me your most special dresses, but you could have sent me the ones I made for you. You could have sent me those.' Muriel began to tear the clothes until the seams popped and zips burst and she flung their tattered rags against the wall. They scattered her perfume bottles as they slid to the floor.

The noise brought Annie running in, surveying the tumble of clothes and her half-dressed mother. 'What are you doing with your dresses?' Annie cried. She tried to wrestle the last one from her mother's clawed hands. 'Not your wedding dress.'

'It doesn't fit me,' Muriel sang, tearing the fabric apart. She rent through the dress and belted down the stairs.

Stopped short when she caught her reflection again, this time in the living-room mirror. The mirror that hung static against the woodchip, its edges painted with a garden in gaudy colours, an arch of roses and a lady in layers and layers of yellow silk that settled over the flowers. Her crinoline lady. Her story companion who held her secrets close. A wide silver sea of secrets in a small front room in a house supposed to be home.

At the beach she had undone her stockings and waded into the water ... there was still sand between her toes. She felt she should have kept going out to sea. Swum all the way back into her past. Back to back streets and park days, grand houses and fresh love. Light breaking through the windows in the town hall on her favourite paintings, longing to be part of them, golden in the spotlight. Back to Canada and war and passion. Dancing, back to dancing, she thought, back to that giddy kipper of a girl dancing in the back yard. Now she could barely get her feet to move. She stamped in frustration. It was not fair.

The light dancing lunacy simmered in her mirror reflection as the radio crackled out a concert by the Halle. Muriel turned the volume right up. She unbuttoned the top of her dress and let it drape from her shoulders as if it was the finest silk. Then she made the first cut on the soft skin of her forearm. The grate crackled and she pushed the razor deeper against her fire-warmed skin. 'Let the light in,' she said. Nonplussed that the neighbours might see over the hedge, through the bay window, and spot her, bare-backed and bleeding.

Annie had run after her mother into the front room and she tugged at the white dress, folded back from Muriel's sharp shoulders. 'Cover yourself up, Mum. The whole world can see!' she said.

Muriel shook off her daughter and pressed the razor in once more. Jim was greeted with the sharp tang of fresh blood that leaked across the rag rug when he stepped through the front door, and with the sight of his wife stripped bare to the waist. His daughter wrestling to cover her up, Billy hiding behind the kitchen door. He spun back out into the cool night and limped to the phone box to call the doctor.

August 1956

Sunday church bells chimed. Muriel's eyelids fluttered like the wings of small Cabbage Whites circling her white Whit Walk dress. She was a young girl again, struggling to hold the banner aloft marching between the dirty crowds. They jeered at her. 'Look at that tatty girl with the dirty gloves and frizzy hair!' She pushed them back with a lace-gloved hand. It was important to keep her dress clean after all the effort her mother had made. She turned into Albert Square as the bells rang loud and the crowd surged, squeezing the edges of the parade. Muriel tried to twist away, but she found her body was paralysed, wrapped in white cotton, in wash-day bright sheets.

Muriel woke from her dream to a bright light streaming through a nearby window. Not her own window with its flowered curtains. She was not that bright giddy kipper of a girl, but a woman. And captive, her arms bound in strips of white. She heard the church bells ring again. A familiar sound in an unfamiliar place. Had she died? she wondered. No, heaven would not smell like damp walls and stale urine. She suddenly felt a deep and unheavenly shame: the smell might be coming from her own body. She tried to move to escape it, but her body was as heavy as a bulging sack of coal. There was a figure all in white by the window. Could it be an angel?

She called to it, her throat burning. 'Who are you? Where am I?'

The figure answered in a gentle voice. 'Oh you're awake, Mrs Burns. Did you have a good sleep?'

A young girl dressed in white swam into Muriel's focus. It was a young angel. She had called her Mrs Burns. She was Mrs Burns, Muriel remembered that much. 'Why can't I move?' Muriel croaked. The figure moved towards Muriel like a tentative deer, keeping away from the bed as if she was a little afraid of her.

The girl fluttered a hand to her neck, touching her finger across a red mark branded there. 'You were a bit wild when they brought you in, Mrs Burns. We had to restrain you until you calmed down. You've got straps on your wrists and ankles, I'm afraid.'

Muriel cringed in shame. She would not want to harm an angel. Her eyes darted over the walls, the rumple of sheets and down her body. She was dressed in a pale blue cotton gown, like biblical robes. Her hands felt like one of Jim's thick leather belts was strapping her down. She turned her head to the girl. She could see her clearly now. The white clothes she had thought were angel's robes were a white cap and pinafore over a dark dress with white cuffs. A uniform. Muriel sank into the bed, disappointed, despairingly realising she must be in a hospital. Had she had an accident like Jim? She could remember the beach at Morecambe, but she had no memory of getting home. Had she been in a car crash?

A moan leaked from Muriel's mouth. 'What happened?' she asked.

The nurse hovered by her bed, unsure. 'We're not supposed to chat with the patients,' she said, staring at the door.

Muriel followed her gaze. It was a solid door, painted with thick white gloss. Jim had painted hospitals. Where was he now? The door swung open and the nurse stepped smartly away from the bed as a doctor entered, older than her Dr Hopton, and balding, his white coat buttoned up like an orderly. Muriel had the feeling she wasn't in Withington Hospital. The nurse stood to attention, her hands pressed to her side and her thumbs lined up with the seams of her uniform.

The doctor snatched up Muriel's notes. 'Were you chatting to this patient, Nurse Evans?' he said.

The nurse looked down at her shoes. 'She's just come round from the Luminal injection, Doctor. I don't think she's feeling too bright.'

He flicked through the file. 'The drug will give her a decreased level of consciousness. She's not meant to feel "bright".' He gestured with his pen to the nurse's neck and Muriel winced at the red welt there. 'If she had behaved when we brought her in instead of fighting, biting and scratching like an animal, we wouldn't have had to inject her, would we?'

He talked as if Muriel wasn't there. She wasn't sure she was there either. She wanted to shout, to make them understand. 'I'm so sorry, I'm sorry if I hurt you ...' but the words were caged inside her head. No one would listen to her anyway. Tears leaked down Muriel's face. She suddenly wanted her mother. She wanted her father. She wanted Jim and Annie and Billy and Harry.

The doctor handed the notes back to the nurse. 'Give her another dose to see her through the night,' he said.

'Could she have some food first?'

'You can feed her something small at six. You need to straighten this bed too, Nurse Evans. The wheels are crooked – Matron will be after you.'

As soon as he'd left, Evans took pity on Muriel and tentatively dabbed her patient's tears with her own handkerchief. 'Now don't cry there. You can go home as soon as you're better.'

Muriel tried harder to push her words out. It was such an effort – they were leaden as cannonballs in her mouth. 'When?'

The nurse pulled away and switched back to the official line, correcting herself. 'When you're not a danger to yourself and others,' she said.

'I didn't mean to hurt anyone,' Muriel said, straining at her straps. 'Please can you take these off?' but Nurse Evans was already on her way out of the door.

'They'll come and take them off in the morning. You can get up and have a little walk round the airing court then. Get some rest now. I'll bring you a cup of tea and something to eat at six.'

Muriel let her head fall back to the pillow, defeated. 'I'm not hungry.'

'You will be later.'

She closed her eyes. If only it were all a dream, and she would wake up in her bed at home, listening to the buses trundle past on Royalthorn Road, the clank of milk bottles on the step, Billy plucking at his guitar, Annie rushing to work and Jim thumping up the path. She wanted Jim. She wanted him back in her bed.

Was that why he had sent her away? Did he know her love was cracked? She was sorry. If they would just let her home, she would try harder to mend it. She drifted in and out of sleep until she was woken roughly by a different nurse and propped up, her arms still bound. She was fed warm bread and milk on a spoon like an invalid. A bedpan was slipped under her backside and the corner of her nightdress caught beneath the rim as she filled it. A wet urine stain spread, darkening the blue gown.

'I'm sorry, can I change, please?' Muriel muttered.

Her request was ignored. This nurse did not chat. She shuffled her heavy-set body away, slopping the bedpan across the room as she went. 'You'll get a bath and change on Wednesdays like everyone else,' the nurse said.

*

Muriel's angel returned the next morning. She settled a tray at the end of Muriel's bed and opened the blinds. Muriel blinked. It was early morning, the light pale and wistful. August's high heat would not burn until midday. A good day for a walk in the park, a good day for dancing, a bright, outside day. Her mind began to flicker. She had slipped in and out of half-sleep most of the night, unsure if she were trapped in a dream or a nightmare. She did know that she needed the toilet again and strained her head away from the pillow to ask.

'Please can you untie me now. I need to use the toilet.'

'Do you promise to be good?' the nurse said.

What else could she promise? She was as helpless as a child with a nurse who was barely older than her Annie. She nodded. The straps were unbuckled and slid away. Muriel rubbed at her wrists as she tried to shove herself up the bed, but she didn't seem to have the power.

'Where's the bathroom?' she asked.

Nurse Evans checked her watch. 'Just down the hall, but you'll have to be quick before the doctor comes. They should have moved you to the main ward last night and unstrapped you there, then you could have used the bucket like everyone else.'

Muriel sensed the nurse was just doing her job, but she had hoped for a little more sympathy. 'I could use the bed pan again if you want, but last night my nightie got soaked.'

Nurse Evans twisted her mouth and softened. 'Well I can bring you a change of clothes after breakfast, but you'll have to wash yourself – I've got ten others to do before exercise.'

'What exercise?'

'It's just a walk around the yard.'

The yard. Muriel knew they had yards inside institutions. She felt a flutter of panic. They must have locked her away. She tried to remember why her brother Leslie had been put in hospital that time. Had the same thing happened to her? Would they leave her in there for being a bad girl?

'Am I in prison? What have I done?' she asked.

The nurse looked nervous again. Questions would draw her into a conversation, conversations got her into trouble. 'You're not in prison, you're in hospital. You've going to have some treatment to make you better.'

Muriel checked her body. It all seemed to be there. Nothing was hurting or missing. There was no rash, she had no fever. 'Am I ill?'

Nurse Evans didn't answer. She helped Muriel to a single toilet down the narrow white corridor before breakfast was brought on a trolley: two slices of bread and marg on a small green plate and tea from a giant pot stirred up with a big spoon, milk and sugar thrown in. She was given clothes that looked like someone else's: a vest and undergarments that did not look wash-day white, a loose, shapeless dress and beige slippers with one hole in the left toe.

The nurse apologised. 'The clothing's communal, but I think they're clean.'

Muriel stared at the pants in horror, having just enough of the wherewithal to protest against wearing someone else's knickers. 'I can't,' she stuttered.

The nurse proffered the clothes again. 'If you don't dress, Muriel, you'll have to stay in bed.' Muriel slipped the clothes on in full view of anyone passing the room, not thinking to ask for a brush for her hair. There were no mirrors to see what she looked like. Her dress was straightened. 'Now you can go outside.'

Nurse Evans led her past wards where patients were lined up like dolly pegs on the line, strapped or asleep in parallel beds. Others shuffled by, leaning on the walls for support. They looked like veterans of a war, traumatised and helpless. Muriel kept her head low and avoided any eye contact. She followed the nurse's feet to a padlocked door and let herself be slotted into the fidgeting queue beyond it. It was a line made up of men and women, all bare-legged, all with slippered feet like hers. She noticed the woman in front of her wore footwear of cerulean blue and experienced a brief pang of envy.

The padlock was undone, which caused a current of excitement to ripple along the line and more urgent fidgeting as the door swung wide. The line snaked forward into an enclosed courtyard below arched white windows, like blank eyes staring down on the inmates. Muriel trembled and rubbed her bare arms. A cardigan would have been nice. She stumbled towards a small patch of grass where the sun broke through, but before she could reach it, the woman with the blue slippers claimed the space and lay longways on the sunlit grass. Her brown flowered dress draped like a painter's model's around her knees and the slippers blooming on her feet. Her eyes were wide and staring under her shock of white hair. Muriel watched her for a while. She felt the urge to lie down beside her and stretch in the warm morning sun like a cat. Would the woman notice if she swapped their slippers over? They looked a little too small for her anyway. The other patients trundled on, not speaking to each other, but talking to themselves in a babble of voices. Muriel followed, round and round in circles, until finally the carousel was stopped, and they were led back indoors.

The exertion had proved too much for some – they looked for places to perch or lay prostrate on the hard benches below the windows. Others lay corpse-like along the corridor floor. The staff left them there and shepherded those who could still move into a large room with long barred windows and more white walls. The surplus of white was beginning to hurt Muriel's eyes. There were no other colours, no pictures and no mirrors. She sidled up to a male nurse who was serving tea from the big pot, a burly man with a badly shaven chin. He looked a little like her Jim. She stifled a compulsion to slip her hand in his paw.

He noticed her. 'Hello there, you new?' he asked, and suddenly mute like the others, she nodded. 'Hungry?' She nodded again. She wasn't really, but she was grateful that someone had spoken to her and she just wanted him to keep talking. 'Well, lunch is at twelve thirty, not too long to wait, then tea at six, bed at seven, that's how it works. You'll get used to it soon enough.'

She could not fight the impulse any longer and grabbed his hand, finding her voice. 'I don't need to be here. Why are you keeping me? When can I go home?'

The nurse pulled away from her. Shouldn't get too close. His job was to keep an eye on all the violent men clustered around a far table, not entertain new patients. He left Muriel staring after him.

She watched one of the men rise from his seat. That made the male nurse hover, expectant, nearby, but the man was too defeated to be violent. He turned away and wiped the tears that covered his cheeks on the corner of a curtain and sat down again. Muriel swayed, overwhelmed. Silence flooded through her veins. She staggered and having nothing to hold on to, she fell. The other inmates watched her topple and watched her being carried out. She woke later in the half-dark, her surroundings shifted. There were five other beds nearby and a bucket in the middle of the floor. Nurses floated beyond the locked door.

*

When the orderlies brought the breakfast, there was none for Muriel. She waited until they were preoccupied with other patients and the drugs trolley and slipped out of her bed. She skirted the stinking bucket in the middle of the ward and made her way to a bathroom. Unsteady on her sandbagged legs, she found the end cubicle and climbed onto the toilet seat to peer out of the high window. There was nothing to see, just the promise of sun through opaque glass that was gridded with wire. It would not open.

Nurse Evans had told her visiting days were Wednesdays, but she did not know what day it was or how long she had to wait, or even if anyone would come to visit her. Had anyone gone to visit Leslie when he was in hospital? She was ashamed that she hadn't; she had been too busy wrestling with her own demons. She staggered back to bed, waking later with plasters across the crook of her elbow and her arms hurting like they used to when Flo delivered her dead arm punches. She had been given more injections.

When Nurse Evans appeared by her bedside Muriel was relieved to see someone who seemed to care just a little more and had, if not a kind word, at least a softer one than the rest of the staff. 'The doctors are coming to see you, Muriel – let's tidy you up,' she said, hesitating as the shadow of the ward sister's winged hat fell across them. A sister that acted least like an angel, embittered and indifferent to those in her care, Sister McLellan.

'I'll say who needs tidying up on my ward. Dr Winstanley won't care what she looks like,' she snapped.

There was no time to argue with her. A doctor was beside Muriel's bed and holding court to a group of students that looked about the same age as her Billy. Surely that wasn't possible?

The doctor narrated her notes as if she were exhibit number one. 'This lady has been displaying classic signs of schizophrenia. We have given her Luminal injections to calm her violent outbursts. She's been demonstrating some manic tendencies and hearing voices too.'

Muriel heard all his words and tried to make sense of them. She'd thought the voices were a part of her: didn't everyone hear them? And she couldn't remember being violent, but she remembered the red welt on Nurse Evans' neck. They said she had done that.

The doctor continued, 'As she has displayed this erratic behaviour for some time, we're trying ECT this morning. Please prepare your patient, nurse.'

Muriel tried to interrupt with one coherent word. 'Why?'

No one acknowledged her.

Nurse Evans fished in the pocket of her pinafore as soon as the doctor had left. 'How about a cigarette, Muriel? It might help to keep you calm. Then I'm going to have to put the straps on you again, but don't worry, they won't be too tight this time.' A lit cigarette was pushed into her mouth and the straps fastened before Muriel had the chance to protest. 'When it's all over I'll get you a nice cup of tea,' the nurse said.

Muriel was rattled down corridors to a set of double doors. The remnants of the cigarette were removed from her mouth and she was pushed into a small room, the walls white and blank like all the rest. Three or four people waited, all in white coats and cotton masks. Muriel feared they were going to operate on her without anaesthetic. What were they taking away?

She was almost relieved when someone took her hand and wielded a syringe. 'This will help you relax, Mrs Burns.'

Everyone wanted to give her something to make her relax. It seemed kind, but her arms were numb, and they hurt. Hurting wasn't kind. The drug did not put her to sleep, just made her detached. She found she was crying again. She wanted to get up and run far away from the bad place, but she was strapped to the table with legs that wouldn't work. Then they made it worse. They put something in her mouth like a stick. 'It's a good job they took your false teeth out, Muriel. Keep still now. This is to stop you biting your tongue,' someone said. They put a mask over her nose, and Muriel inhaled the smell of rubber and sharp chemicals. Padded electrodes were stuck to her temples. Her nerves prickled and danced across her chest as panic churned her gut. She twitched. A huge jolt shook her body, lifting her off the table. Finally flying, she twisted away. She would have danced off the table if she could have, but firm hands pressed her down. Then the doctors stepped smartly away, like a crowd in awe of a movie star, waiting to view the person between the smile and the flashbulbs. Muriel's glare burned into her audience. A vast jolt rocketed through her body. She spasmed into a convulsion, struck with a violent thunderstorm of soul-frozen fear, her tongue bark dry, fingertips slack. They did it to her again, and again. Made her dance like she never had before.

*

The electricity recharged every synapse and briefly bestowed a euphoric lightness which had made her feel hopeful in the dark. Sleep was hard to find. She spent the night watching the comings and goings of the nurses and the restless dreams of her fellow inmates. In the early hours she had managed to use the bucket. It wasn't so bad, she reasoned, squatting over it on strengthened thighs. She'd had worse. The shock treatment must be what they brought her in to hospital for. She'd had it now, so they must be letting her go home. By morning she was well enough to put her own teeth in and to eat some of the leathered toast she'd been given. It was a brief slice of peace that was disturbed by Sister McLellan sailing back onto the ward in her tall hat, clapping her hands.

'It's bath day today! Nurses, get the patients up, please.'

Muriel was disappointed. She hadn't finished her toast, her tea was cold and congealing by her bed. A tiny memory flared. Hadn't a nurse told her bath days were Wednesdays? Were Wednesdays also visiting days?

'Is it Wednesday?' she asked and slid to the edge of her bed, keen to get the routine done in the hope it would be followed by someone coming to visit and fetch her home.

The bathroom was large, airy and lined with tubs, their previous occupants disappearing round a far corner, naked and dripping, as rangy and dilapidated as horses being led to the knacker's yard. Numbed to the embarrassment of seeing so many naked men, she let her fellow inmates shove past her. They swarmed into the bathroom, shedding their hospital gowns and stepping into the dirty water before it had drained down the plughole. 'Close the bloody door,' someone shouted. 'At least let's give the next lot clean water.'

The staff panicked and herded them back into the corridor where Muriel waited as the baths were filled again. She let herself be led to the farthest one and climbed into the tepid liquid, sinking below a grey tide mark, barely caring that the scum was from another body. She had the sense that it had all happened before. It was not as pleasant or as fun as Victoria Road Baths, with its huge steaming tubs lining the landings around the gala pool, and her sister Flo swimming lengths below, but she was getting clean. She hugged her knees and let her back be roughly scrubbed, hair tugged and combed through with coal tar soap. There was no Amani or hair oil here. A jug of cold water was tossed over her head to rinse away the soap and she was hauled quickly out of the bath, naked and shivering, into a side room to be dried and dressed.

Muriel leaned on the back of a chair as a nurse dried between her toes. She watched the sunlight trace the pattern of a window on the wall and, for one moment, imagined the light was a mirror and she was back in Mrs Belmont's salon making ready for the ladies to model her bias-cut silk gown.

'Are we dressing for a dance?' she whispered.

The nurse frowned. 'Dances are Saturdays, love. Arms up now.'

Muriel caught sight of a greying slip as it was pulled over her shoulders. 'Is it a Saturday then?' she said.

'It's Wednesday.'

'Of course, it is, and Wednesday is visiting day?'

The nurse yanked a brown patterned dress over her hips and did not answer. Muriel was sure she had seen the dress on the woman with the blue slippers in the yard. It must be her turn today.

She was let into the big room and returned to the barred

windows time and time again in the hope of spotting someone. The glass was greasy, smearing the scattered flower beds outside into an otherworldly blur. Lunch rolled in, a pale stew of washed-out meat. Still there were no visitors. Restless, she took herself off to a side table to watch a dark-haired woman playing patience. The repetition and familiarity of the game brought an instant of lucidity. Jim played patience, counted out four cards, dealt a layer over, put the aces to one side. She snatched away the two of hearts to place it on the three and the woman snatched it back, catching the back of Muriel's hand with a ragged nail. She withdrew, wounded, nursing her scratch, and paced the room, watching the imprint of the windows on the opposite walls and trying to decipher if the sun was passing high or low above her prison. There were no clocks, the sun was high, so it must be afternoon. Surely visitors would come in the afternoon?

The burly nurse rattled a trolley into the room, followed by a straggling line of others. Neither patients nor staff, they looked as nervous as wild rabbits smelling the stench of a hungry fox nearby. Muriel caught sight of a redhead amongst them. She would have run to her daughter if her legs were working well enough, but all she could manage was a frantic wave until Annie came to her and drew her to a vacant table underneath the barred window.

Muriel reached across with trembling hands and took hold of her daughter's young, peachy skin. 'Have you come to take me home, Annie?'

Her daughter dipped her head. She wouldn't meet her eye. 'I can't today, Mum. You haven't finished your treatment yet,' she said.

Muriel looked at her in horror. 'I have! I've had it! I

217

don't want that again, please, Annie … don't let them do that to me again.'

'Do what?' Annie asked.

Muriel gripped her daughter's wrists hard. 'It was terrible, Annie, it frightened me.'

Annie untangled her hands. Her mother was hurting her. 'You mean the electric shock treatment? They put you to sleep first, don't they?'

Muriel shook her head violently. 'No, I was awake the whole time.'

'That doesn't sound right, I'll speak to the doctor. It's all right, Mum, no one wants to hurt you. Maybe just one or two more treatments will make you better.' She reached into her bag. 'Look what I have got. I have brought you some Pond's, and I thought you might like an orange. I brought you a scarf too.'

Muriel stared at the small blue jar, the bright orange, and the patterned fabric. She snatched the scarf up and tied it quickly over her head. 'They gave the woman in the bed opposite me a haircut this morning because her hair was getting too long. A basin cut. It stripped her of all dignity. I'll keep this scarf on in case they come for me. Thank you,' she said.

Muriel disrobed the orange, and arranged the segments and peel like a flower on the table between herself and her daughter. She poked at the segments with her finger, the citrus tang scythed through her befuddled mind. 'Where's Jim?' she asked.

Annie folded her arms. She knew this was coming. 'Dad started as a telephone operator at Withington on Monday. You were the one who wanted him to go for the job, remember? It's his first week, so he couldn't change his shift, but he sends his love. It's hard to get here, even for me. I had to take two buses, just for a five-mile trip. I told work I had a doctor's appointment.' Annie sighed. Her mother was often flipping between her awareness of reality and her fear of it. Sliding off at a tangent into her own world. It was hard to remind her of what was real and to get her to see beyond herself. She had hoped a few days in the hospital might improve things, but little seemed to have changed. Annie tidied the orange peel into a neat pile. 'Do you remember Dad used to work here, Mum? Silburn's painted the whole place.'

Muriel chewed on a piece of orange, letting the sweet juice relieve her dry mouth. She did remember Jim coming home with paint-caked overalls and dropping flakes on her clean rag rug. She wouldn't mind that now.

Annie went on, tempting her mother into the real world with facts. 'It's over a hundred years old, this hospital, isn't it? The nurse told me there are nearly three thousand patients here.' Muriel followed Annie's nod to the door. Nurse Evans smiled back at them. 'She seems nice, doesn't she?' Annie said.

Muriel swallowed an orange segment. Was Nurse Evans nice? She was kinder than the rest. Muriel's mind was briefly settled and clear enough to think. She leaned forward. 'Why am I in here, Annie? What happened?' she said.

Annie leaned forward too and dropped her voice to explain. 'You came back from your day out in Morecambe and you were very quiet. Dad thought you wanted to be on your own, so he went to the pub. Just after, you lost it, Mum.' She scraped the orange peel into her bag. 'I had to stop you from cutting up all your clothes, then you cut yourself and we had to call a doctor.'

Muriel slumped back in her chair, arms folded. She remembered the beach, did not remember cutting herself. She squinted at her daughter, one eyelid drooping, Annie's red hair a smudge like bright blood blooming in the white room. 'I didn't cut myself, I've never done that,' she said. 'Why would I do that, Annie?' She was uncertain now. There was a memory of something sharp, a white dress, shadows flickering. She felt afraid, tiny in the big room.

'I don't know, Mum, you frightened Billy,' Annie whispered, as if it was a terrible secret between them.

Muriel pushed her hands through her hair, rocked back on the chair. Like butter on baking parchment, she could not absorb what Annie was telling her. She had no memory of making the marks that were fading to a whisper on her skin, she could not scare her son and would not feel guilty for something she didn't do. Maybe they had made the story up to get her in here. They were all in it together. 'Those doctors talk about me all the time, they said …' Muriel stumbled over the words. It was no good, it had gone. 'They told me something, I can't remember the word they used … oh, it began with an s?'

Annie blinked at her. 'Schizophrenia, you mean?' The doctors hadn't told her that. 'They told us it was a nervous breakdown, like Uncle Leslie had. That's why you're here, to have some treatment and get better. I told that nice nurse over there that you can sew, and she said you might be allowed to make a few cushions for the day room. They've got a garden too – that's good, isn't it? Maybe you can go out there, she said they grow all their own veg, and there's a little farm with chickens and pigs. Dad would like that, wouldn't he?'

Muriel did not answer. Her daughter was talking as if she would be in here for a long time. She gazed down at the pile of orange fragments on the tabletop, assaulted by a memory so strong she could smell it. She and her flame-haired little girl hitched to her shoulder, laughing into her favourite mirror above the sideboard. The crinoline lady painted in the corner, her face hidden by her bonnet. They had told stories to that mirror. Stories to chase away the questions. When Annie had run in from a street ball game. Tommy from number six had told Annie her mother was ill. Picked the scabs on his elbows as he bounced the ball away from Annie's waiting hands. Muriel could see the little devil from her bay window, teasing her daughter. 'Your mum's not well, is she, ginger nut? What's she got, scarlet fever, mumps? Our Freddie had mumps last year, he went blind.'

Annie had run in crying. 'Mum, are you ill? Are you going to go blind?'

Muriel had swept her up and hugged her tight. 'I'm all right, Annie, look, see, nothing wrong with me. There we are in the mirror ... shall we go and dance with the lady in the garden?' she said and waltzed Annie round the front room.

Muriel fingered the bandages on her forearms, felt the pinch and itch of healing skin across her shoulder blades. The memory rushed back in and battered her then. No wonder they had locked her away. No wonder her daughter looked so afraid of her. Muriel was a hollowed-out woman with the tenant of madness squatting within.

*

There was no breakfast again. She knew what that meant.

*

Breakfast was allowed. Muriel was so relieved she didn't have chance to appreciate the fact that she was let outside into the garden. Led by a male nurse who checked the name tag on her clothes and walked her past the other patients that were working alongside staff. Weeding, planting and loading wheelbarrows. The nurse gave her a hoe and instructions to work a small patch of soil at the edge of the hospital grounds. Hidden behind the vast web of low buildings that stretched across the fields. They gave her the blue slippers. She had not seen their previous owner for days. Perhaps she had been allowed to leave.

The dry earth flicked into her slippers and settled between her toes as the sun burned her neck, but she didn't care, she was outside and almost happy. The warmth and the breeze and the smell of roses turned in the August heat before the drift of autumn. She wandered alone, further into the garden, until she came to a greenhouse where others were potting up green shoots.

The man she'd seen wipe his tears on the curtains was tending a large waxy plant in the far corner. He smiled when he saw her. Beckoned her over. 'Banana plant,' he said proudly.

*

On Saturday Muriel was woken by the rattle of a teacup on a saucer. Nurse Evans brought her breakfast that day, but the fact she was being given something to eat no longer made her feel less anxious. It could all be a trick to make her relax before they wheeled her down the corridor again. She lay squinting at the ceiling, unsure if she should put her teeth in or if the food would be suddenly taken away. She didn't trust them.

Her angel nurse interrupted her worrying. 'Your daughter told me you like dancing and I thought you might like to know there's a dance today.'

Muriel could not imagine she would be allowed to take part, or if she could. 'I can't dance now – that thing they do makes my legs hurt.'

The nurse cast about to see if anyone was watching. When she decided there wasn't, she perched on the bed. 'Now you'll be all right, Muriel, your legs won't hurt anymore. You had the last treatment on Thursday and I heard Dr Winstanley say you could go home next week, if you take your medication and come back for treatment if you need it.'

Muriel hugged her tightly. 'Oh, thank you, thank you so much.' The nurse quickly extricated herself from her patient's grip before anyone saw and smoothed her pinafore. 'Will you be going to the dance?' Muriel asked.

'No, it's just for the patients. It's in the big room this afternoon.' She leaned in, sharing her secret. 'But I am going to the staff dance tonight. I've a got new dress too.'

Muriel put down her tea. 'Then will you come in before you go, let me see it?'

'I'll try, yes.'

*

The weekly patients' dance was an occasion at which the nurses mostly watched. It was staged as a ceremonial event to escape the miserable blandness of the everyday. The burly nurse unlocked a cabinet against the wall to reveal a hidden record player. He pulled a stack of shiny black discs in crumpled dust covers from the shelf below and put one on, balancing the needle gingerly over the grooves. Loud music blared across the room and bounced off the walls. Muriel recognised it as the rock and roll her Billy loved, the guitar and drums, and a treacle-voiced singer, not much else. She hadn't danced to it before, but she had wanted to, and there was always a first time. She could learn a new dance to teach Jim when she got out. She tapped her slippers to the beat and watched the nurse. He'd started shaking his right leg as if he was being given ECT himself. Some of the men jerked alongside him until someone yelled over the din, 'Take the Elvis off, Geoff, you're getting them too wound up. Why don't you put a nice waltz on instead.' Geoff groaned and switched the record over.

The softer sound of Henry Mancini & His Orchestra drifted from the cabinet. The men retreated to one side of the room, the women to the other. The music had already made its dent in Muriel's soul: she remembered how to dance. She could dance all the way home. She waltzed across the room, catching Geoff unawares, and pulled him along with her. She demonstrated back steps and spins, even though she took the lead, and it was difficult to spin in slippers. Others slowly followed; they coupled up and shuffled along. But when the music stopped, they dropped hands as if they were infected and retreated to their corners. Muriel wished Geoff would put Elvis back on again to liven them up. She drifted to the day room early, disappointed, and stared out of the window as the strains of Mantovani echoed down the corridor.

Roused only when Nurse Evans came to show her dance dress. Lemon yellow with cap lace sleeves and a full skirt. The nurse twirled to show Muriel how it flared. 'Do you like it?' she asked.

Muriel smiled. She did, she was thrilled.

*

Within a week, Muriel had slipped into a hospital routine where time meant nothing. She was not sure how long she had been in the institution or whether Annie had visited once or twice. She knew no one else had. The week felt like a year. After two treatments, she resigned herself to the terror and locked away the experience, grateful for the small mercies of simple sewing tasks and light gardening that she was given. She had almost forgotten what Nurse Evans had told her about going home so it was a surprise to be taken to Dr Winstanley's office instead of him visiting her.

'Mrs Burns, we think we can continue your treatment as an outpatient. You can go home today. An ambulance will take you this afternoon.'

She could hardly believe she had heard him right. Nurse Evans took her back to the ward to help her pack her few things. The white shirtwaister she had been admitted in had gone.

'Where's my dress?' Muriel asked. Then she remembered the cuts on her arms. Blood on white cotton would not come out unless it was soaked straight away in cold water. She expected no one had thought to do that.

'You can keep this one, Muriel,' her nurse said.

Muriel looked down at the drab brown dress. It was the same one the lady with the cerulean slippers had worn. Was that her life now? Muted, devoid of colour in a second-hand dress? She could not wait to get home to her own family. To wear her own clothes, sleep in her own bed and eat the food she wanted.

There was no grand welcome when she got there. Jim waited at the front door, as she had waited for his ambulance over a year before. He hugged her carefully, as if she were a chipped ornament with hairline cracks that might split any moment. She did not pull away as she might usually have done, she just wanted to step over the threshold and close the door. Be home, be safe. There were no other visitors that day, there was no whisky to be slopped into chipped mugs or home-made cake to celebrate her homecoming. There was no party. Jim did make her a cup of tea, and she noticed he put it in a cup and saucer. He'd got some biscuits in, malted milk, not her favourites, perhaps he couldn't find them, but she was glad he'd made at least a little effort.

'Thank you,' she said, as she lowered herself to the vinyl three-piece, glancing about the front room to check everything was still in its place. The house was spotless. Annie must have dusted.

Jim laid an old shoe box in front of her. 'I found these while I was tidying.' Muriel lifted the lid on her collection of photographs and postcards. 'They're the paintings you like, aren't they?' he said. He placed her postcards across the coffee table like he was playing patience.

The pictures brought her a moment of elation and she leaned towards them, lost in a delirium of their faded colours. She knew the names of the paints Ford Madox Brown used, had learned them long ago, and repeated them, pointing a jagged nail as she named them. 'Reds – carmine, sienna, umber, vermillion, madder.' Jim drew a breath through his teeth. She glanced up at him and draped herself along the sofa in her brown dress, weary. 'They are the names of the colours, Jim.'

He sat beside her in his chair and a silence settled between them as he read his paper and she dozed. After a little while, he shifted. 'I'll run you a warm bath, Muriel, and I'll send Billy to the fish shop for tea, so you don't need to worry.' He paused as he limped across to the stairs, bent and kissed her stale forehead. 'I'm sorry you had to go there, love, I'm sorry I didn't visit. I couldn't get away from work. It's good to have you back. I'm glad that you're better now.'

She kept her eyes closed, heard him shout up to Billy as the shadows danced between the curtains of her eyelids.

January 1958

It was one of those clear days in late January when the sky had shed its Manchester white and nothing but clear blue dazzled above them in Alexandra Park. The sun took off its winter coat pushing the promise of some spring warmth through Muriel's frosty bones. Muriel sat on a bench beside Flo. She counted six daisies unfurling by her boots, she had six sticks the length of her little finger secreted in her coat pocket. She pushed her hands deep into the seams and counted them again, a new strategy to settle her mind. Her time in the Lancashire lunatic asylum seemed another world away.

'They should have kept you in another week,' Flo said, pleating her coat about her.

Muriel was inclined to disagree with her sister about the length of her stay. 'It doesn't matter one week or six months – I had to go back to it,' she said.

'To what?' Flo asked.

'The house. I had to go back to the house.' Muriel leaned towards her sister, whispering her theory so none of the park strollers would overhear. 'It was the house that did it.'

Flo flipped her coat collar up. 'Your hospital stay had nothing to do with the house, Muriel. You're getting confused again,' she said.

The council had started to modernise the houses on the Wythenshawe Estate with new kitchens, new boilers and top-loader washing machines. Muriel thought the new appliances were alien contraptions that she couldn't understand; they made her anxious. All that disruption. A settled house was what she needed. The flitter of childhood moves had made her long for a static refuge. Modernising her home had taken away its familiarity. The new appliances were cold and smooth, and they had removed her mangle. The fire had no coal, no black dust crystals to squeeze under her nails. It made her mind an unsteady dancer wobbling on the balls of her feet.

'I can hardly work the new gas fire you've got. How am I going to manage when they put one in our house?' Muriel said.

'It's not hard, you'll learn. I hear they're putting in central heating for the next phase. Think of that! No more coal fires ever and no need to wear a vest indoors!' Flo said, delighted by the modern comforts.

Muriel pushed back against the park bench. She had liked the dancing flames of the coal fires and she couldn't imagine Jim without his vest. Flo's dolt of a husband had succumbed to a stroke the year before and the sharpness of her sister's grief had temporarily sliced through Muriel's muddled mind. From time to time she reached beyond her self-obsession and saw someone else's pain. She spent more time with her sister. She nudged Flo on the park bench, felt her elbow disappear in the hollow of her coat. 'You're getting too thin, you know. You need to look after yourself more now that Albert's not around,' she said.

'I'm fine, stop fussing,' her sister said. 'You're the one that needs looking after, always have been. How is your hospital treatment going? It is helping, isn't it?'

Muriel closed her eyes again. She hadn't told anyone that she had stopped going. She hated it. Even when Harry had the time to go with her, she cried and begged not to go. 'But it's for your own good,' Jim had said. They all did. It didn't feel good. When letters from the hospital dropped onto the doormat, she hid them. She expected the doctor would be round next, wondering why she hadn't been.

Muriel counted the sticks in her pocket again for comfort and whispered into her lap. Her words gathered speed and she addressed no one in particular. 'I'm too frightened to go home today in case the same thing happens to me again. That modernised house makes me ill – I can't move. I hate the kitchen … I can't cook the same in it or get things dry. The cat has gone, and I am frightened we'll get more mice. I suppose I know there are worse things, but I can't help it. I look at the work I need to do, and I just come to a full stop. I hate that house now. It's making me ill. I wish they had left it alone.'

Flo covered and squeezed her hand. 'Don't be daft, Moo. You can't be frightened of a house.'

Muriel leant against her sister's bony shoulder. 'But I am. It's the dark nights and short days too, they don't help.'

'You'll settle down, you'll see,' Flo said.

Muriel had settled, like sediment in cheap wine, but it did not take much to stir her up.

She left Flo at the corner of Royalthorn Road and made her way back to her own avenue, noticing the cracks across their concrete path as she slipped her key in the door. Last summer's heat had brought an ant swarm up through those cracks, millions of tiny black bodies battering against her bay window. Muriel had cowered, terrified, in the back kitchen, until she could bear it no longer and tore round the side of the house snagging her cardigan in her rush to get to the phone box and call Harry in a high-pitched whine. 'Please come right away. I can't go back in there. There's a plague of ants possessing the house. Please, Harry, come now,' she begged. He found her locked in the downstairs toilet quoting passages from the Old Testament. Harry fetched a shovel from the coal store and battered the flying ants until Muriel emerged from her hiding place, inconsolable and incoherent.

Harry rang Jim at work. 'You should come home right now. I can't console her. She thinks the house is crawling with ants. She's shouting about it now, sees them everywhere. I don't want to leave her on her own, Jim. I think you best fetch the doctor out again.'

The doctor arrived the same time as Jim, the two of them advancing in a pincer movement from the front gate and the concrete drive. Jim made it to the door first, hoping to calm his wife before an outsider witnessed her mania. It was too late, she was failing before the mantelpiece, striking the wallpaper as if it were covered in black specks as Harry watched, helpless. The doctor delved in his bag for a bottle of pills and between them they persuaded her to take some with a cup of tea.

He drew Jim aside. 'I've given her a sedative for now, but she really needs to go back to Prestwich for regular treatment, Mr Burns,' the doctor said, surveying Jim's false leg and drawing conclusions: an incapacitated husband whose wife was not able to provide the full care he needed. He'd seen stoicism and pride in many of his male patients before. They were unwilling to do what was necessary. 'I don't know how you put up with it. You could have her put back in hospital for a while.' He rolled his sleeves down and put his jacket back on. 'Or you could leave her?'

Jim was shocked at the suggestion. Marriage was for life, in sickness and in health. Muriel had been there for him – he would not betray her now. 'Have her committed for ages? I can't do that, I love her,' he said, and that was the end of it. Muriel was wrapped in her own world and it was hard for her to see that her husband's loyalty was more than duty, it was love. He rarely told her so.

New medication brought about a lull in her mania, but Muriel was still vaguely absent. School ended for Billy and technical college called. Engineering, he thought. He loved to take things apart and put them back together. Annie had gone to Canada. Bravely and carefully organised her move while her parents were preoccupied. Reasoning her mother was more settled, she followed a friend at work who had taken an assisted passage, secured a job and a passage on *The Corinthian*. She longed to leave, like her mother had years before. Muriel did not go and wave her daughter off at Liverpool docks as her family had done for her. She mourned the loss of her daughter in the moments when she was aware of it, quiet moments watching *Come Dancing* on the television, or reading her Bible. She consoled herself that at least Annie was with Jim's family in Ottawa and had fulfilled the ambition Muriel once had. Missing her brought her life a little more into focus. She daydreamed of her vivacious paintings, seeing her daughter sailing across the sea from The Last of England, and hoped she would find someone who would protect her from life.

The winter wind had bitten through her thin coat. She hung it in the wardrobe and fingered the worn astrakhan collar. It was time for a new coat. A small surge of positivity and productivity drove her to a dusty shoe box below her Singer sewing machine. One of her Butterick patterns was double-breasted, she was sure of it. Maybe with a bolt of flannel from the market she could make something in the Cossack style. She carried the box downstairs and turned the radio on to listen to the Light Programme. Charlie Melville was playing some new jazz from America, a gravelled voice singing 'Mack the Knife'. She liked it. Liked listening to the story the lyrics told. The danger and menace about a shark and his sharp teeth. The Bible lay for once neglected as she sorted through the patterns in her box. The comfort that brought, the warmth of the fire and the medication soon lulled her to sleep in Jim's chair.

An unexpected peck on the forehead roused her from dreaming. There was a whiff of hops on her husband's breath. 'Hello, sleepy head, better shake yourself, we're going out dancing,' he said, his shirt gaping. He was sturdy now in his beige cardigan and as burly as that nurse in Prestwich she barely remembered, and almost as badly shaved. He shifted the weight off his false leg and half smiled, expectant.

Was Jim really asking her to dance? The radio was still on and jazz tinkled around the front room. They would never get around the settee. 'You don't dance, Jim,' she said.

'Mickey has got some spare tickets for a concert at Belle Vue. I thought you might like to go. He'll drive us there.' He folded his arms across his chest, pleased with his idea.

It was too much for Muriel, too improbable. She crossed and uncrossed her legs. Her calves burned from the heat. 'Why would I want to go anywhere with Mickey?'

'Come on, it's a dance, Muriel. When was the last time you had a chance to go out dancing?' he pressed.

She granted it was a temptation. She gathered up her patterns from the floor and began to stack them back in her shoe box when she noticed the four quarters of a black-and-white picture of a young woman in bias-cut silk. She reassembled the jigsaw, placing the ragged edges together on her lap. She did not remember she was the one who had torn up the photograph from Mrs Belmont's. Her younger self gazed back from her knee, fragmented but defiant. Muriel dropped the sections back in her box underneath the patterns, vowing to glue them back together the first chance she had. She had not felt like dancing for a long time. She was still unsure. Perhaps Jim would change his mind.

'The place will be full of youngsters dancing the jive. I can't jive,' she said. That was not quite true. Annie had shown her how in the kitchen. She got the spin and a little of the bounce, but there would be no way Jim could swing her up in the air or send her twirling, and she wasn't letting Mickey near her. Anyway, she was far too old for jiving at forty, surely? 'And you won't like the music, Jim,' she pouted. She'd heard Belle Vue had become a rock and roll venue and some nights there were skiffle bands. 'Besides, you're not dressed for it.' That was her final salvo.

Jim loosened his work tie. 'I'll get washed and changed then. Tonight's a special night at Belle Vue, Louis Armstrong & His All-Stars. I think you'll like him – they're a big thing in America.'

Muriel slid to the edge of her seat, poised with excitement. 'Louis Armstrong? Really? There's a coincidence, I've just heard him on the radio. I do like him,' she said.

'Well he's on tour and this is his only night in Manchester. Come on, love, let's go.'

'What about Billy? I haven't made his tea.'

'I'll leave him a few bob for a fish supper,' Jim said.

'But I don't have anything to wear.'

'What about the dress you wore to the races last summer?'

When Harry had driven them to Chester Races on a family day out. Muriel had worn her best polka dot dress, let her hair blow wild in the warm breeze and laughed like the giddy kipper dancer she once was. Her excuses weren't cutting through Jim's resolve, and the jazz on the radio finally dissolved her last objections. Sometimes she found lost moments of happiness; she could make tonight one of those moments.

Muriel rummaged for her dress in the depths of her wardrobe. It smelled slightly of mothballs and she worried that it wouldn't fit anymore, but it fell neatly over her new girdle when she slipped it on. She snapped on some stockings and pushed clips in her hair to restrain some of the frizz. Smoothed Pond's cream over her face and hands, found a vortex of red inside a metal lipstick tube and rubbed her little finger inside, blotting it on her dry lips and pressing the last of her 4711 cologne behind her ears. When she returned to the front room, Jim had poured her a sherry from the Christmas leftovers. He'd shaved, changed his shirt and combed his hair. Muriel caught herself in her mirror above the sideboard: her reflection looked something like her old self.

Jim took her hand. 'You look nice, you look like Elizabeth Taylor.'

She laughed at the comparison but appreciated the compliment. 'Hardly, Jim.'

'Will you be all right tonight?' he asked. She knew what he was implying. Would she behave? He was taking a chance that she would stay steady by his side while her insides fizzed. Jim leant forward and kissed her on a powdered cheek. 'I'm proud to take you out, Muriel Burns.'

She nodded. 'I know.' Outside, a car horn beckoned.

'You're going to need a coat,' he said.

'I'm not cold,' Muriel answered. She shone enough as she stepped onto the avenue to brighten the winter night.

*

The new Bavarian ballroom at Belle Vue was more modern than The Ritz and Muriel admired the balconies festooned with fairy lights and the sprung maple floor, reluctantly accepting Mickey's offer of a cigarette and a gin and orange from the bar.

'Impressive, isn't it?' he said, noticing her admiration for their surroundings. 'It cost enough to build. Thirty thousand, I heard.'

She took her glass from him. 'Do you have to know

everything, Mickey?' His hands were shiny, polished like the floor. 'No gloves tonight? Won't that put off your dance partners?'

He ignored her barb. 'It won't put you off, Muriel, when I'm the only option for a dance partner – Jim can't dance. You look lovely tonight by the way.'

She stepped away from him. It was typical of Mickey to go one better than Jim in his compliments. Lovely … was she worthy of love?

She found seats amongst the tables facing the stage. Jim followed with a second gin and orange. There was something that struck her as familiar in the crowd, the clutches of people smoking and chattering, an energy and vibrancy she'd seen before. It was as if they were posed for a painting. She hadn't seen so much colour in a scene since before the war, since her town hall murals. New man-made fabrics meant clothes were rainbow hues and full skirts swirled, slashed boat-neck tops revealed girls' sharp collar bones. Muriel felt outdated, old and dull by comparison. Ford Madox Brown would paint her brighter, make her modern and place her in the centre of the scene.

She tipped her chin to the roof. 'Those chandeliers look like trifle bowls,' she said to Jim.

'Do you remember they made the world's biggest trifle here?' he said.

The ballroom was just one of the Belle Vue entertainments both their families enjoyed through the generations, along with the greyhound track, speedway, zoo, and theme park with its roller coaster. She acknowledged their shared history with a squeeze of his hand.

Sometimes they agreed on shared memories and she warmed to him when he gave her what she wanted. 'Thank you for this,' she said.

There was a loud fanfare from the stage as Louis Armstrong & His All-Stars were introduced. The curtains swished apart and the band launched into their music with passion and precision.

Muriel was entranced. 'This was the one on the radio today!' she said, tapping her feet and singing along. '"When the shark bites, with his teeth, dear, scarlet billows start to spread ..."' She drained her glass of fragrant sweet gin, unsure if it was her third or fourth as dancers flickered past their seats. She was lifted, each nerve tingling, goosebumps on goosebumps forming on her forearms. The medication battled to rein in her mania, but the combination of music and gin won out. '"Never a trace of red ..."' she sang, and clapped her hands, bounced in her seat.

Jim shifted. He'd lit the touch paper. Perhaps it was time to stand back as his wife laughed out loud in a burst of pure, unencumbered joy. He allowed himself to think that she was just happy, not volatile. 'We should buy this record, Muriel, and get our Billy to play it,' he said.

She rewarded him with a kiss on the cheek, leaving a stamp of red velvet. 'They're a marvellous band. Shall we dance?' He shrugged. Muriel was momentarily disappointed. She had known it was unlikely he'd dance with her, certainly not to fast beats. She wouldn't let the dance floor go unfilled. Desire made her decide. She stepped alone into the space beside the stage. A flamboyant move that was noticed by Louis and won her a special smile that flared her confidence. She could still do it, she could still dance. The music would keep her safe as she spun, sparkling in the spotlight, the centre of attention.

She dropped, sweating, back into her seat and Jim handed her another glass. He was happy to see his wife happy. The evening rumbled on with edges undefined. There was more dancing, and a lot more drinking.

She woke much later with Jim snoring beside her in her own bed. She could just make out the outline of his false leg, resting against her dressing table. She had no memory of getting home, she couldn't remember getting to bed, or what might have happened there, but she would keep his company for the chance to sleep. Jim left for work before she woke up, and when she did, it was with a thick head. A cup of tea, her medication and an extra fizzy glass of Alka-Seltzer settled her stomach. She felt as if something had shifted. Perhaps she wouldn't mind if Jim came to her bed some nights. They could make it every Sunday: she could go to church in the morning, and dance in the evening.

February 1969

In her early fifties, it was as if her face began to fold and hide her features. Age caught up and overtook. Her eyes grew hooded, the skin heavy and drooping, haunted bruises pouched below. Her cheeks curved around a nose that held her Max Factor powder in its large pores. Once plump lips turned inwards, thinned, while her body went the other way. She'd knead her stomach in despair, with hands bulbous and arthritic, nails like mint imperials and fingers tanned with nicotine, disappointed in the softness of her whole. Edges blurred, she dissolved and became an invisible woman to all but family. Dressed in muted Terylene prints and sensible shoes, she wore tights of American tan instead of stockings. The years ploughed onwards dragging Muriel behind, turning the desires she had as a young woman into elusive dreams.

Jim watched his wife and decided to act. He took her into the city on a trip he hoped would jog happy memories and settle her worries. It was a concession on his part to sacrifice the safety and solitude of his own car and accompany her. They rarely took the bus together. Muriel liked to sit upstairs, and Jim could not climb stairs. She sat silent beside him on the lower deck, staring out of the window and chewing on the chain around her neck, its gold cross pendant lying flat on her tongue like a communion wafer.

'There's concrete everywhere now, it's all so grey,' she said.

'The new buildings are filling in the gaps for the ones that were bombed, Muriel. It's progress.'

She remembered warm ochre stone. 'Well I don't like it and there's so many people, the pavements are bulging. Looks like there's a march brewing.'

She felt herself a rattling marble in the crowds as they walked through Piccadilly Gardens. Her hands were cold. She had left her gloves on the kitchen table. She slipped her hand in Jim's, looking for familiar landmarks amongst the sea of faces in the new Manchester. She spotted the clock of the town hall floating above the streets and picked up her pace, practically dragging her husband along Princess Street.

'Let's go in the town hall.'

'That was my plan,' Jim answered, staggering and breathless as he stumbled to keep up. 'I thought it might cheer you up.'

Muriel pushed open the door into the lofty main hall, as eager as she had been as a young girl at her dance competition. Her epic murals hung silent and unchanged. Their stories static, as hers had moved on. She had taken a different path from those childhood dreams. Her mind fizzed into another of her unpredictable moods, the light, ebullient moments that contrasted with long days of heaviness. She could let her mind loose for a bit in the town hall beneath her paintings. They understood. She had learned to see the features of her seesaw head as well as the transparent paper templates of her dressmaking days. Yet try as she might, she could not pin the pieces of her personality together. There were times when she welcomed the excesses of her maladjusted mind and this was one of them. It gave her permission to live snatched moments of an ecstatic life. Her favourite paintings provided a flashback to her giddy kipper childhood that she was afraid to let go. She marched towards them on light feet, lifted, like she was returning home.

She spun a pirouette under the high ceiling burnished gold amongst the blue, encircled with the names of all the places Manchester had traded with. Places she had never been.

'It's so quiet in here, but they're all so noisy,' Muriel said, puzzling Jim.

He looked about him. 'We're the only people in here. What do you mean? Who's noisy?'

Muriel laughed and gently punched his arm. 'The paintings, you daft ha'p'orth. Remember they're called murals, you said it sounded like Muriel. I used to think that too. I used to wonder which painting I would like to be painted into if I could.'

She stepped quickly along the panels until she came to a medieval scene: a woman on horseback with attendants. The workers in the foreground were handling fabric like they were the skilled dressmakers from Mrs Belmont's. Flemish weavers watching the arrival of a queen. They offered her boughs heavy with May blossom, pale against her Lincoln green gown. Muriel stopped and studied the painting, reminded of the May Queen she had been. She pushed her hands into the pockets of her cardigan. She had been the centre of attention too few times in her life.

'If that's the queen, where's the king?' Jim said, limping level with her.

'She doesn't need a king,' Muriel answered.

Her mind had quietened again, overwhelmed by the riot of colour. But then the room tipped. The murals began to twist, the figures grotesque and mocking. Her chest tightened as heavy hod bricks of melancholia pressed down upon her shoulders. It would catch her sideways like that when she least expected it. Muriel shuffled to a bench and lowered herself down to the wood, just as hard as she remembered. The benches lined the walls in the same way they had when she'd sat there as a young girl, waiting to show off her skills. The memory jumped out and startled her. She got up and followed Jim as he wandered around the hall, his neck craned at the paintings.

'It must have been a lot for one man, painting this lot. Such a big job, it would take years. Be like me painting Withington all on my own,' he said.

Muriel thought of the elderly Ford Madox, creaking his ageing limbs into difficult positions as he painted from his platform. 'The painter was getting on a bit too. He brought his wife with him as he worked on these.'

Jim laughed. 'Why on earth would he do that? I wouldn't take you to work with me. Too much of a distraction!'

'He needed to keep an eye on her,' Muriel said. 'I think she had a drink problem.'

'Ah well.' He squeezed her shoulder. 'In that case.'

Muriel shrank beside him, suddenly heartsore for something. She nuzzled into the stale-ash smell of his cardigan. 'I'm afraid, Jim.'

He squeezed her hand. 'What are you afraid of? I thought you liked these paintings. Come on, tell me more about your Ford Madox and his drunken wife.'

She muttered into his sleeve. 'This was one of his last paid jobs. They were broke, before it came along.'

Jim nodded. 'I know that feeling, Manchester was lucky for him then.'

'Maybe.' She twisted her lip, smudging her lipstick. She read aloud the caption on the town hall wall below the last mural. '"Something to brighten the age and quicken the pulse – teach the people that Manchester has a history of which they can be proud,"' she quoted. What of her history, could she be proud of it, littered as it was with missed opportunities? A sudden blast of organ music electrified her body and she clutched Jim's hand in panic. 'What the hell's that?'

'It's all right, love, there's an afternoon organ recital. I thought you might like some music.'

She breathed out, releasing the shock, and settled to listen to the lively notes as they rang around the hall. It was hard to see the organist; his head was dwarfed by the giant pipes that reached like stalactites to the vaulted ceiling. The sound echoed, matching the paintings' vivacity. They shone radiant, lively and divine with their warm and welcoming colours. Muriel felt a temporary peace rest upon her.

*

Muriel had fallen into a roaring grief after her mother died. It cracked open the fissures in her mind and she had sunk back into dark cloud days when she felt she was pushing through a great tide, unsure of her destination, or if she wanted to get anywhere. Harry was a kind comfort. He tried to take her to familiar places and disturbed her diurnal rhythm one early summer morning when the May blossom was bright on the avenue. He had brought the car round and suggested a drive out, a trip to Booths Hall. She didn't need much persuading. But it wasn't until they had been in the car for nearly an hour that Muriel realised they had been travelling for some time, moving north, not south. There was something familiar about the route they were taking, but she couldn't quite place it. It caused her a gnawing anxiety.

They had pulled onto the new motorway when she thought to ask. 'I thought we were going to Booths Hall.'

Harry changed gear and kept his eyes fixed on the outside lane. 'I'm trying out this new route. Got to stop off somewhere first – I've got a removal delivery up this way next week.'

Harry took any job he could find and had started working for a removal company in between his shifts at Ringway Airport. They pulled into a car park beneath a dark green yew that had probably been planted the day they laid the first bricks of Prestwich Hospital. It stood like a defender of the ground. Muriel panicked. Her brother had betrayed her. She would have leapt from the car right there if she could, but she couldn't find the handle.

'Why have you brought me here, Harry? You promised we were going to Booths Hall. I didn't want to come here.

I'm not going in.' Silent tears of terror slid down her face. She gripped her handbag so tightly the clasp clicked and unclicked rapidly like the switches on the dreaded ECT machine. She began to shake.

Harry attempted to placate her. 'It's all right, Muriel, it's all right. I told you, I've got a job up here. I was just trying out the route.'

She didn't believe him. 'Take me home,' she demanded.

He unbuckled her seat belt. 'Let's just have a look around, shall we? I never got to visit you when you were here and you told me there's a garden, like an allotment. There's lots of people about, isn't there? Patients can come to the hospital just for an hour or so, you know. Have their treatment, then go home. Outpatients, that's what they are. Like the outpatients' department at Withington that Jim painted. Have you thought about coming here for a quick treatment then going home afterwards, Muriel? It would just be like going to the doctor's. I'd bring you, I'd wait for you and take you home.'

She stared straight ahead and ignored him rattling on. There were a few people meandering beyond the tree, walking in and out of the front doors. They didn't look like inmates. The doors kept swinging open and shut, letting them in, letting them out. She could see they were not locked, but she had been locked in and the experience still terrified her.

'I can't come back, I can't,' she said.

'Not even if it makes you better? Well enough to have days out every week? I could drive you anywhere you like, Muriel,' Harry said.

She would not look at him. He couldn't drive her anywhere she liked, could he? He couldn't drive her across the sea to Canada to see Annie, couldn't drive her to Booths Hall as he'd promised.

Harry tried again. 'Why don't we just have a sit in the courtyard there for a bit, then we'll go on to Booths Hall. We could stop at a pub for lunch,' he cajoled.

She shuffled out of the car, wary that their short walk would lead somewhere she didn't want to go. She allowed herself to be led as far as the outer gardens, until, like a dog refusing a walk in the rain, she parked her haunches on a bench by the rose beds and refused to budge. 'I'm not going in there, you can't make me,' she said. Deaf again to Harry's entreaties, she retreated into the folds of her green jacket and tucked her calves under the bench and worried a hole in the knee of her tights.

He tried one more time. 'Are you sure now? They won't make you stay, you know.' He had developed the plan alongside Jim, who had managed to call Muriel's doctor and arrange an outpatient appointment for her. Now that Harry had got her there, he could see it was useless. The windows of Prestwich were watching them from behind the low hedges and lichen-covered paths. Muriel already felt trapped. He prised her from the bench and took her back to the car. Perhaps next time he would have more success.

Muriel glared at her brother from the passenger seat. How could she trust him again? 'Are we going to Booths Hall or not?' Harry started the car and swung south.

At the entrance to the long wooded drive a security guard emerged from a small shed and flagged them down. 'Good afternoon, do you have an appointment up at the house?' Neither of them remembered the gate being guarded.

Muriel regained her confidence in her eagerness to see Booths Hall and spoke up. 'Harry and I are part of the family. The hall belonged to our granny's side, the Cowburns,' she said.

'I know the name, madam,' the guard said, 'but nobody lives here now, it's offices.'

Muriel's face fell. This was to be a day of disappointments then.

Harry leaned across her. 'Could we have a quick look round anyway, mate? We won't be any trouble.'

The guard shrugged and waved them on. 'Park up at the front of the house,' he said.

Muriel beamed at the familiar frontage. The warm yellow-stone columns, doubled either side of the porch, the red brick and polished sash windows. She strode from the car to the porch with a sense of purpose and ownership and tentatively tapped her feet on the colourful mosaic tiles.

'You were just a little lad last time we were here, Harry,' she said, pushing her palm against the solid door. It was firmly locked. 'I would have left the door open all the time if I'd lived here.'

Harry led her away around the side of the house before anybody came out to tell them off. Down some stone steps to a small fountain that bubbled clear water onto the lily pads. Muriel watched the golden fish flash between them. Behind, a row of low buildings had been constructed across the side lawn. Girls with tiny skirts and shiny shoes, carrying sheaves of paper, scuttled between them and reminded Muriel of Annie. She'd be at her office in Ottawa. She felt the tug of loss as she thought of her daughter. Harry was already striding off down the hill. She followed.

'Do you remember the lake, Harry?'

'I remember our Leslie. The bugger pushed me in,' he said.

'I saved you,' Muriel declared. It wasn't quite the truth. Flo had been the better swimmer and got to him first, but Muriel had tried. Who was saving who now? She trotted after him. 'We could roll down this hill, Harry, you used to love that.' She laid herself horizontal and began to turn, over and over down the slope.

Harry looked around to check nobody was watching. Then he lowered himself to the grass and followed her, nearly losing his glasses in the process. Muriel's stomach somersaulted as she rolled, sparks of sky and grass flashed past and she stopped at the bottom of the slope, laughing. Leaning against Harry in their little rebellion. She had grass stains all over her skirt, she didn't care as Harry bundled her back up the neat lawns to a stone bench by the roses. Muriel pulled a petal from a tight bud of a yellow rose and put it in her pocket.

'The lake does look lovely.' Harry nodded. 'But I don't think you can walk round there now, it belongs to someone else,' Muriel said as she shredded the petal in her pocket and contemplated the view. The sunlit, sharp green grass with its new-cut smell, the glistening lake, gravel paths and the house behind. Booths Hall could have been hers. It should have been. What a different life she would have led. She would have pushed her personality into its creaking floorboards and hung original Ford Madox Brown paintings all along the hall. She wanted to stay.

'I don't want to go home, Harry. I don't want to go back to that house. I can't bear it anymore,' she said.

Her brother reached for her hand. 'But it's your own home, love, you've made it nice, and Jim and Billy are there, people who love you.'

It wasn't quite enough for her. 'Not Annie, though, not my daughter,' she muttered.

Harry was surprised by his sister. 'You miss her that much? You've never said.'

'Of course I do. I miss our mum too. Everyone leaves.' She was helpless to stop the sudden acute pain in her chest. A heavy, tight weight Muriel recognised as the familiar pain of loss. Annie was gone, Billy was more out than in, performing with his band and working as a young engineer, and Jim was at work or out drinking with Mickey. She was battling her demons on her own with only her faith and medication to arm her. When she was alone the spaces in her mind made the most noise; she had to fill them with something. Most times she craved company when she had wanted her own space for so long.

Muriel did not know that Harry had written to Annie, a kind and honest letter with a cheerful tone, letting her know her mother was all right. Yet Annie detected an undertone of concern. She knew Billy was too young to cope with a distracted mother, and their father was incapacitated. Her friends had returned to Manchester and prompted by a sense of duty and a touch of homesickness, she made plans to come back. Muriel was pleased when her daughter returned, yet so absorbed by the self-interest created by her illness, she could not see the sacrifice Annie had made for the family. She did not remember her own crushing disappointment on her return from Canada.

Annie recognised the fragility of her mother's mind and knew the only recourse was more treatment at Prestwich. She was the only one to confront Muriel with it and to make an outpatient appointment that she would not let her mother escape. When the date arrived, they sat in the kitchen and Muriel refused to go.

In desperation, Jim resorted to tactics of emotional blackmail. 'Annie came all the way back from Canada to help you with this treatment. You don't want her to go away again, do you?'

Annie washed her cup and re-stacked it in the cabinet. She had been ready to come home, but she didn't want to contradict her father.

Muriel sat clutching the edge of the table, looking between them. 'But I don't want to go,' she said.

Annie squatted beside her. She spoke to her mother as if she was calming a child. 'It's all right, Mum. I'll be right there with you. We could go to the gallery after, you'd like that. Take your tablets now, that will help.'

She dosed Muriel with more medication and fooled her back into Harry's car. Annie sat next to her in the long hospital corridor while Muriel wept. A young nurse with black eyeliner like a bird flapped towards them.

'Where's my Nurse Evans?' Muriel asked. 'She was an angel.'

'She left ages ago, Mrs Burns. No angels here now,' said the bird nurse. She bustled Muriel away before she had chance to run.

The room was the same. A blank theatre with white cold walls. Muriel folded herself inwards and numbed her body down in resignation as they fixed the pads to her temples.

Annie kept her promise and took her to the gallery afterwards where Muriel, mute, wandered the plush corridors, inhaling the layers of oils, colours, figures as if they were a freshly opened bottle of cologne. The therapy had given her a brief sustenance, strengthened her senses and resolve for recovery, although she would never admit it.

*

Annie had returned to a thriving city. She found work easily and soon met someone. A relationship blossomed and she brought her new boyfriend home. Muriel was lucid enough, post-treatment, to recognise the importance of the visit. She cleaned the house from top to bottom. She bought iced buns from the bakery and made a fresh pot of tea. Made the tea too far in advance and it lay stewing on the draining board as she was distracted by the pages of her Bible, so by the time the front door went at three in the afternoon she was lost in the tiny print. One of her occasional hallucinations had emerged from the pages, surprising her. It sat beside her.

When she went into the front room to introduced herself to Annie's boyfriend, she told him.

'Jesus visits me sometimes. He's in the kitchen now, sitting at the table in his robes. They're always so clean. How do you think he keeps them so clean?'

The young man smiled politely. 'Maybe he uses Omo.'

Muriel grinned. She liked this one. She set a fresh pot and the best china on the coffee table. Jim moved across the living room to turn off the television, standing squarely on Annie's boyfriend's foot with his false leg as he did so. The young man barely winced and Muriel took his silence as a sign. He had passed the test.

*

There was talk of marriage before long and a date was set for June. Muriel heaved her old black Singer down the stairs and covered the kitchen table with oilcloth to help her daughter make her wedding dress. It was the only space in the house big enough. She could not bear the thought of the material becoming marked with butter or pantry scraps and when Annie opened the back door for fresh air, Muriel shut it.

'We can't have ants crawling all over this beautiful white crêpe, Annie, and wash your hands before you cut those patterns.'

Hands were washed, and washed again before Muriel was satisfied they were clean enough to handle a bolt of fabric that unrolled like a crust of iced snow across the table. She offered Annie her new pair of dressmaking scissors. 'Do you want to start cutting the sections we've pinned, and I'll sew the bodice?' she said.

'I can do it myself. I can manage, you know,' Annie said.

Muriel tried not to show her hurt. She expertly threaded the bobbin and ran a trail of stitches over a piece of scrap fabric, her head bowed and her words muffled by a mouthful of pins. 'I thought you might like some help. I made my own wedding dress.'

'This is different,' her daughter said.

Muriel lifted her hand off the wheel and let the stitches run to a stop. Annie was right. No one in their family had the money for a white wedding dress before the war. A wedding was a subdued and simple affair. This was hardly going to be extravagant, but it was different. It was better.

She watched her daughter as she deftly pinned the paper templates across the fabric. Annie had inherited her creative talent, and her father's practical skills. Muriel fed the fabric through her fingers; it would need fully lining or it would snag on her daughter's soft skin. She felt herself longing for some of her old skills, frustrated by her lack of contribution to the wedding. All she could offer was a cut from what she collected for weekly housekeeping, allowing Annie to save enough to buy her dress fabric for fifteen guineas from a shop on Oldham Street.

Muriel hoped Annie and her new husband would have a better start in life than she and Jim had. One thing was made clear, her daughter would not be living at home. They had already found a flat to rent in Chorlton and would be saving for a house. At least they would only be a bus ride away.

Muriel supervised Annie's cutting and pinning of the pattern, tapping invisible stitches under the silver pressure foot of her machine as she sewed, her mind cast back to the fusty room above Mrs Belmont's. Her friend Margaret had passed away years ago, and she'd lost touch with Joyce. The dressmakers had never made a wedding dress, not even a dress they could keep. Annie had cobbled together the sections from old Butterick patterns for hers, adding modern touches like a straight skirt and a boat neck and a train that flowed from the shoulders. Flo had offered to buy the veil; Muriel could stretch to the shoes. Something borrowed, something blue, something new. Each one of those promises would be kept, even if Muriel had to make some of the purchases on tick. All her energies had gone into Annie's dress and getting herself well. It was exhausting. She pricked her finger on a pin and took a sharp intake of breath through clenched teeth. 'Give me strength,' she muttered and sucked the bead of blood, the tang sharp on her dry tongue.

'You okay, Mum? You've gone pale,' Annie said. Her mother had been stable for some time now, but there was no telling when a storm might come.

Muriel refilled her mouth with pins. 'I'm fine, I can still help. I'm not useless yet,' she said.

*

Muriel would need to buy her own outfit – there was no time to make it. Two weeks before the wedding she had two essential tasks to undertake. She chose the most pleasant first. Early morning she took the bus up to the new shops in Benchill. Spinelli's allowed purchases on credit. She knew this, because she had bought from them before. It was a scorching June day, and as she alighted from the bus, she stopped to watch a young boy poking a stick in the soft tarmac of the road outside the shop. She could smell the bitter smell of warm tar. The weather would need to cool for the wedding day, else everyone would melt.

Muriel pushed open the door of Spinelli's bringing a satisfying tinkle from the little bell above it. Really there was no need to announce her entrance: she was the only customer.

A compact lady with a black beehive advanced through the racks towards her at a trot. 'Good morning, Mrs Burns, you're nice and early today. Now do I hear your daughter's getting married soon?'

Muriel did not fail to notice the glint in Mrs Spinelli's eye. She'd seen the same look on Mrs Belmont's face when a bevy of ladies descended on the shop with an occasion coming up. Muriel was easy prey. 'In two weeks, at St Luke's.' She drew herself up and held her handbag to her chest. She could do this with dignity, even if she was on a limited budget. 'I thought I would see what you had in before I popped into town and had a look in Affleck's.'

Mrs Spinelli smiled again: they both knew the game. Muriel was as likely to buy a high-end outfit from Affleck and Brown's department store as to take a taxi home. Both were out of her reach.

'I'm looking for a dress with a jacket,' Muriel said.

She perused the rails, Mrs Spinelli in tow like lint on her shoulder. Muriel kept her focus. She wouldn't be passed off with cheap rayon, not for her only daughter's wedding. She stopped at a pale blue shift with a long sleeveless jacket. 'What about this? Have you got a larger size?'

Mrs Spinelli plucked it off the rack and spun it round, measuring it up against Muriel with pursed lips. 'It is very elegant, but bare arms for a wedding? Perhaps something with a little more decorum suiting a lady of your years.'

Riled, Muriel almost told her where to stuff her decorum. 'I think the bridesmaids are wearing blue anyway,' she said.

Then she saw it, her perfect dress. A shift in off-white with short sleeves, so not entirely bare arms. It was covered in huge, treacle-toffee-splat giant polka dots. She loved polka dots – her own wedding dress was printed with tiny white ones. Her favourite navy-blue best dress had polka dots the size of the bottom of teacups. The ones on this dress were almost as big as saucers. Perfect. It was smart, but a little giddy too – you wouldn't miss her in it. There was a matching coat with a polka dot collar. She negotiated a discount for both and bought some long white gloves to match.

'If this heat keeps up, you won't need to wear the gloves,' Mrs Spinelli said, ringing up the bill. 'I had gloves just like them when I was a little girl, for first communion.'

Muriel inspected the gloves as the shopkeeper wrapped them in white tissue and put them on top of her bag. 'I did too, not as long, though, our Flo got the long gloves. They weren't for communion, they were for the Whit Walks.'

Mrs Spinelli nodded. 'Yes, I have heard of those. Everyone went, did they?'

Muriel bit her lip, thinking of her next trip. She would need to march there soon, or her determination would wear thin. 'Not everyone, but there were lots, thousands of people. Thank you for your help, Mrs Spinelli, but I must get on now.' She made for the door, tinkling the bell again.

'Of course, there's so much to do before a wedding, especially as mother of the bride,' Mrs Spinelli said.

Muriel left before she was drawn into a longer conversation. Her next task was hardly traditional pre-wedding preparations for the mother of the bride, and she didn't want to share it with anyone. It had to be done. She had had no breakfast but she bought herself an ice lolly from the newsagent's in defiance of the instructions that had come in her hospital letter, and held it carefully away from the precious cargo in the Spinelli bags at her feet. It was lemonade flavour. The ice melted quickly on her hot tongue, sugar sweet.

The bus pulled up with a wheeze of brakes and a belch of diesel and Muriel dropped the stick on the pavement and stepped aboard. She would need to change to another bus at Piccadilly to get up to Prestwich. The doctor had made her a late-afternoon appointment. Harry had promised to meet her there and bring her home in his car.

The severe Victorian buildings of Prestwich were half hidden by cherry trees and conifers. The last of the May blossom clung sparsely to the branches, frilled like her white Whit dress, and drifted in stained trodden piles underneath the benches in the courtyard. Outpatients entrance was one building away from inpatients. Muriel knew there were still wards behind the line of conifers, dark green shadows that hid barred windows. As she waited in a corridor brightened by paintings and a vase of fresh flowers on the sill, her stomach tightened at the knowledge that just a few feet through a locked door there could be a patient strapped to a bed as she had been. The familiar prickle of nerves drove currents of electricity through her arms. Her hair stood on end before she had the treatment. She picked up a magazine beside her chair and flicked through the pages, pausing at an advert for a pair of Clarks kitten heels in blue. Where was the woman with the cerulean slippers now? she wondered.

A nurse opened a door. 'Mrs Burns, they are ready for you now.'

Muriel put the magazine down, tried to stop her hands from shaking and wiped her damp palms on her skirt.

'You can put your things in the corner,' the nurse said, and Muriel placed her Spinelli bags under the chair behind a green screen. She slipped off her clothes and donned the cotton hospital gown. She shut her eyes, closed off the world outside and concentrated on the blank white walls. She was never ready for this. She endured it because the wedding was next week. She had to be at her best for her daughter.

When the wedding day arrived, Muriel dressed upstairs. She covered the small, bare patch near her left temple where the ECT pad had slipped with a careful curl and pinned it under her pill box hat.

Jim was waiting in the front room. He hitched up his braces and kissed her gloved hand. 'You look like Queen Elizabeth,' he said.

She was gently wounded that he no longer thought she looked like Elizabeth Taylor, but she'd take the reference. 'Don't be daft,' she said.

They commanded regal attention when they left the house. The whole avenue came out to wave the wedding car off, a long cream Ford Zephyr that Harry had sourced from a friend with white ribbon stretched across the bonnet. Muriel rode with the bridesmaids in a less impressive Morris. People pointed as they passed and the girls, the grooms' sisters, waved back, laughing, like they were in a royal parade.

She took a seat on the front pew at St Luke's as she waited for her daughter. She lowered herself carefully to the cold stone floor and pulled her gloves on and off in fervent prayer, rising as the organ music changed, and she heard the unmistakable thump, thump, thump of Jim's leg coming down the aisle with their Annie. Muriel kept herself together all the way through the service and the photographs.

She relaxed at the reception in the Scout Hut, watching Billy strike six chords on his guitar as the room erupted into a whirl of jiving bodies and his band commanded the stage. Flo pulled Muriel up to dance. She slipped off her jacket and felt the love that had been stuck inside her complex mind coming undone like the zip on her dress. Before they surrendered the floor to the younger and more energetic dancers, Jim appeared by her side. She stepped away from him on the dance floor as she always did, but this time he took her hand.

'May I have this dance?' he asked.

Startled, she accepted. The tempo of the music slowed and feeling languid, Muriel leaned her body into his, letting Jim lead with his staggered step around the floor.

'Jim, you never dance, but you're doing all right. You must remember those lessons I gave you at The Raby – step, touch, and glide,' she said.

'You were a good teacher,' he said, and they danced a slow half-limp and slide around the fringes of other couples, who were stuck together with the attraction spell that weddings cast.

Muriel watched them over her husband's shoulder. 'Why do so many people get together at weddings and funerals?'

'Maybe those times remind them of being alone, and perhaps they don't want to be alone,' he said.

Muriel understood that longing, but she still needed time on her own to think about the changes ripping through her life.

When Jim returned to the bar, she slipped outside and rested against the hut as the evening fell on the smoke-dust summer night. The Scout Hut windows glowed like sugar pane in a ginger house, department-store bright. Muriel lit a cigarette and watched the only guests who had escaped from the adults make their own game with a lost tennis ball from the courts next door. Five children stood in a circle nearby, and the tallest, possibly the oldest, gave the instructions.

'Throw the ball to each other. Drop it once, you're chipped, drop it twice, cracked, and if you drop it three times you're broken, and you're out.'

Annie had played such a game in the avenue when she was little. She had run in crying when Tommy from number six said she dropped the ball when she hadn't, and she was just as cracked as her crackers mother. Muriel had boxed his ears for that. She stubbed out her cigarette, watching the dancers through the window. Here was her life, played out in the small landscapes of South Manchester. She was still on the outside, looking in, but she thought she could live with that.

December 1972

Seasons passed until one cold Christmas and on Boxing Day Muriel and Jim went to visit Harry and his quiet wife. Muriel drank too much sweet sherry and she livened up her brother's front room by slipping a shiny new disc from its dust cover and putting The James Last Orchestra on his new turntable. She swayed around the living room, cigarette clenched between the fingers of her right hand, her feet flirting with the music and the carpet. Pulled her brother up to dance in his cardigan and braces and forgave him his clumsy arm position, letting him place his hands on her shoulders and hold her steady. They laughed as they traced a conga around the front room in front of Jim, who moved his leg out of their way, and the timid May, who tapped her teacup in time. Several glasses of Advocaat later, Harry drove Muriel and Jim through the green open fields of Cheshire to Annie's new house in the true suburbs.

Muriel opened the wrought-iron gate at the end of the driveway. 'They've done well for themselves, haven't they, Jim? It's a nice place to live. The only thing that worries me is that pond at the end of the garden. They need to keep an eye on her while she's playing out,' she said.

'You worry too much,' Jim said.

She did, with good reason. The houses were built around a pond. Annie and her husband couldn't swim – who would save her precious granddaughter? The dark water of Booths Hall lake would have swallowed her brother Harry, if she and Flo had not been there to save him. She shuddered. She would not let her worries overtake her and become the obsession that dampened her moods. She clutched the bag of presents she had specially wrapped for Alice and rattled the door knocker.

A month earlier, Annie had taken some part-time work and left her daughter with her mother. Muriel was delighted with the responsibility. She planned to make the hours she was given bright and memorable. She got up especially early to make sure the house was clean and shelved her few delicate objects out of reach, locked the drinks cupboard and rummaged through the cutlery drawer for her paring knife. She would show her granddaughter how to make potato prints.

The small blade glinted in the dull light and Muriel trembled slightly. She wrapped the knife quickly in a clean tea towel from the pantry and placed it on a higher shelf, taking a moment to calm herself. No madness would creep like ants through the back door while her granddaughter was in the house, she would not let it, she would fight to keep it from infecting another generation. Muriel hurried into the front room to escape those thoughts and turned the radio on. She pushed the volume right up, wrapped her cardigan about her and let the music scare away any clustering worry, practising a few dance steps across the bay. Perhaps she could teach her granddaughter to dance.

It was early morning. Too early to leave a child standing outside her front door in the shivering cold. Muriel had not heard them knock. She was singing along to the chorus, imagining herself leading Alice as a young woman out under the chandeliers of The Ritz. How the audience would admire her granddaughter in her fine white dress. 'Her nan made that for her,' they would say. 'Finest silk. She taught her to dance too. Muriel Burns, remember what an excellent dancer she was?' Muriel stepped into her bay window. She raised her arm in half-salute, her hand turned, and her head dipped under her frizzy hair. She laughed at their praise, lapped it up. She did not hear the next knock.

Outside, Annie's hand tightened around her daughter's. She moved one shuffle closer as her mother knocked again. Muriel saw the first slaps of rain hit the bay window with her floral curtains wide open. If Jim had been home, the curtains would have been drawn; he didn't like people staring in, didn't like them to see what was going on in his own front room, behind the privet hedge.

She noticed the figures on her doorstep and shook her head sharply, once, like an electric pulse, and finally let them in. She left the radio blaring and the fire blazing, newly lit, its hot, sparking orange stories dancing on the black coals, heating the vinyl sofa and making the room smell of warm plastic. Muriel pulled Alice into the front room. She knew the child liked watching the flames in the fire; she liked the soft bristles of the grate brush and the shine of the brass dustpan. If she was good, Muriel would let her play with the hearth set. Annie marched across the room and switched the radio off. The music died and she pushed her daughter over to Muriel like a reluctant gift.

'I'll be back soon, sweet pea,' Annie said and bent to give Alice one soft kiss on her forehead. Then she was gone.

Muriel could see the child biting back a ball of tears lodged in her throat. She grabbed her before the tears burst and swung her high, hefted to her shoulder, straining the muscles across her blades. 'Now then, no tears, we'll have a lovely time, won't we?' Muriel said, urging the question into a statement. She knew the child was unsure of her, just as she was unsure of herself, but she would try to be steady. Muriel's face folded into creases as she smiled. 'Look at you, angel, what can you see from up here?' The child had a better view from her shoulder. The custard-thick paint along the shelf, yellow with tobacco, little pottery knick-knacks, the sideboard and above it the mirror, hung from its dull chain, static against the woodchip. Muriel pointed to the mirror and smiled at their reflection. 'Look in the mirror, Alice. I used to tell your mummy stories about the lady in this mirror.'

The child pointed to the figure painted in layers and layers of yellow silk, eternal behind her bonnet. 'That lady?' she asked.

'Yes. That lady in her garden, the crinoline lady. Do you think she's smiling at us behind that bonnet?' The bottom edge of the mirror was painted with a garden in gaudy colours, an arch of bright roses and within it a lady, her face hidden, in layers and layers of yellow silk. Her huge crinoline skirt settled over the bright flowers. Alice placed her hands either side of her nanna's face and Muriel felt the air freeze like the sugar frost on the lawn that morning. The two sides of a generation captured between the mirror and the front room.

Muriel lowered her granddaughter into the chair by the fire and watched her swing her feet at the end of her bare legs. Bare legs on a cold day. Annie had put Alice in long socks to make up for the short dress, a smaller version of Annie's cold-defying mini. Muriel could understand the sacrifices young girls made for fashion, but she could see the goosebumps like a naked chicken on her granddaughter's legs. Annie looked up at her expectantly. She would be wanting a story. Muriel usually told her stories about the crinoline lady in the garden mirror, the large house she lived in and the servants who waited on her every wish, but she suddenly felt lost. Like she had drifted into the mirror herself and the story words clogged in her throat. The child's eyes drooped. She would be tired, it was still early. Perhaps she needed a little sleep.

'Why don't you have a nap now, Alice? We'll put the radio on, it's *Listen with Mother*. I'll get you a blanket,' she said. 'Stay there, don't move.' Muriel rattled up the stairs and snatched the candlewick off her bed, remembering something she had meant to bring downstairs. She rummaged in the back of the dark wardrobe for an old shoe box and pulled out her dusty dance shoes, wiped them briefly with the bedspread and hurried down the stairs again. Her granddaughter's head was nodding, heavy with the words from the radio, her eyelids loaded with fire warmth. She opened her eyes as the fire threw glowing sparks like fireflies onto the rag rug. They glimmered and almost caught before Muriel stamped them out with the black shoes on her hands like puppets. She poked the fire with the brass poker, squatted in front of Annie and levered the lace-ups off her granddaughter's feet.

'Your great-granny used to say you could tell a person by the shoes they wore,' Muriel said, and pushed the shoes over Alice's feet like Cinderella. Her toes rattled inside them. Muriel frowned and perched back on the edge of the coffee table. 'They don't fit you yet. They were my dancing shoes. Never mind, maybe next year.' Alice dropped a shoe off her toe and watched it lie dusty on the rug.

Muriel draped the candlewick around Alice and tied it at her shoulder like a dress. 'There now, you're dressed for the ball. Shall we dance?' She pulled the child to her feet. 'Give me your hands. If you stand on top of my slippers, I'll teach you to dance.'

The child balanced on her feet and Muriel lifted her legs in a clumsy waltz, her granddaughter attached like a puppet. They glided around the green vinyl three-piece and the coffee table, across the bay window where the moon was still visible in the pale sky. 'Look, Alice, you can see the moon up there.' Muriel pointed out its lunar light as they waltzed past the sideboard where Muriel paused, a little breathless. 'Sit down again, love. I want to show you something else.'

She unlocked the drinks cupboard and felt behind the dusty bottles for a shoe box, its edges stained and split. Muriel put the box on the coffee table and lifted the lid, drawing out postcards that she placed like patience cards in front of Alice, pointing a finger at each one, her nails broad as mint imperials.

'These are my favourite paintings. Aren't they lovely, Alice?' The child looked at the faded colours and the frowning faces of the tired-looking people and shrugged. 'Maybe they're not bright anymore, like the pictures in your story books, but they used to be. I bought them a long time ago in Manchester Art Gallery. Ford Madox Brown was the artist who painted them. He used lots of red, crimson and carnelian – that's the colour of bricks.' She pointed to the faded red on a lady's bonnet, as pink as her granddaughter's inner lip. 'He painted the town hall murals. Has your mum taken you to the town hall yet?' She was babbling. Alice looked a little scared. Muriel creaked her knees to the floor, her tan tights stretched over them, so she was level with the child.

'Muriel's?' Annie asked.

Muriel laughed. 'No, your grandad used to say that too. Murals. I could take you to the town hall one day. Mind, there's no trams now, but we could catch the bus. Do you like the bus?' she said.

Alice nodded. 'On the top deck?' she asked.

'Of course,' Muriel said. There was still something left in the bottom of the box. She passed it to Alice delicately, between a clean finger and thumb. It was a photograph of a woman, her black hair on white skin like Disney's Snow White.

'Who's that?'

'It's me when I was young,' Muriel said. A point above her left eyebrow began to pulse with a sharp knife-thrust of pain. 'Younger than your mum is now. I worked in a dress shop. I was a dance teacher too.' She paused, unsure of how much the child had understood. She put the mended photograph of herself in the bias-cut silk dress, draped like a goddess in Mrs Belmont's studio, back at the bottom of the box.

'Nan, I'm hungry,' the child said.

Muriel took her into the kitchen and sat her beside the table. She flicked her granddaughter's bunches. 'Good job your hair is tied back in bobbles, might get trapped in the mangle. I used to have nightmares that your mum's hair got trapped in it and she was pulled through, rolled as flat as pastry. Imagine that!'

Alice put her hands over her bunches as her nan disappeared into the pantry. She did not know what a mangle was and scanned the kitchen for some monster that might snag and tear her hair. Muriel fetched a plate on which she had made a floured barm cake, thick with yellow marg that squeezed out of the sides. She laid it in front of Alice who bit into it until it leaked down her chin. Muriel wiped Alice's face with a dishcloth and pulled the paring knife from its tea towel.

'Do you know how to make potato prints, Alice?' The child pushed the barm cake around the plate and shook her head. 'No? I didn't think so,' Muriel said, laying newspaper sheets across the Formica. She thumped a pile of spuds into the sink and began to scrub them until clean and tumbled a few onto the table.

One was heart-shaped. Alice chose that one. 'It has eyes.' The child pointed.

'Looks like a face,' Muriel said, and sliced through the heart potato with her paring knife. She showed Alice how to carve into the spud, made a star on hers with sharp corners and triangles. She held the knife carefully in her granddaughter's hand as Alice made a square on her half with nice neat edges. Muriel dropped the remnants of the barm cake into the bin and rinsed the plate off. She sprinkled it with white flour and mixed a spoonful of red food dye and water into a paste. Red dye like red blood, she thought, and made sure she had put the paring knife back in the drawer.

'They call this red food dye cochineal. It's crushed from beetle shells,' Muriel said. A lone ant scuttered across the newspaper. She pressed her finger over it as if it were a stain. 'I'm not having any of them ants in the house.' She pressed her hand over the child's and showed her how to print her potato shapes across the newspaper. Shapes soon hid the print and Alice's fingers were stained red.

'Let's wash your hands, then you can have a treat,' Muriel suggested.

The red stain was difficult to remove from her granddaughter's skin and she did not want to scrub too hard. She fetched the butter dish from the pantry and rolled the last of it with a blunt knife, dipping the curls into the sugar bowl. 'We used to have this in the war, instead of sweets,' she said as she fed them to Alice, thinking what entertainments she could conjure next.

The day was brightening outside. Weak light bathed the empty coal store and the patch of path beside it. 'Those dance shoes are too big for you now, Alice, but one day soon they'll fit and then you can dance like me,' Muriel said.

The early winter dark was creeping down the avenue by the time Annie knocked at the door. There was no answer, but laughter rolled around the side of the house and she tiptoed round the corner. Muriel and her daughter were dancing on the path. Muriel sparking bright steps in her dance shoes, breaking out wash-house beats into the pale Manchester sky.

Author's Notes

A story grows from the tiniest seed. In this case, it was an overheard conversation at a family event as my uncle described clattering down the stairs when he was a child to find his mother, (my nan) mid-breakdown in front of the living room mirror. I grew up surrounded by family stories, but this one was new, and I started to wonder, who was the woman that was my nan? A woman I had only experienced as old (she would have been the same age I am now). I took some family history, some truth, and I made the rest up into a short story around that event and sent it off to a competition. It won, Wasafiri published it under the title *The Crinoline Lady*. They offered me an Arts Council bursary to work with The Literary Consultancy and a mentor to make the story into a novel.

It is a novel in so much as it is a work of fiction woven from family stories and my imaginings of what happened in the gaps between them and historical research. Some call it autofiction, some a novel in biographical form. I suppose this is my disclaimer. Muriel may share a name with my nan, but she is a different character. I took the skeletons of fact and overlayed them with the flesh and mind of fiction.

For research, I relied on the oral history of my family. I tried to visit Manchester Town Hall to see Ford Madox Brown's murals, but it was closed for renovations for seven years, and I couldn't wait. Maybe one day. Other ideas and settings were gleaned from local history books like *Victoria Baths* by Prue Williams, *Looking Back at Moss Side* by Chris Makepeace and a bit of the history of dance in Manchester in Dave Haslam's *Life After Dark*. *Lancashire, Where Women Die of Love*, by Charles Nevin, *A 1950's Housewife* by Sheila Hardy, *Women's Leisure in England, 1920-1960*, Claire Langhamer. Ford Madox Brown's work came from You Tube tours of the Manchester Town Hall Murals (or Muriel's) and the book *Into the Frame* by Angela Thirwell.

It has taken a long time for the story to get to this stage and I would like to thank all those who helped it on its journey. My lovely second cousin Sue Williamson, who claims the title of the real family historian, she gave me so much detail and background, and to my Great Uncle Harry, (Muriel's brother) the last of his line, who I managed to get to chat to before he passed away. To Aki Shiltz and the team at The Literary Consultancy for your patience and wisdom, and for some great workshops, to my mentor during that process, Kerry Hudson, a brilliant writer who really understood Muriel. To the team at Story Terrace who have helped put me in touch with so many people to get their life stories out into the world. Thank you to Dr. John Hopton of Manchester University, who helped with research and allowed me access to his paper on Prestwich Hospital in the twentieth century, *A Case Study of Slow and Uneven Progress in the Development of Social Care.*

To all my friends, and Jackie and Jackie, who read some of the early drafts, and Louise who bought me balloons when the initial short story won the Wasafiri Prize. To the Writer's at Talliston House, where I was Writer in Residence, who also saw a few early notes. To my mother, Muriel's daughter, thank you for letting me create this story and for your stoicism, support and love all my life, and my father, who pointed out there were some great stories in his family too. (That's for another book) To my brother Rob. Thanks to my other half, Stuart and for my wonderful Izzy and Joe and to my nan, Muriel, of course.

https://www.joolsabrams.com/
Twitter: @joolsdares

This book is printed on paper from sustainable sources managed under the Forest Stewardship Council (FSC) scheme.

It has been printed in the UK to reduce transportation miles and their impact upon the environment.

For every new title that Matador publishes, we plant a tree to offset CO_2, partnering with the More Trees scheme.

For more about how Matador offsets its environmental impact, see www.troubador.co.uk/about/